DANCING

DANCING WITH GHOSTS

By

Emily Gillespie

[signature]

LEAPING LION BOOKS

Toronto • 2017

Dancing With Ghosts
Copyright © Emily Gillespie 2017

This book is a work of fiction. Names, characters, places, and incidents either are the products of the author's imagination or are used fictitiously, and any resemblance to actual persons living or dead, events, or locales is entirely coincidental.

www.yorku.ca/llbooks

Library and Archives Canada Cataloguing in Publication
Gillespie, Emily, author
    Dancing with ghosts / Emily Gillespie.

ISBN 978-1-988170-06-0 (softcover)

    I. Title.

PS8613.I4923D35 2017   C813'.6   C2017-900758-0

Cover Design by: Carlyn Atkinson

Foreword

This isn't a true story. In fact, this isn't even my story, although it was in part inspired by life, like all stories.

This story was inspired in part by my efforts to navigate the metal health system in different communities in Ontario. Even for educated, relatively privileged individuals, trying to access mental health supports is atrocious. It's about banging and screaming at doors in a system where you have little chance of being meaningfully assisted. There's a general lack of funding, lack of transparency, and lack of dignity in trying to get help. The more privileged you are, the more agency and sway you have in attaining vital services.

Every piece of paperwork you fill out, and every one-off doctor's appointment people manage to get after long wait-lists, is framed in the narrative of lack of resources. People are asked to prove that their case is worthy. Money speaks. Funding speaks. What health care the government prioritizes says volumes about who is valued. I'm fucking tired of excuses.

This coming-of-age tale also emerged from frustration with works that normalize and romanticize rape culture and abusive relationships, especially when combined with mental health.

I want to write words that you will spill coffee on, may the pages be wet and creased. May sunscreen smear the words, and may you take them with you. This isn't some crisp virginal text—never was. Take my story and set it free. I'm not responsible for this story any more than Patricia is. Late at night, in the space between awake and asleep I become Patricia, and Patricia becomes me. Think of her when you are bored, busy fucking nameless people in forgettable places, and wondering who their ghosts are and how long until you become one.

–Emily Gillespie

PART 1

CHAPTER 1

I don't know where to start, so bear with me. In case you aren't Alice, I guess I best explain; Alice suggested I write my story. She told me that everyone had a story and that once I started writing I would know what I needed to say. I'm not going to tell you where I'm from. Those little details don't matter in the end. I don't want you to start making guesses about my identity. *And besides, this isn't just my story, I'm sure parts of it belong to you as well.*

Who is Alice? Well, that's kinda hard to explain, and I'm not good at this sort of thing. She is a blur of blue hair and ink, a bittersweet smile—a devious girl, always pushing back against the way the world works. I stumbled into her after Derek and I were over, but I'm getting ahead of myself. You don't even know who Derek is.

Anyway, because of the stuff with Derek I was hesitant to get close to this girl—this creature—but still she had a way of getting in. She would ask questions of me that everyone else didn't even think of. She had this graceful yet defiant presence, and our closeness just seemed natural. She always said that she liked how raw I was. Hesitant, yes, but present. And a dreamer like her. I can't imagine my life, or the last few months without her. I'm blushing thinking about her reading this. Anyway, I'm starting to ramble now, so I better get on with my story.

Perhaps it's best to begin on the first day of school; I suppose that's when it started. My story revolves in part around a guy named Derek. I don't mean to make this about him, but it seems so much goes back to that boy. If I knew what he'd bring into my life, I'd have stayed far away, not even giving him a second glance on that first day of class.

So this is what happened, and if you aren't Alice and happen to be reading this, well, I don't know how you got this, but bear with me, and maybe I can share my story with you, too. Perhaps you can make more sense of this than me.

"What is the meaning of life? To live is to suffer, or is suffering a consequence of living that we must make sense of? Is pain what connects us to the divine? These are questions that people, particularly philosophers, have been struggling with since the beginning of…"

My attention shifted from the professor, a balding man of an unclear age in a grey suit, to a boy two rows ahead of me. Golden thin dreadlocks hung past his shoulders, covering a tweed jacket. I could just make out his backpack with an array of buttons that advertised various social causes ranging from animal rights to fair trade. I saw the beginning of a tattoo on his neck, but it was partly concealed by his clothing. I wondered what it was.

He sat transfixed by the professor. His mouth twitched, and his hand moved as if he was resisting the urge to say something. I wanted to know what he was thinking. He moved his hand towards his head and began absently playing with his dreadlocks. The motion seemed so natural that it appeared as though he didn't even realize he was doing it. As he shifted in his seat I tore my eyes away from him, afraid that he would notice me staring.

I turned my gaze to the rest of the lecture hall. I was sitting in the middle of a row near the back. Each row was made of orange, cracked plastic chairs that looked like they belonged in a 1960s bowling alley. There were small desks attached to each chair. The carpet was a dark blue, stained with salt and chewing gum. The bright overhead lights produced a dull hum.

The lecture hall sat around 300 students; most of the seats were occupied, as was to be expected for a first year course in September. I looked at my peers, some urgently writing what the

2

professor was saying while others looked at their cellphones in their laps. The professor waved a copy of *Man's Search for Meaning* and I suddenly realized that I missed the last few minutes of the lecture.

"Your reflection on this book is due next class. Don't forget to include your student number and the course code on the first page of your reflections."

We debated and reflected on the meaning of life, but in this class I was nothing more than a number. Of course, I couldn't expect my professor to know who I was among my nearly 300 peers, but still...I was 0519341 firstly, AKA Patricia McCormack. I was just another consumer of education. I gathered my bag, throwing my pen and paper inside carelessly while I waited for my row to exit. In their haste to leave, fellow classmates pushed me up the stairs. These people were all strangers to me—fellow student numbers. I scanned the crowd for the guy with the dreads, but I couldn't find him. I didn't know why I was searching for him in the first place—I wouldn't have anything to say.

That was the first time I saw him—a glimpse of a body in a crowded lecture hall.

I exited the air-conditioned school and suddenly I could feel the heat on my pale face and arms. I had to squint to see where I was going on the still unfamiliar campus. The gentle breeze dishevelled my frizzy brown hair, and I tried to tuck it behind my ears to keep it out of my face.

It was a warm day for September, the temperature reached the mid-twenties, and the occasional leaf was starting to turn, reminding me that the warm days were numbered. A few groups of girls sat on blankets, their textbooks set aside as they chatted. I passed a group playing Frisbee. Guys made a scene of catching lavish throws, as girls with pin straight hair and bare legs made over-exaggerated displays of approval. As their laughter drifted past me, I tried to imagine myself playfully flirting like they did, but then again I've never been one of them. Despite the sunny day, I quickly walked the five minutes to the subway station and descended the stairs. I was distracted and didn't have my change ready as I approached the gate, and a line formed behind me as I looked for the correct coins in my wallet.

Crap, hurry up, Patricia! I thought.

People brushed past me to the other turnstiles as I obstructed their path. With clumsy hands I dropped my change on the floor, scrambled to pick it up, and at last made it through the gate.

I needed to go to a bookshop further downtown before I met my friend, Elyse for drinks. I took a moment to read the signs and orient myself. Which way was I supposed to go? Again, I was jostled as people hurried by. The station was filled with students wearing backpacks and business people carrying briefcases, each rushing a different way. I reached the stairs and was nearly pushed down by the flood of people. I paused for a minute, not caring that I was in the way. I was dizzy, hot, and needed to catch my breath. The colourful wall advertisements on the subway shook as the floor slipped from under me, and all I could feel in my bones was the vibrating train.

What am I doing here? I asked myself as I found a seat on the crowded subway car. This had become a familiar question in the first two weeks of class.

You are here to go to school, I reminded myself.

You waited four years for this chance.

You wanted to leave home and get away from small town life.

You decided on the city over the local community college, and now you are stuck in Toronto.

The subway conductor called out the station and startled me, but I quickly fell back into my thoughts.

Just finish first year, no matter what, and then see about staying. I told myself this day after day. I needed to give it a shot before deciding if it was for me. The image of my student number flashed in my head. The voice in my head that I was trying desperately to block out reminded me that indeed, I didn't belong here.

But maybe, if I tried hard enough, maybe I could belong.

I started to think about the philosophy lecture, and what the point of it all was.

"Are you sure you really want to leave, sweetie? It may not be too late to sign up for classes at the college, or do another term of high school?" my mom asked.

I sat on the floor of my bedroom folding clothes and stuffing them into my suitcase. I looked at my mom; she was dressed in high heels and a business suit. Like always, late for her job at her real-estate office. Her question suggested concern, yet resonated with the other questions she and my father asked over the course of the summer—questions that subtly implied doubt in my ability to succeed away from home. My mom shrugged and kissed me on the forehead as she straightened her hair. Conversation over.

My parents are respectable people, but they do the minimum of what is suggested in parenting books. They went to parent-teacher interviews when I was younger, tried to help with homework, asked how I was doing, and encouraged hobbies, healthy eating, and exercise, but they were, and still are, distant. They're both successful in their careers, and their careers always come first. I'm a neglected project, like expensive piano lessons that one felt obligated to go to because one was paying for them, but interest had long since faded. I have an older brother who already left home. I, the second child, completed the image of their successful, upper-middle class life.

"How was school?" my father would ask at our daily family dinners. I long since learned the quickest answer was expected before they hurried on to talk about their respective days at the office.

Don't get me wrong, I love my parents, but we've grown to be more acquaintance than family, with each of us over polite in acting out our respective roles. That's why I found my mother's doubt a bit ill placed. She knew me only on a very superficial level. My anxiety and depression shaped her impression of me...shaped everyone's impression of me.

I've learned to be self-sufficient and rely on them very little for emotional support. Nonetheless my mother's concerns, that my father echoed, added greater pressure to succeed.

I remember in grade ten or so being in a really bad place. I was depressed and didn't know how to deal with my feelings. I was having trouble eating. I didn't want to go to school. All I wanted to do was lie in bed and cry and read all day. It got to the point where my mom couldn't exactly ignore it, so she awkwardly asked what was up. She found some expensive counsellor online. I went to his office a few times, but he wasn't really helpful. His background was more focused on adults and leadership training skills than depressed, frustrated youth. After sessions my mom, or sometimes my dad, would ask how many more I thought I'd need, but that was the end of the discussion. Talking about mental health was clearly a conversation that they weren't comfortable with.

I vaguely remember one Saturday lying in bed, feeling rather indifferent to the world. My mom was banging on the door and reminding me that her parents were coming over for lunch.

"Smile, chin up, don't look so moody, and don't mention counselling," were her hurried instructions to me as she yelled from the kitchen as she finished the salad. "And wear something nice!"

So yeah, my parents are good, but distant, people. I never really had the, *come-here-let's-talk-about-your-problems-over-hot-chocolate* type of relationship with either of them. Smile, keep it inside, and get by. If you weren't okay, fake it. They were wrong; I get that now. But yeah, my parents and I, we don't really talk.

"The next station is…" the static voice of a robotic male over the loud speaker startled me again. I tried to remember why I was thinking about my family. During those high school nights filled with tear-soaked pillows, I promised myself the chance to start again. I would make friends; people here don't know my history.

I will succeed. I have to succeed.

My anxiety and depression were vicious cycles that seemed determined to consume me. Regardless of my actions, it moved on like an invisible force that shaped my life without my consent.

It was like a riptide or tidal wave or whatever it was called, forces of nature that pulled you in. If you want any chance of surviving you had to let your body go limp. Don't fight it, or you won't make it up in time for air.

Unless of course you want to die, what do I know?

Maybe that's better than floating adrift so far from where you started, always just waiting until it's safe to swim to shore. Every time you make it to the beach you are safe for a moment before being pulled back in further. You can see the little figures in the distance on the sand, searching for you, but you are too far away to call out.

But it's never really safe is it? There are always sharks and god knows what else under the surface. And you want them to come rescue you, but you know the ocean may get them too. Another headline about a man going to rescue a child, and they both die. *They both die.* He is better off leaving her. They are better off leaving her.

My head is under water, counting the fragmented seconds. My eyes are squeezed shut, and my teeth digging through my cheeks. I wait until my brain shuts off from lack of oxygen. This is it. And I'm not sure if I'm mad at the water or if I'm thankful. It's over and I never had a choice.

I kinda get what Alice meant when she said depression is terminal. With weak arms and burning eyes, coughing up a lungful of saltwater as you wonder if it's worth it to drag yourself to shore again. Your legs are cut by the coral. What they didn't tell you is that beautiful things can make you bleed, too. And then you try to make up for it by pretending that you love the ocean, and you wonder if anyone sees through the lie. Maybe you're better off turning away from the beach and running back to the water. Predictable demise. The only real option is to relax your body and go with the current.

I told myself I would do well in school and work towards my Journalism degree, that I would like living in this city that it would be okay. Bearable. *It had to be okay.* I am now realizing that that last thought appeared more as a desperate plea than a promise.

What they don't tell you in the "it gets better" rhetoric is that this shit is terminal. Alice and I are lifers.

A backpack brushed past me and I remembered my surroundings. Most of the seats were taken and a few folks were standing. There were a couple of students with backpacks, either absorbed in conversations or looking at their phones. A young mother sat near me, singing to her baby in the stroller as she tried to force her other child to stay still. Why would anyone every want to have kids? You don't know what hell you are putting them through by bringing them into this world. In the seat beside me was a guy in construction boots, holding a hardhat. Another man in a business suit and tie stood impatiently by the doors. A young couple sat across from me, whispering and leaning into each other. I wondered what their story was. How did they meet? Were they happy? As the stops were called and people entered and exited the subway I couldn't help but think about the different paths everyone was on. Had the man beside me always wanted to be a construction worker? Did the young mother have a loving partner at home?

What did they see when they looked at me? Did they just see another young student on her way home from class?

My stop was called and I exited the subway into the sunshine. I was underground for ten minutes, but it felt much longer.

CHAPTER 3

Depression and anxiety created a wall—a wall that continually divided me from my peers. I lived in a different world from my high school classmates. Most girls were concerned about clothing, boys, and weekend parties. I wasn't. The occasional mention of grades, careers, and families emerged, but I had trouble relating. Not to make them sound shallow...I wish I could be interested in those things.

There were fleeting moments when I did care, but most of the time I was consumed by a weight I can't even being to explain. It's not so much a desire to die, but rather a lack of energy to go on living. Heavy. Tired. Empty. Alone. I wish I could focus on smaller things, but the cheap slogans about taking life one day at a time and not sweating the small stuff have always sounded empty to me.

Every school day felt like a losing war against the clock. I am so all over the place—from kind of okay, to empty, to having thoughts race in my head. I couldn't get it to stop. It never stopped. Sometimes I'd start thinking about something, say the bullies in high school who were always ready with an insult, and the memory would play over and over again in my head, despite willing myself to think of other things. I knew the basics of cognitive behavioural therapy. I had my positive self-talk lines ready, willing to rationalize my way through. I could tell myself how it wasn't my fault and that they were just picking on me out of boredom and that what they said had no merit, but even now this positive mantra was always overcome by the words, *ugly, awkward, boring, stupid, nerd, loser...*

It's hard to describe unless you are in the midst of this unbearable thing—this depression—this toxic circle. When I emerge from that darkness, it's dangerous to think my way back in. Sometimes it seems like this all must have happened to someone else. Not only am I isolated from my peers, but also from myself. Disjointed. Always trying to get back into my body. My mind wanders, but my body is stuck.

I used to engage in *normal* conversations with the few people who tried to talk to me, but the inner battle was draining. I could put on a smile and pretend to care about schoolwork and what movie was coming out on the weekend, but trying to care was exhausting.

It was hard to relate to people who didn't carry this weight. Sometimes, I just stared at the clock, waiting for the next five minutes to pass. Society is so eager to try and throw people into binary categories: gay or straight, black or white, young or old. For me, there is only depressed and everyone else.

But those who carry the same weight as me are also dangerous to grow close to, so I've learned. I was hard to connect with, or so the few boys I went on infrequent dates with in high school nicely told me. I heard this every time they explained why they were no longer interested. They had trouble relating to me. I either spoke too much or too little. I was inconsistent. I wasn't like the other girls they spent time with. It was okay though; I wasn't really interested in dating. High school boys bored me anyway. My laughter always felt forced and I worked too hard to smile. The interactions were just empty and too much work. On top of that, the comments from the students at school always had a way of following me on my dates.

I had a few friends in high school, but no one really to speak of. There were a few girls I could share lunch with, call when I was stuck on homework, or occasionally do something with on the weekend. These connections were forged out of recognition of isolation and outsider status. We kept each other company, but they weren't friendships built on inspiration, and I doubted we would remain friends when it was no longer convenient. I didn't tell them about my demons and they didn't tell me about theirs. We never really made it beyond polite conversation. I guess that was one thing that I really learned from my mom—*don't air your dirty laundry*, or something like that.

We decided on different universities, and that was the end of our little group. It was an ending that didn't come with a fight or hurt feelings, but rather a fade away type of finish that would only be recognized in a year or two when we realized we hadn't talked to each other in months.

I don't know why I'm boring you with this part of my history. I guess I just wanted you to understand.

Anyway, new city, new chapter, and I was hoping to leave most of this high school life behind. Like I said, no one here knew my history. No one knew me as the girl who got called names in the hall and was pushed around.

But where was I? Elyse. Elyse was the energetic redhead that lived two doors down in the dorms. She's pretty *normal*. Not normal as in boring, but normal as in she had her shit together. Her laughter wasn't forced; her interactions with others seemed genuine and easy. She was the opposite of me. Despite this, we had an instant connection. It's hard to describe, but when I met her at residence orientation I just knew we would be good friends.

She said she felt something too. Neither of us could really say why. It was just a feeling. You probably think I'm crazy by now—a girl made of fleeting feelings and memories, no substance. But for the first time ever I connected with this interesting popular girl. It was like the *freak* sign on my forehead was invisible to her.

After navigating through the subway, I met with Elyse at a pub. As we waited in line for a table we listened to the guys in front of us talk loudly about the Blue Jays and guess the bra sizes of the girls at the bar. Normally, this crowd would have made me uncomfortable, but with Elyse by my side I felt like I blended in. We eventually got a table and began to talk about school. Elyse was a psychology major so we only had one class together. The talk drifted to plans for the weekend, and finally to the guys in the bar. Elyse had her eye on a guy sitting a few tables behind us who happened to be in one of her classes.

"Isn't he cute?" Elyse whispered. I couldn't see his face properly and only caught occasional pieces of his conversation about baseball. Elyse commented on a few other guys in the bar, but none of them appealed to me. My thoughts returned to the guy in my philosophy class. The boy whose name I didn't know, yet I could picture his dreadlocks cascading down his back. My face turned red as I thought about playing with his hair and touching his face. A stranger.

Elyse talked about her family. She was really close with her mom who was a third grade teacher. Elyse's mom was her motivation for going to university since she wanted to be an elementary school teacher just like her. She talked about missing her mom, little brother, and golden retriever. I was comfortable listening, feeling that she respected my privacy and would not pry when I didn't talk of also missing my family. I liked that about Elyse. She seemed interested in me without needing to know my entire story.

Our friendship seemed mutual. I know I'm getting ahead of myself, but for the first time it felt like I had actively recognized and chosen a friend rather than stumbled into them out of some type of shared convenience, though that sounds awful to say. Although her life seemed easy, for some reason I never found her tiresome. When we parted ways that night, I briefly felt like some of her energy had been shared with me.

CHAPTER 4

The weekend came and went. Elyse and I went to karaoke with a girl named Brittany, who was in Elyse's Psychology class. On Monday morning I stood looking at the calendar, trying to get organized for the week. I scribbled in gym time that I knew I may or may not commit to, and I decided that it would also be a good idea to book an appointment with a school counsellor. I was feeling okay; actually I was feeling pretty good. I made a few new friends and was on top of my schoolwork. Those doubts from the subway seemed far away. But I still knew what things could get like for me, and I thought that maybe it was a good idea to set up supports in case I got overwhelmed with school or anything else. Like I said, I try and outrun my depression and anxiety. *Proactive. Self-care*—those hip terms.

Aashi is my floor don. She seemed friendly enough. She was a dark-skinned girl with pretty brown hair. She's an upper year student, studying political science or something like that. Anyway, I think her job was to serve as a kind of substitute sibling and role model. Dons lived in residence and helped students navigate the first year of school. Aashi mentioned the school's free counselling program during the orientation weekend and gave us all colourful, inviting flyers with the contact information for the counselling office. I booked an appointment for the next day, although I hadn't gotten far with the past counsellor. However, this time it was of my own volition—not something I did because my mother suggested it as a quick fix.

I wondered what Elyse would think, but assured myself that no one else would ever know. Besides, she wouldn't care.

The counselling office was filled with an array of brightly coloured posters advertising various forms of help. The poster nearest to me was for group therapy for eating disorders, and another flyer advertised a group program for people who wanted to stop gambling. The office was hopeful and extremely cheerful. A few motivational posters also covered the walls. I remember one in particular that was a picture of a waterfall and some quote about relaxation.

I approached the secretary as she got off the phone and noticed a sign on her desk that mentioned this was short-term counselling. This meant that students were allowed a maximum of ten appointments. I wondered what would happen if someone needed regular supports. Was this all you got? I asked the secretary about the number of appointments.

"Don't worry, dear; the counsellors determine how many appointments you will need to resolve your problem," she responded. I was a bit thrown by her response. I just wanted to put supports in place *if* I needed them.

Be proactive. Let others help you. Of all the places I've had to prove myself, I was angry that I might have needed to defend my case in this "safe space" that was designed to help.

She asked me for my student number, then handed me a pile of papers. Flustered, I quickly wrote down my name and basic information because my appointment was supposed to start in five minutes. The bottom line of the paperwork was that something needed to have happened relatively recently that was significantly affecting my ability to function. There were no checkboxes to ask for basic support, never mind ongoing help, or more general life concerns. The paperwork asked what the issue was, what could be done to resolve the issue, and what said resolution looked like. The last question asked how I felt about filling out the questionnaire. I wrote "frustrated." I mentioned that I had an array of things that I wanted to address and saw no straightforward solution, or clear answer as to what said resolution would look like.

"You always ask for too much of people," Derek would later tell me. Too much.

The other part of the paperwork was a checklist about my life in the previous week. It included a five-point grading scale, with two positive responses, two negative responses, and a neutral. The first set of paperwork demanded that I present one clear problem, while the checklist asked for proof that this problem affected my quality of life the week before. It asked questions such as: how are you sleeping? Are you satisfied with your friendships? How is your concentration?

I was having a good week. The simple checklist did not reflect my need for yearlong support. It did not touch on the roller coaster of anxiety and depression that had shaped my life for the last few years.

"Who are you, tell us your story, but you must define yourself according to the template we've given you," it seemed as though they were saying. I felt like it was telling me to come back when a close friend or family member died, or after a school shooting. Only then could I clearly state in the paperwork about how I, along with the rest of the school, fit the "template." Tell us how traumatized you were by the shooting. Write about how it affected your mental state in the past week, and make a guess as to how many appointments you will need to return to the previous state—the pre-shooting state. The "normal" state. It was a little more complex than cause and effect. Was I supposed to apologize if my problems weren't big or clear enough?

I entered the actual counselling appointment feeling like I needed to prove myself and give them a good reason as to why I was there. I was greeted by an attractive male who was only a few years my senior. I think he said his name was James.

I was nervous. I assumed that after the paperwork I would have the opportunity to form a relationship with my appointed counsellor. I hadn't realized that the paperwork was followed by a series of intrusive questions from an intake counsellor like James.

He told me that his job was to decide if I was an appropriate fit for counselling.

I was there. I wanted help. I needed help. Wasn't that enough?

He thumbed through my papers. "I noticed that you don't mention having a disability, or a mental health diagnosis. Yet it seems that you are asking for mental health related supports, if I am to understand you correctly?"

"Y-yes. That's right I guess," I said, but I could tell this already wasn't going well. "I'd like some form of consistent support system. I don't have any formal diagnosis, and I'm not really interested. I just want to make sure that I have resources if, if I need them."

"I see," he tapped his pen against his notepad.

I continued to try and explain why I was there. I was frustrated that he was making this about whether I had a diagnosis. I stumbled, repeated words. My face was turning red. Fuck.

"I have a series of questions I'm going to ask. This will take about thirty minutes. Try to answer as truthfully, and with as much detail as possible. Try not to pass on any questions. It's essential that I get a full picture of the circumstances. Okay, Patricia?"

"Yes," I responded, seeing as I was given little choice. The intake counsellor wasn't who I would be seeing regularly. It was exhausting trying to have people understand me and I very rarely made the effort. It was clear that we had a timeframe that did not correspond with the nature of my possible responses.

"So, what's your family like?"

"Middle-class, my parents are together…good careers…"

James wrote something and glanced at his watch like he was timing each answer. If this was a game maybe he should have pulled out one of those timers with the coloured sand. That'd have made this a bit more fun. I could have won a prize for the question I answered with most detail in the quickest time.

"Can you tell me a bit about your relationship with your mother?" he prodded.

I wasn't there to talk about my family, and I certainly didn't want to talk about my mom. Couldn't we get to why I was there?

"Oh, well…umm…you know, pretty typical I guess. She's in real-estate, so she's rather busy, but she makes time to help me with schoolwork and stuff, encourages my hobbies…really pretty average relationship," I muttered in response.

"Have you or your family ever been involved with the criminal justice system?"

What? I wanted to sputter, but I shook my head.

He continued to ask about my education and previous experiences with counselling and mental health. I fought to sit still, feeling like a specimen under his scientific observation. I struggled to keep my voice and face neutral. I wanted to stand and stretch, to crack my neck and fingers.

I might have been comfortable talking about these things with my counsellor, but the intake appointment made me feel vulnerable. I was tired and started to zone out, giving "yes" or "no" answers to questions that required explanations.

"Have you ever been abused or assaulted?" He was looking at me, probably taking into consideration my physical reaction as part of my answer.

What? I wanted to say again, but I didn't. Of course I didn't. "I'd rather not talk about this. I'm here to establish some long-term supports while I'm at school. I don't really feel this question is relevant."

"Yes, I see. But anything may be relevant. Please answer the question, Patricia."

I just stared at him. No longer caring about politeness, I said, "I'm…well I'm…getting tired of explaining myself in the few seconds allotted per question just…just to have notes on record."

"Please answer the question, Patricia," he repeated, that time a bit louder.

I just looked at him and shrugged.

He asked a few more insignificant things and then scrunched his face as he looked at the paperwork, as if trying to solve a difficult math question.

"What would you say your central goal is in counselling? What main problem is your reason for coming here today? And what would successfully addressing this issue looks like?"

"Well, that's the thing. It's not one thing. It's everything. And I don't have a problem, per say. I just think it would be helpful to have supports in place and someone to talk to regularly, especially when things get challenging," I tried to assert. Things always got challenging; I could go from okay, to overwhelmed, to totally indifferent in a matter of minutes.

"Okay, well, can you try and articulate the central issue? And what would resolving said problem look like?" He was frowning at his paperwork again.

"I just want someone to see regularly. I'm in a new city. I often feel up and down, anxious, and I just want supports. I...I can't give you only one issue and...and the resolution. That's not why I'm here." I waved my hands as I spoke. My voice shook as I tried to stay calm.

"Yes, but according to the terms of short-term counselling..."

I stopped listening. "I understand resources are limited, if I get a set number of appointments, can't I just take my eight or ten allotted sessions or whatever, and spread them throughout the year?"

He sighed. "It's up to the counselling professional you are paired with to do as they see fit. I can't really make that recommendation. It's at their discretion." It sounded like he was reading from a memorized script.

I was incredibly tired and frustrated. I could potentially meet and be paired with a counsellor, only to have them tell me they will only meet with me once or twice. I was already being told that my problems weren't big enough. They were basically telling me to either come back with another problem, or when I was in a complete crisis. Only then would they help me, and send me on my way.

"I really need you to be able to describe one clear problem, and the steps towards resolution, or unfortunately your file won't have adequate information to be considered."

I just looked at him. I had nothing else to say and he knew it.

"We also have group therapy options that may be a good fit for you. There are groups of about eight students who workshop issues to address things they are dealing with. I also think that seeing a doctor for medication is a good option. If you have a chemical imbalance, there is only so much that psychotherapy can do, and having the medical intervention can also be helpful. Are you sure there isn't something I can put on the paperwork? Why are you really here Patricia?"

Yes—why? I felt like screaming back at him.

Oh yes, they could have stuck me in a group with eight other people, and I would use less of their valuable one-on-one time. Better yet, they could have offered a diagnosis and drugs. All about cutting costs, right? The doctor would see me, decide what was wrong, give me drugs, and I'm out of the way.

I looked at him with his notes out, computer screen blinking, waiting to try and process me through the system. I realized that this wouldn't work at all. He wanted me to beg.

I was a second away from crying or screaming, perhaps both. I mumbled something like, "this isn't for me," as I got up quickly and hightailed it out of the office. I rejected him before he could reject me. That's a lesson I keep learning—to pull away from people first.

He started to respond, but I was already out of his office. As I ran past the secretary, she tried to ask me if I need another appointment. Screw that. *Proactive.* Right. It was okay though. I was doing okay, and I didn't need them. I could never need them. I kind of regret not being more forceful, this wasn't my fault, I deserved help, but I really didn't think they knew how to help me.

CHAPTER 5

University fell into a basic rhythm and I got so busy with school projects and social outings that I eventually put that awful experience out of my mind. I went home for Thanksgiving weekend. I went out for coffee with one of the girls from high school. I had a nice, but quiet, visit with my parents. They asked the standard questions about school and what it was like living in Toronto. My parents and I already emailed each other once or twice a week, so there wasn't really much to share.

It was nice to have a chance to see my older brother, Todd. He works as a human rights lawyer at a non-profit organization that supported refugees. My parents applaud this and boast about it to their acquaintances. I mean, I think it's great work, too. I definitely don't have the personality to be a lawyer.

Todd is nine years my senior. The distance in years means that we didn't really grow up together. He felt more like my senior than my equal, and we skipped the sibling mischief and shenanigans. On occasion he was assigned as my babysitter when my parents went out on weekends. Since we both no longer live at home, our interactions now seemed to be more of an exchange between adults.

My parents went out on Saturday night, so Todd and I spent the night in. He asked me about my interest in journalism, and we talked about how much he enjoyed his work.

The conversation quickly switched to new friends, and I mentioned the connection I felt with Elyse. I also told him about Brittany, who to be honest I'm still not quite sure about. She's friendly, funny, and smart, but there was something about her that put me on edge. She seemed to have this need to compete for attention, and she always had to be the best at whatever she, Elyse, and I were doing. Brittany really made me feel self-conscious for not drinking as much or sleeping with as many people.

Anyway, back to the conversation with my brother. He asked me about Kara, a girl who was in my introduction to journalism class that year. She's serious and reflective, and we spent a bit of time together outside of the classroom, though she's fairly busy between school, a part-time job, and living with her boyfriend. It was nice to spend time with Todd. There's a lot about me that Todd didn't know. He left home when I was pretty young, so he missed the details of my teenage life. Things like depression and anxiety weren't talked about in our family, so I tried to hide these things as best as I could. In a way I wished we were more open, but talking about serious subjects was hard when you've been raised to only talk about the surface things. Religion, politics, sex, and health didn't make for good dinner conversations.

It was a display of uncharacteristic openness when Todd told mom he was gay. I only knew this because I was walking towards the kitchen when I heard them talking. I will admit that I lingered, hidden in the hall. When he revealed his secret, mom sighed in response and made some statement about how weird it would be at Christmas dinners. They sat in an awkward silence. No other negative comment was made, but there was also no display of acceptance. Todd left home a day early from his visit that year. I assumed my mom passed the message to my father. Todd didn't visit home again for a few months, and our parents' relationship with him was overly formal and polite for the next year or so. Eventually things returned to *normal*, but it was very clear that any further discussion of Todd being gay was unwelcome. They very rarely acknowledged John, my brother's fiancé. The country club gossip would have to focus on Todd's successful career as a lawyer, and not his love life. I was pretty young when all of this happened, so we never talked about it.

I took the bus back to the city at the end of the weekend. Later that week Brittany and Elyse came over to hangout and watch a movie. Elyse started to talk about her holiday as she rearranged my pillows.

"It was really nice to see my family. I'm glad I went home, but now the wait until the Christmas holiday is going to be even harder. I got to spend a day with my grandparents, which was nice. My grandma is eighty-nine and——" she was cut off by Brittany.

"I went shopping in the States with my mom. She bought me this designer bag, she wanted to buy the knock off, but I convinced her the real label was worth the extra two hundred dollars. Oh and she got me these shades…"

"What about you, Patty? How was your visit? Did you get to see your brother?" Elyse inquired.

"I'll be right back, I just need to use the washroom." I slipped out and headed down the hall.

When I came back Elyse was still sitting on my bed, but Brittany was hovering over my desk calendar. She looked at me, unashamed at having been caught snooping.

"So, how's counselling?" she asked with a bit of a smirk.

I was shocked. Did she actually want to know? Or was she just trying to find something to gossip about? Elyse didn't comment on the conversation, and when I shrugged in response Brittany didn't reply.

As we ate popcorn and watched the movie, my mind kept returning to the calendar. It was dumb of me to write something private in a visible place. But still, why did she need to look at my desk and comment? What did they think of me? I tried to tell myself that it was no big deal. They didn't know anything, and even if they did, I was sure they would accept me.

It's no big deal, I tried to reassure myself.

That night was the first night in months that I couldn't sleep. I lay in bed replaying the scene from the counsellor's office over and over, getting increasingly angry at the lack of support.

I need to make it through the school year, I reminded myself.

Then, I thought about Brittany's snooping and felt something towards her I couldn't quite place. Why did she need to spy? And what was with that comment? And why did Elyse say nothing? Is she trying to remain on good terms with Brittany? Did she think that I should be the one to defend myself?

I was probably over-reacting. My peers and family used to tell me that I needed thicker skin. That was back in elementary school, before I learned how dangerous it was to express my feelings.

I eventually fell asleep, but I woke a few times in the night. I dreamt that Elyse, Brittany and I were in the counsellor's office.

CHAPTER 6

his isn't a love story.
Even if it starts out as me explaining the story of how I fell in love. But that, that story didn't last for long. I can tell you all the ways my experience of falling in love was unique, but in reality my story may just be part of one universal fall.

Derek is the name of the guy with the golden dreads from my philosophy class. I silently watched him for weeks. I promise I'm not a creep. He mainly kept to himself and often doodled as the professor spoke. Derek occasionally took part in the class discussion, making a comment or starting a debate that went beyond the intellectual level of most people in the first year class. Unlike some of the other students, it didn't seem like he was trying to show off. Derek's comments often resulted in an excited response from the professor, which would start a conversation that I gave up trying to follow. Later, I replayed what Derek said in class, trying to make sense of it.

One day, their conversation diverged from the meager introductory course content to a debate about whether ethics are universal or relative. They started talking about ethics in relation to culture, and whether it was justifiable to apply universal, as in Eurocentric ideas about gender relations, to all cultures.

They discussed female circumcision and whether it was violence, or a cultural rite of passage. Did we really have the right to intervene and critique this practice, or was the Western response based on our different ideas about sexual liberation? Derek argued both sides, so it was hard to tell what he believed, but I could tell the professor was impressed by his contributions.

The lecture was drawing to an end, and most of the class ceased to pay attention. The professor returned to the discussion of Plato, along with Socrates and Aristotle, as being one of the founding fathers of Western philosophy.

The professor cleared his throat and said, "Work in groups of two or three, and using Plato's text, explain in simple terms what he was saying. Formulate a response to his ideas, and consider the modern relevance and application of the text. The response should be three to five pages in length, using only your own ideas."

I thought it didn't seem too difficult until my classmates began to shuffle around in search of people to work with. I hadn't talked to anyone in that class. I normally arrived to lecture just on time and stretched my legs during the break, avoiding social contact with my peers. Great, I thought as everyone began to find groups. No one seemed to notice me, and everyone around me was partnered.

I noticed that Derek was just sitting at his desk, looking relaxed and making no effort to find a group. I wondered what it'd be like to work with him. I'm shy; I couldn't just go up to the smartest guy in the class. He would probably think my ideas were stupid. The project would have been easy to do alone.

"Remember, the purpose of this assignment is collaboration, sharing ideas with classmates, and experimenting with co-writing a paper. When you have a group, come to the front and I'll assign you a piece of Plato's text to work with," the professor coughed.

I decided to approach the professor to see if I could work alone. Derek looked at his surroundings as I walked by, as if suddenly realizing he was alone for the assignment.

In a low voice he asked me if I'd like to work with him.

I paused for a second, unsure that he had actually spoke. We quickly introduced ourselves, as if I didn't know who he was. I tried to appear calm, rather than both flustered and excited even though I didn't quite understand why.

We were assigned Aristophanes' Speech from Plato's Symposium and agreed to meet Saturday afternoon at the library to write the paper. We exchanged email addresses and parted ways, having spoken few words, but said what is necessary.

I wondered what talking with him one-on-one would be like. Would his references confuse me like they often did in class? Would I have anything to say, or just feel stupid and like he could have written the paper easier without me? What if he totally forgot to show up and I'm left waiting in the library? Would he think I was awkward or strange?

Relax Patricia, this is just a small class assignment and you know nothing about this guy, why are you so concerned with what he thinks? Despite telling myself this, I read Aristophanes' speech several times and wrote detailed notes before the meeting, hoping I would have something worthwhile to say.

The speech turned out to be about a myth on the origin of love. There was once three genders—male, female and androgynous. Each person's body was double in size, with two heads, two pairs of arms, etcetera. Because of this, humans became too powerful and threatened the Gods. In order to weaken the humans, the Gods split them in half. After this, people longed for their other half and searched the earth for it. When they found their missing piece they were filled with love and they clung to each other, eventually dying of hunger. Pitying them, Zeus moved their genitals so they could be united through sex. If people failed to obey the Gods, Zeus could separate them once more from their other half as some kind of punishment.

I sat, waiting for Derek in the library. I tapped my pen against the desk, my heart pounding in my chest.

Looking back, I realized I was in over my head before he even walked into the library. I was this lonely, bored girl. Derek just appeared as this character—this fantasy—and he excited something in me I didn't even know was there. He became this, this unhealthy obsession. I won't let it happen again, I promised myself that now. My heart can't survive another Derek, or me becoming that person I was when I was with him.

Anyway, I had my notebook and wrote a few ideas about the narrative of monogamy and soul mates. I scribbled something else about love being used as a controlling force. In every story we tell about love, love and power seem to be closely weaved.

I really don't know what to think about the whole "soul mates" thing. I guess it's a nice idea, but that's it. It doesn't make sense that one person was put on earth just for me and that we'll complete each other. Yeah, right. There are just so many random factors to take into account that led to one existing in the first place. What if my parents didn't meet, or decided not to have children? And with so many people in the world what are the chances of stumbling into "the one," unless the earth is supposed to have some magnetic pull that somehow drives us to the other? According to Aristophanes' speech, people have just one other half—not two or three.

I don't know. I don't really believe in fate; I'm trying to be a realist. I don't even know if I believe in love either, for that matter. *Side note for later—fuck love.*

When I say I'm not sure if I believe in love, I really mean love for people like me. The table I sat at in the library was some kind of old laminated wood with generations of lovers' names etched into it. I saw things like this all over my high school, too, but never saw my name.

I looked at the clock. He was supposed to be here ten minutes ago. Where could he be? I hoped he was still coming. I began to anxiously play with the spiral ring of my notebook.

Derek walked into the library casually, nodding at me as he took a seat.

"Hey, how's it going?" He didn't acknowledge that he was fifteen minutes late.

"So, umm, so where should we start?" I asked.

"I actually did some writing on this before for an essay in high school. I'm looking forward to hearing your thoughts on the piece."

Just my luck.

No pressure, I thought to myself before speaking. "Well, it was interesting, but not meant to be taken literally. If it is meant as a universal message about love…well, many people don't have this

28

experience. I think few people are actually connected with their so-called other half...and people only have one? What if you meet them and don't really like the person, or they mistreat you, but you stay because you love them so much? I don't really like the pre-determined narrative of this story, but it's an interesting view of sex..." I started to go in circles, waiting for him to interject and spare me. The speech sounded silly when I read it by myself, but talking about it with him made it seem even more ridiculous. I knew it was only a myth and not meant literally, but still.

Derek's head tilted towards me as we spoke so we could hear each other over the other loud students. I was aware of his body beside mine, from his even breathing and slightly sweaty smell, to the swaying of his legs. I wondered when the last time he showered was. If he could smell my body, period, slight cramps, hormones pouring off my skin. I didn't want to talk about class anymore. I swallowed questions as my mind thought of more things to ask.

"It's a nice idea—other half-stuff, but I don't believe it. Maybe a few years ago, when I was more naïve, but life has a way of teaching you what's realistic and what's fantasy. How do you explain the idea of someone being in love and caring about a person one day, and then deciding to have no part in their life the next?" He paused for a second. "If it went against human nature to leave our other half that the gods tore away from us, then present human action makes little sense."

He's talking about the text, I reminded myself.

The tale of a person who had already fallen, I'm to learn, but I'm getting ahead of myself again.

I was curious about his history, so I took the fragments that were given to me during our breaks from writing. I watched his hand and ink create words on the page. I tried not to stare at his tangled dreadlocks and ink covered skin. He was an exotic and erotic creature compared to the small town beings I was accustomed to.

When we finished working I started to put my stuff back in my bag, reaching for my pen and my notebook. I put on my jacket, not wanting to appear as though I was lingering. I was surprised when Derek didn't move.

"What other classes are you in?" he asked, looking up at me with his clear green eyes.

"Well, Intro to Journalism, English—"

"I'm in English, too. I guess I'm just in a different section than you are. At least I don't think I've seen you in my class."

"Must be." Surely I would have noticed him.

"What'd you make of English? I find the course a bit pointless. It touches on too many genres. It leaves little room to develop a love of literature or creative insight."

"Well, it's still pretty early in the program, so it's hard to say really. I love reading and literature in general, but I'm finding the poetry unit a bit dry. I can't really relate to it, but I'm looking forward to the short story and novel sections. Poetry just seems like it's about counting rhythms and greeting card mass produced sentiment."

"You don't like poetry?" he sounded surprised.

Derek—a fan of poetry?

Perhaps I just didn't *get* poetry.

"It's not something I can relate to, and for the life of me I just can't pay attention to the descriptions of love, roses, sunsets and anger…and trying to memorize rhyme schemes. A, b, a, b, or what have you…" I was frustrated at myself for trailing off. I felt clumsy, my mouth tripping over words. I couldn't articulate my defense.

"What are you doing tonight?" he asked.

My heart pounded and my stomach twisted.

Relax, Patricia, he's just being friendly. I can smell my blood; I can feel my pulse coursing through my entire body, into the old wooden table.

"I have no plans yet, but I might meet up with some of my girlfriends," I responded, hoping to sound like I had a life and also to hide my surprised by the question.

"If you want to understand and appreciate poetry you need to *experience* poetry, not just read it on paper. You need to actually *hear* the words spoken to embody the emotion—to hear the poet's articulation and presentation of their text…"

"Yes," I said, acknowledging that I heard him. I wanted him to continue.

"I'm going to a spoken word event tonight and you're welcome to come. That is, if you feel like it." The invitation sounded casual, like he was just throwing it out there. Given my availability and comments about poetry, I figured he was expecting a *yes*.

I found myself in the library washroom a few minutes later, wondering if that conversation had really just happened.

And so, I met up with him later that night. Heart pounding and hands sweaty, I was tempted to turn around and tell him I was sick. So excited I was nervous, or so nervous I was excited.

What can I tell you about that first evening I spent with Derek? I can't separate what part of the experience was him, and what was the energy——the enchantment of the poetry.

I worried that I would feel awkward, uncomfortable, and undereducated. You know the times when your tongue feels clumsy and you are tripping over the words in your mouth? And what if all the evening revealed was that Derek and I were two strangers doing a dance that made no sense, unable to find shared language? Or maybe we would realize we felt strange around each other, and not the good kind of strange.

But the evening was easy and conversation flowed. Words slipped from my head and into the air and, Derek enthusiastically responded to my comments before I realized I'd spoken. I listened to his beautiful voice—deep, yet soft, and scratchy yet somehow smooth. The word, "fuck" punctuated his intellectual ideas and musing about embodiment. But this sounded natural from his mouth, like it was the only way in the world to speak. He had a language of his own. Some of the words he used would float over my head. I was utterly transfixed. I felt like I had arrived at a destination that I didn't even know I was looking for.

And in that moment, I felt like I was enough.

And in that moment I knew it was already too late. *Yes, I know how this sounds.*

A crowded room. Spotlights. A stage. The smell of beer and sweat. The incredible experience of collective energy. People bumped into one another, drinks spilled, but these weren't like the uncomfortable collisions of rushing bodies on a subway platform.

Rather, there was intimacy as people stood close to one another friends just some that had yet to meet.

Several people greeted Derek as he introduced me. I could feel the question mark that lingered at the end of our introduction, but no explanation was necessary. *Never explain yourself—right Alice?*

I watched, intrigued as each poet made their way to the stage and began to tell their story. The topics ranged from love and heartbreak, to politics and depression. Some were funny, but I liked the heavier ones—the dark ones, the real ones—the most. One person spoke of her experience struggling with depression and subsequent suicide attempts.

How easily it could all be over. That was a thought that had comforted me since my first day of high school—suicide ideation I think they call it.

The audience listened, respectful and quiet, snapping and nodding their heads in encouragement. I couldn't quite describe it, but the energy in the room was electric. Another person spoke of her experience of being raped. I could hear the pain in her voice. The crowd cheered for her, validating her anger and her story. Not that such an experience ever needed validation, but you know what I meant.

Here, private and socially isolated experiences took centre stage. Here, there was room for anger and frustration. I looked at the stage, trying to picture myself feeling entitled to occupy that space.

I could sense him beside me, watching for my reactions. We made eye contact a few times, and I shyly smiled and returned my eyes to the stage.

"Could you ever picture yourself up there?" he asked. "I was watching you and it seems like you are really enjoying this— like you are experiencing the words."

I was flattered by his apparent attention.

"Maybe, but I'm not quite sure it's for me. I don't know anything about spoken word, and I'm not sure I'd enjoy people watching me." I began to think about how anxious I'd feel standing on the stage, sharing my work with a room full of strangers. I didn't even have any work to share.

"What about you?" I asked, turning the conversation to him.

"Yeah, I've done my fair share of spoken word, and I love both listening and performing. I've been away from the city for a few years, so I'm still getting familiar with the scene here. It's an important space to talk about issues outside of academics. Reading about things like Canadian politics and gender equity in the newspaper and debating in academic journal articles is one thing, but actually taking this stage and engaging with narrative is completely different. Psychology textbooks may be able to tell you the science of depression, but here people can enter this space and feel empowered to tell their story——their narrative. To tell you the truth, I'm surprised I even came back to school…"

"What do you mean? About…about school?" I was eager for him to say more.

"Academics isn't really my thing," he paused, looking at me to see if I was still listening.

"Yeah, I know what you mean I think. It's all about showing that you can think in a very specific way, follow instructions, engage with a certain author's ideas, and don't move outside the box. Sometimes it's all just theory, and the real world gets lost," I responded, trying to get him to continue. I needed him to continue.

"Exactly, and it all just turns into this grand narrative about power and becomes really inaccessible. Take a look around; so many of the people on that stage are using it to tell their life stories. This is real and raw—an anger and a response that screams for equity—not just a debate about it." He tilted his chair towards me.

Here was this gorgeous man sitting across from me at the bar, talking about social justice and paying attention to me. I knew I had found someone special.

"You look really pretty tonight," he said, glancing at me as the show finished and people began to leave. Or maybe I just imagined him saying that. I wondered if he could smell me, sweaty from heat of the overcrowded bar. I felt moisture between my legs, but knew it was from my period. Bloody. *Alive*.

The night started as two classmates attending an event together, but by the end of the evening it felt like a date. I wasn't sure if it was a change in sentiment from Derek, or if it was just the magic of the evening and the energy of the poetry. We even stayed for a drink after the show.

As we exited the bar, I turned to say goodbye and started to walk away. With my heart fluttering, I lingered for a second too long...or perhaps just long enough, depending on the story I want to tell. We looked at each other and our lips met for a brief second.

"Goodnight, Patricia," he whispered. Then, he headed for the streetcar.

I stood on the corner for a second, wondering if I had imagined the kiss.

Looking back, perhaps I couldn't find the perfect words to describe him because there was always a glimmer of the surreal——of magic——in our interactions. I felt like if I touched him, even as he stood in front of me he may disappear and simmer into dust. Someday my hand would reach for him, and I'd realize he was never really there in the first place. I'd be left with empty fingers grasping at air. Forgive me as I fumble to describe this man. I know I am tedious at times——a bit too dreamy mixed with whiny. You don't need to like me, but please...just listen.

I waited for the streetcar alone. The street was vacant as people stayed warm inside the bars and restaurants. The news announces shootings on that corner fairly often, but that night all I heard was silence. I've been told that empty streets they too have ghosts.

CHAPTER 7

I was so intrigued by Derek that I sought to collect the bits of his story.

I know, I was obsessed from the start and that gave him this weird power over me. I never said I was innocent in this.

I mentioned him to Kara one day as we sipped tea after class. She didn't personally know Derek, but still, she knew, *of him*, so to speak.

"He's a few years older than us. I guess he did some travelling and soul searching after high school. I hear he parties a lot, drinks a lot, and that he's bad news. But you can't believe everything you hear, can you? I'm really happy for you, if you are happy that is…but be careful," she warned.

"Thanks, and I'll be careful. I'm probably…I'm probably getting ahead of myself. I don't know if he likes me, and I haven't seen him since the poetry night. It's just that he's still on my mind. I know how that sounds, but there's just something about him…" I find myself talking about him when I didn't want to. Shut up Patricia.

"I know the type—out there, creative, strong, free bird, intriguing, almost magical. But really, watch yourself, those are the dangerous ones. If you want safe, stick with boring. I know that sounds bad, but it's the truth," she offered.

"Thanks for understanding. But don't worry about me, I'll be careful. How's Adam?" I asked, inquiring about her boyfriend. Did she find him safe and boring? Of course I'd never actually say that.

Later that day, I ran into Brittany. She was sitting underneath a tree, enjoying the autumn day, with a textbook open on her lap. She was flipping through her music, apparently lost in a daydream. She looked up as I said, "hi," and motioned for me to sit.

"What's new with you?" she asked.

"Nothing much, I'm just heading back from class." I was careful not to mention the night with Derek. I was hesitant to share other intricate details of my life after the incident where she outed me about the counsellor.

The awkward gaps in the conversation spoke for itself. I made an excuse and continued on my walk.

During a break from homework the next night I knocked on Elyse's door. It was easy to drop by friends' rooms unannounced when you lived in a dorm. Elyse greeted me at the door with a tube of mascara in her hand, holding it like a wand.

She smiled at me and exclaimed, "Patricia, I'm so glad you came by! I was disappointed when Brittany said you were too busy with assignments to go out tonight. Did you decide to ditch the homework? Personally, I think we're more fun than some dead, old theorists."

At first I was confused, and then realized what happened. I went along with it, pretending that I declined the invitation and that I was actually too busy with schoolwork. I was embarrassed and frustrated that Brittany excluded me, but I really didn't feel like starting a conflict, so I just let it go. I didn't like to go where I'm not wanted.

"I better get back to my homework, and leave you to getting ready," I said, and hurried back to the safety of my room.

I'm sure Elyse was confused by my brief visit, but that was okay. I just needed to be alone. I sat at my desk for a long minute and thought about everything. My mind lapsed into memories of high school, but this was different. I was in a new space with new friends. It was a new chapter, so to speak. I couldn't repeat what happened before…I just couldn't.

I closed my eyes, letting the memories of hurt wash over me for a minute before trying to bring myself back. So what if Brittany didn't like me? She was one person, and at least I realized this before becoming better friends with her. But, despite trying to control it, my mind could not and would not rest. The voices of the bullies from high school continued to weigh on me. What if Brittany thought I was awkward, boring, or stupid…was that why she went out of her way to exclude me? Did I even care what she thought?

I spent so much time trying to keep everything together, putting all the little details of my life in boxes. Sometimes the walls I try so hard to build come crashing down and everything gets tangled…things like the past and present, realistic fears, versus the ones I imagine, unable to tell the difference. Sometimes everything is just too real——too raw. Some people could just brush things off like they are of no consequence, but for me things are heavy. Things stay with me. The past isn't always something that stayed in the neatly marked container I tried to place it in.

I went over to my kitchenette, put on the kettle, and opened my homework.

Concentrate, I told myself. I looked at the syllabus for my journalism class. The next assignment was rather simple. I had to pick a topic, find a local expert and interview them. Then, record the interview and present it to the class. I had no problem finding topics I'm interested in, or doing background research. Interviewing someone might be okay, if I was really prepared. But presenting this to my classmates? The pain in my stomach and chest reminded me that this exceeded my comfort zone.

Relax Patricia, one thing at a time. But the more I thought about it, the more I questioned my decision to study journalism.

I enjoyed asking questions, always wanting to understand the *why* and how about the workings of the world. I loved writing and telling stories. But was I really prepared to make a living talking to people? I was okay if I had time to think of responses, or was comfortable with a person, but being put on the spot made me anxious.

I'm in the wrong program. Seriously, why did I pick a career that involved interacting with people?

You aren't giving yourself enough credit. I tried to respond to the doubting voice in my head. *I just need to make it through this school year. I can easily change programs later. I just need to make it through this year.*

I just wanted to find my old sleeping pills. They would keep me under for the day in miserable, half-lucid dreams. I wouldn't be able to stay awake, but I also wouldn't be able to properly sleep either…but I would still be alive, so that was something.

My legs couldn't move. I couldn't get dressed because my arms were heavy. My eyes were swollen and vacant from crying. They scared me when I accidently caught a glance of myself in the mirror.

If you've experienced depression you are likely nodding beside me, and if you haven't…well, I doubt you'd get it. You would probably just tell me to, "go for a walk." It's bullshit when people say things like that. Only those who have been where I am could know what it's like. Anyone else doesn't fucking get it. And they shouldn't pretend like they do.

I woke to the sound of my alarm clock, but I closed my eyes and lay as still as possible. Sleep tempted me to return to its oblivion, but I wasn't tired. I was nothing. I wasn't sure how long I lay still before getting up and turning off my alarm.

These waves of depression left me feeling like my body was an alien. This was not the body that I inhabited yesterday. My stomach would growl, but I'd feel little responsibility for my body. The cry of my stomach seemed far away—a detached part of me. I knew in theory I should eat. Any thought of trying to move my heavy legs, of standing, of walking across my room, of going to the washroom, of pouring cereal, and trying to eat the cereal as it became dry paste in my mouth was exhausting. I couldn't. Eating seemed impossible. Something so easy was completely out of my reach.

It was almost nice——this lack of caring, a cure for the constant flood of thoughts and anxiety that invaded my body.

I rolled over and looked at the clock. If I was going to make it to my class on time I needed to be out of bed in the next twenty minutes. There was no way I was going. This would be the first class that I missed. While yesterday, the idea of skipping class would've seemed like a big deal today it was of no consequence. There was only right now and this space where I had no motivation to do anything, except perhaps keep breathing and keep still.

Later they'd ask if I wanted to die—I don't have energy for that either.

Midafternoon, I got up to eat. I went for something simple since I didn't have the energy to consume food, let alone prepare it. Food was life and pleasure, and when I was in a state of lifelessness, the idea of eating food that was exotic, complex, or even unhealthy, lost its appeal. I had little desire to lift my head from the pillow; the idea of anyone ever eating something dripping in grease like pizza was absurd. *Maybe you understand.*

I decided on toast. Dry. Eating this in a better state was unthinkable. I sat with my plate in my bed, slowly picking at the dry lump, willing myself to swallow bite after bite. I left the crust. I chased the toast down with tap water that somehow seemed stale.

When that task was completed, I decided that maybe I'd feel better if I got dressed. I took my pyjama pants off and started to dig through my drawers for jeans.

What was the point in getting dressed? It wasn't like you were going anywhere today.

I gave up, and in my underwear I curled into the fetal position. I spent the rest of the day drifting in and out of sleep.

Indifferent.

Immobile.

Almost comfortable.

CHAPTER 8

Derek was friendly in philosophy class, but made no mention of Saturday. I started to wonder if I imagined our "almost date." I was hoping that we'd spend more time together outside of class, but I didn't want to impose. I know, I know, just go for it, girls don't need to wait for guys this century. But still, I didn't know if the date was a onetime thing that came about because of the poetry and the beauty of the night. If we spent more time together would we have anything to talk about beyond school? Kara implied that he was a bit rough and worldly. I hoped he didn't view me as naïve and simple against the backdrop of his life.

Sorry, I know I already told you this, it's just important. People tell me I say sorry a lot, so I should probably stop. But I *am* sorry. I'm sorry I'm sad. I'm sorry I'm in the way. I'm sorry, I'm sorry, I'm sorry.

I spent the next few days thinking about whether I should ask him to do something, but my thoughts never evolved into actions. I pulled out my phone and composed texts to Derek that I didn't send, erasing them, and writing them again.

Saturday morning I was surprised to find an email from him that invited me to a concert at a local bar. One of his friends was playing, and he and a few others were going.

When Saturday came, I was introduced to his group of friends. I wasn't really sure if I was his date, but it was enough to be in his company.

We never talked about us; we just kind of fell together. Looking back, it's hard to even say how; it all seems so surreal. Sometimes I wonder if I imagined him. An odd pairing that never had a conversation about our romance, as if talking would somehow break the spell.

What do you want me to tell you? About poetry readings and late night debates at coffee shops? Or what about picnics in the park during the last crisp days of fall? We lay on a blanket, huddled together and drinking apple cider from a thermos in High Park, surrounded by a watercolour of falling leaves. We absorbed the last rays of autumn warmth, the sun glistened through the trees, and we looked like a happy couple from a magazine. Or, should I tell you about how we snuck into abandoned buildings, just to look around? That was me, always chasing forbidden stories that hid below the surface. Maybe I could be a journalist after all. Or, I could tell you about how we stayed in bed late on Sunday afternoons in the fall? He was a good partner at first, coming by with food, when he could tell just from my voice that I wasn't okay, and couldn't leave my room. He'd just come and be with me, I didn't need to do anything. We enjoyed each other's physical closeness, talking, sharing, and sometimes drifting back to sleep.

But don't let me distract you; this isn't a love story, but instead the prelude to chaos.

Sometimes I felt really stupid. Surely he'd go for a more interesting girl? Maybe one of the girls in dark clothing, with black eyeliner and bodies like canvases covered in ink, and faces filled with holes from piercings. Intriguing girls. Ironically the ones that seemed most captivating were the ones that didn't need you at all; they didn't even want to know your name.

I tried to convince myself that I meant more to him than a simple placeholder. He asked my opinion on different subjects and seemed excited to hear the answer. Despite my fears, our conversations flowed easily. Our different experiences and worldviews merged together and his wisdom deepened my intellectual knowledge.

I'll admit I often measured my interactions with other people by how much they tire me. I'm not so much an introvert as I find being in certain people's presence exhausting. I actually have a time limit in my head for how long I can spend with people. Brittany for instance might be three hours; Elyse, perhaps a day. Having my guard up was my natural inclination with new people, but I easily relaxed with Derek. An entire weekend could slip by and I wouldn't feel the need to return to my isolated space to collect myself away from his company.

"There's an open mic night later this week at The Bar. The theme is Critical Responses to Mental Health. According to the poster, they're welcoming spoken word performances, music, and dance," Derek mentioned one day as we were having coffee after class. He had to raise his voice to be heard above the ruckus of the coffee shop.

"I'd like to go. When is it?" I responded. I was still eager to do anything with him.

"Saturday. Actually, I was thinking that maybe you'd be interested in performing?"

"I don't know. Performing isn't really my thing. Even if I want to it's only a few days away. There isn't much time, and I don't know what I'd say." Not to mention my thoughts on having an entire bar looking at me.

"I remember what you told me about your experience trying to access counselling. You have so many ideas about the mental health system; why not give it a shot?" He was both offering me a challenge and suggesting that I could do it. I saw the corners of his mouth twitch, an almost smile flirted across his face.

"I've seen how excited you get during the poetry events we've gone to, and I think you may really enjoy the opportunity to be on stage. I'm not telling you what to do, but if you feel inclined," he continued.

I responded to Derek's dare by writing a poem about the school's counselling policy. Normally prone to staying within my comfort zone, Derek had a way of understanding what I desired, and helped push me outside of my boundaries.

I met Derek outside The Bar on Saturday, and I told him that I wrote something. He whispered that he was proud, and put his arm around my shoulder. For a minute before we headed inside, I felt completely safe. My stomach twisted and turned at the thought of standing in bar full of people and sharing my "art." Derek had this calm manner, like he'd lived and experienced so much that the idea of stage fright seemed trivial. I wondered if anything was capable of making him anxious or angry; his stoic manner suggested that he somehow evolved to a space beyond these emotions.

His calm was the antidote to the rollercoaster I was on. I guess what they say about opposites attracting was true. Until I met Derek, I laughed at all the clichés about love, but there I was feeling like my brain had reduced itself to existing in terms of clichés and romantic movie lines.

My spoken word performance actually went rather smoothly. Derek coaxed me into performing when I was tempted to cross my name off the list. Time slowed as I made my way to the small stage, scraping chairs aside, squeezing my body as I navigated through the crowd, holding my breath. I exhaled when I reached the stage, as if my lungs in that instant learned to not need air. I scampered up the stairs, feeling even clumsier than usual and out of touch with my body as the room turned to watch me. On the stage, I felt both my legs and voice shake, and I wondered if people could understand anything I was saying. I reflected on my life and doubted myself in a way that only people who've made themselves vulnerable in a public space might understand. I completed my piece and people politely applauded. I was met by Derek's embrace.

"I knew you could do it," he whispered in my ear.

Despite the ease of our relationship, I sometimes questioned why Derek was with me. I know I already said some of this—I just wanted to get it all down, to help you understand. Not that you can understand. I wondered if I was exciting and worldly enough for someone like him. Was I just an experiment with dating the girl next door, serving as just another experience on his list of colourful adventures? On my good days these thoughts were silent, but during the times when anxiety shaped my every thought, I couldn't help but wonder…

You've probably been waiting to hear the *good stuff*, like if I was a virgin before I met Derek. Not that it's really any of your business, but I feel like sharing. I can see my mother flinching as I write this. I can hear her saying, "there are some things that are meant to stay behind closed doors, Patricia." I bet I'm one of the only girls in my high school that completely escaped an awkward sex talk with their mother. My parents trusted that the school would cover the safety aspects, and the rest was something that polite families just didn't talk about.

There really isn't much to tell you about *losing my virginity*. As if virginity is something you have that can be *lost*, like a misplaced wallet on the subway that can be found in the lost and found box. Whatever. I didn't fall for that romantic coming-of-age bullshit. Perhaps that's why I had trouble getting along with my high school peers.

Blake Serancio. He was in my eleventh grade biology class. We went on three or four dates, to the movies and ice-skating and such. After dating for a month or so, he invited me over to watch a movie when his parents were out of town. Prior to this, we kissed, and his hand awkwardly made its way to my breasts, unable to go further in the public space of a park. *Not that I was sure I wanted to go further. Not that I was sure I didn't want to go further.* You get what I mean.

After we watched the movie, he gave me a tour of the house that concluded in his bedroom. A well-planned tour destination, I assumed. He sat on his bed, and I joined him. He put his arms around me and touched my chin, pulling my face toward his. Instead of the passionate kiss he tried to create, our faces bumped, and we stumbled into each other. There isn't much to tell, it was no Harlequin Romance scene.

We pushed a pile of dirty laundry aside on his bed. Clothing got caught on glasses as shirts came off, we fumbled with belt buckles as if we were learning to get undressed for the first time. Excited by the opportunity, he was too rough with my body, twisting my nipples with his fingers, excessively using his teeth. His hands made their way up my legs, and when he found my clitoris he began to rub, but he applied too much pressure. I wanted to hurry up and have sex just to stop him from touching me. I thought about telling him to stop, or getting up and going home. His hands found my slit, and he inserted a finger, then two, but my body didn't respond to his presence, and his fingers felt uncomfortable against my dryness.

I can't believe I am telling you all of this.

"Are you sure you want to do this?" he asked as he fumbled with the condom wrapper and lube.

I nodded, and he slid inside me. The sex was unremarkable. I lay on my back, and he gave a few deep thrusts before he lost control. It wasn't particularly painful, and I didn't bleed, but it wasn't enjoyable either. My body was too unsure and tense about the new sensation to relax and enjoy the experience.

"Sorry, I didn't mean to finish, you just felt so good," he blushed.

We stayed there in a tired heap for a few minutes before I called my parents for a ride. We had sex three or four more times. It was a bit better, but I still didn't see what the big deal was. Our encounters were defined by hesitance and hiding from parents. About a month after we first had sex, he started seeing someone else and we stopped talking. I didn't really mind.

This all seems like so long ago now. Sex was marked in my memory as something that was okay, but not particularly special, or even enjoyable. I remained further untouched until I met Derek.

I'm not sure how much I should be telling you, but I trust you. And besides, I'm supposed to be a part of this generation of so called liberated females, so I suppose it's okay.

Derek lived off campus, and his place was our oasis. It was a small one-bedroom basement apartment. The lack of light made it a bit dreary, but the downtown location was ideal, and it was so nice to be off campus. Besides, I could never picture Derek crammed into a dorm room, being encouraged to go to group activities with the other first years. He was only a few years older, but I felt that his slow, thoughtful, yet optimistic view of the world could be lost in the misogynistic party residence culture.

Where was I? I've such trouble keeping track of what I'm telling you. Oh yes, Derek's apartment. It was cozy. It had a small kitchen, which we often found ourselves in, waiting for pots to simmer, or sitting and talking over a cup of tea. Derek learned quite a bit about food during his travels, and I enjoyed dishes with names I couldn't pronounce. I watched him throw spices I'd never heard of into bubbling pots. Always cooked from memory, never using paper or measuring devices for that matter, but his food was always delicious.

Derek claimed to be a minimalist, trying to only own necessities, but his apartment overflowed with items that reflected his interests. He had an extensive record and CD collection, and his walls were covered with music posters. In his small living room he had a large bookcase. The first time he invited me over he explained that he only bought books that really touched him in some way. Wandering around his apartment I felt like I was walking through a museum of Derek's life. The only thing missing was pictures. He only had one album of his travels, but the pictures were of places, not people. There were no photos of his former lovers, or his family for that matter. He also had quite the elaborate liquor cabinet. His place was messy, overflowing with artifacts, but still fairly clean. His furniture was used, but well taken care of. His decorations were colourful.

We were dating for two weeks or so when we found ourselves in his bedroom. Well, I saw his room the first time I was over, but you know what I mean.

My lack of experience was at the forefront of my mind, and I was worried that I would somehow disappoint him. I sensed that it was going to happen today, even before it started. He rubbed my shoulders, how cliché—I know. I relaxed into him, wanting the impossible—to be one with him. The entire experience was comfortable; I trusted him and felt safe. He slowly took my clothes off and admired my body, gazing at me as if I was some magnificent landscape, and he was seeing something other than what I see when I look in the mirror. Clothing was strewn on the floor. He slowly kissed my entire body, his lips gently brushed against my neck and breasts. Applying just enough pressure, and I melted into his skin.

His hand reached lower, but he stopped first and whispered, "may I?"

I nodded, and he found me dripping. I reached down and felt his hard cock underneath his jeans. He was thick against me, but I wasn't worried about it hurting. I unbuttoned his pants and reached inside. He helped me slide his pants down, and his shirt came off. I silently admired his body and stroked him as his hands continued to discover me.

I made little whimpering noises of pleasure that I didn't know I was capable of making. I closed my eyes not wanting to move.

"We don't have to go any further, if you don't want to. It's a privilege just to touch you," he whispered.

"I want you, Derek. Please," I responded. For once I knew exactly what I wanted. He moved his hands from my clit and continued to kiss my entire body. He gently brushed his lips against my neck, then my breasts, then stomach. I responded with little gasps of pleasure. I wondered how far he was going. My heart beat wildly, excited and nervous—a tangle of emotions, but excitement dominated. Looking down, I suddenly became conscious of my hair, and hoped that he didn't mind.

"Your body is beautiful," he whispered, as he looked at my pussy, and began to kiss my clit as he inserted his fingers. My head was against the pillow, legs open, fingers digging into his back, eyes squeezed shut with pleasure. He rubbed his hard cock gently against me and I bit my lip to stop myself from begging for him to slip it inside.

"Are you ready?" he asked, pulling back in order to look me in the eyes.

My mind had a flicker of doubt. He looked in his dresser for a condom as I waited. *What if I'm not as good as the other girls he's been with? What if I'm not loud enough or my face looks funny?* But I pushed aside any lingering worries and decided that this was about Derek and I.

The first thrust filled my entire body with pleasure that I can't begin to describe. We moved together slowly, yet brimming with excitement. We kissed, long lingering, forgetting everything else, even our bodies for a minute. Then we pulled back to look at each other. I watched his face as he moved, getting faster. I wanted Derek to be everywhere at once. I wanted him to go faster, but I didn't want it to be over. I know how this sounds, but I would've been perfectly happy with my life if that moment—that tangling of bodies—could have lasted infinity. And this wasn't just about the sex; this was about us being together.

I looked into his eyes. His face was so serious and concentrated on our movements. I pulled him closer, and felt my muscles tighten on his cock and a rush of sensation that I couldn't quite describe, and I was greedy for more. I lost track of time.

"I'm close," Derek murmured as I lay quivering, having come a second time. "Is it okay if I come?" he asked. I watched Derek's expression of pure pleasure, as he let go. He gently kissed me on the lips and we held each other.

We lay there, naked bodies dripping with sweat, perfectly content. I finally understood what all the sex talk was about. I relished in the afterglow, feeling high from my experience of bodily pleasure and amazed that I could feel that way. We eventually drifted to sleep, and I woke the next morning to sunshine streaming in his window, and Derek at my side.

I could tell you of the weeks that followed after that first night, of goodnight kisses and massages, snuggling together in the morning. I could tell you about being half-awake and rolling over and him reaching for me as he whispered, "you're beautiful." Or what about the times when I was bleeding, and I told him "it's ok," but he still wanted to make me feel good.

I could tell you of our evolving sex life, how I kept thinking this was it—this was the best experience of my life, but then the next time we made love, or whatever you want to call it, it was somehow better than the last. Our nakedness went beyond the physical. We embraced our so-called flaws. He revealed the stories behind some of the scars that covered his arms. I asked about his tattoos, and he told me of distant places and his friends who were tattoo artists and had helped to sculpt this body that I loved. Our bodies became familiar; we were no longer ashamed of our noises, our smells.

This is bliss, and on this journey that I'm on, it was a high that I know couldn't last. This paradise, it just had to fall. *Otherwise, I wouldn't have much of a story for you, would I?* None of us would really have a story. Who wants to read about happily ever after, more like happily never after? Best-sellers and hit radio songs are made of pain. Heartbreak is the only real universal experience.

Sometimes he did oil paintings, making canvases come alive with landscapes of places I've never been. The paint splattered his clothing, but he didn't mind, and he went out with drops of green and orange on his pants and hands stained purple. He enjoyed the comforts of home with a book or paintbrush in hand, but was also restless, hands tapping, legs swinging. Always ready to travel, never content in one place. I should have realized—realized he wasn't looking for a travel buddy.

How do I describe him? Interesting, compelling, inspiring, daring. This magical creature represented the potential for a different world, an alternative way of thinking, being, becoming. The fact that he existed at all—this, loving, open-minded soul— made me think that maybe there was some good in this world, or order to this universe. I can't quite get this description right; maybe you need to place a hand on him to understand this—this energy about him, to look him in the eyes and experience it somehow. And those eyes—light and present or dark and vacant. Inviting, loving, scary, terrifying—gone.

I guessed part of the problem was that I idealized him. How were we ever to be equals, when he fulfilled my fantasy if only for a minute? I never intended to fall for him. I just realized that it was happening, and that I was on an irreversible path. I was swept downstream by a current and I was too weak to swim, or perhaps I didn't want to.

Derek knew how to push back, to ask questions of people and situations, to challenge social convention, but still somehow conform just enough to get by. You know, there are rules about how to break the rules. He was popular without trying to be, as if he didn't intentionally create his following of friends. Derek seemed to value his space and independence, so he was left with balancing his popularity and trying to retain this wall of solitude. He was extremely intelligent, but not snobby, and despite my different life experiences, I always felt that I could relate.

He was a bit wild at heart, a free spirit, beautiful chaos. This was why I loved him, and this is why I knew I shouldn't. Just living in the moment. His very existence was a footnote reading: *sooner or later I'll break your heart*. It wasn't a question. It was a promise.

Derek was somehow light and heavy at the same time. He was never someone to take tomorrow for granted, so to speak. Sometimes, he acted as if actions had no consequences. He enjoyed bodily pleasures, food, sex, and recreational drugs. Tomorrow for him was just another philosophical concept. He taught me to be grateful for the present. To feel more, talk less. To be. I learned more from him about life and being myself than I did in the classroom that first semester of university. Then again, he cost me far more than the price of tuition for that first term. I know it sounds like I'm memorializing him while writing this down...this character in my history.

He was carefree, but at the same time he had this serious demeanour, never smiling. His presence was paradoxical, suggested that one could be jaded and playful at the same time. His extra indulgence was to offset the hopelessness and insignificance he experienced against the larger picture of world events. Sometimes he made vague references to pain, to struggle, and it seemed that he had already lived, and I could not help but wonder who or what already broke him. A girl, I was to later learn. *It's always a girl.* But I could never ask for his story unless he was willing to share. Stories are the most expensive things to ask of another.

I was careful not to show how much I cared because, like an injured bird, I didn't want him to feel trapped and take off. But still, I think he knew. I remembered the first time he told me he missed me. I was away for the weekend to visit my brother, and I was surprised when he sent me a text saying that he couldn't wait to see me, and that he missed me. I thought maybe, just maybe, he was safe to miss.

I know it sounds like I'm rambling, but I wish I could make you understand what a man he was, but I'm afraid he was better with words than I am. I can picture you rolling your eyes at my description, as I do now when I think back to Derek. Perhaps you'll never understand what I saw in him, but that's okay.

To outsiders, we may have seemed like an odd pairing. He was worldly, giving off the faint aroma of sweat and almost earthiness from his dreadlocks. I wondered what girl made them, whose hands played with that hair, delicately weaving the strands together. And then there was me, the girl who would make a good movie extra—background material. I was plain, pale face, average build, and fuzzy brown hair. An anxious, sad, and directionless small-town girl. Awkward, shy, but somehow resilient, eager to become more. Even though he was only a few years older than me, his face seemed aged by his experiences. My education resulted in an arrangement of facts and logic. Book smarts, so to speak. His intellect and thoughtfulness was in part informed by his travels and whatever else his life had involved. There was still so much I didn't know. Will never know.

He referred vaguely to his world exploration with a story here and there, offering fragmented memoires, but was careful to never create a coherent map. He'd list the continents he'd travelled, and maybe the countries, but he never answered when I asked about the cities he'd lived in, leaving spaces as big as countries to represent the void of his story. Maybe he didn't think I was worthy of his story, or perhaps he didn't want to make himself vulnerable as he fumbled over the details of his life.

I got the impression that a girl was with him during his travels. *The girl*. but I never clarified, partly because I felt that I'd be prying, and in part because I didn't want to know.
Sorry if I'm a bit vague when I speak of Derek. My memory of him is starting to grow faint, something I never thought I'd say. It's embarrassing really looking back at how caught up with him I was. I don't care to remember some of the details. I know how I sound—infatuated, whiny and insecure, but you don't need to like me. You just need to listen. When I try and think of him late at night, I lose my words. He feels outside of the realm of linguistics. I struggle to capture the words for all the emotions he made me feel, most of which don't have names. I read somewhere about the limits of the English language: too few words to describe feelings. Yes, perhaps I'll blame this struggle I'm having on the confines of the English dictionary.

CHAPTER 9

Decomber arrived cold, snowy and without my permission. It felt like the first day of school had just passed, yet suddenly my calendar was full of end of term assignments and exams.

I saw Elyse and Brittany less as the term continued. Elyse tried to contact me, but I didn't feel at ease with the two of them. Again, this might be my self-confidence issues and depression. Elyse and I got together once in December. She was pretty busy, and started dating some new guy and working at a coffee shop. Kara and I talked sometimes over tea after class, but the winter and workload made social opportunities less frequent.

I tried to get to know more people in my residence building. Aashi was kind and seemed interested in my life, but it was hard to decide how sincere she was when interacting with me was part of her job. She came by with flyers for events, and I attended a few. I joined the other first year students in our residence recreation room for an ice-cream sundae one afternoon, and another time for a movie night. I tried to be friendly with my peers, but everyone showed up in small groups and seemed more interested in free food than getting to know each other. Sitting by myself and trying to interact with half-interested people caused me anxiety. I stopped trying to make more friends. Besides, with school I didn't have much spare time, and I felt that I had little to contribute to their conversations about who got how drunk last night, and what colour hair dye stayed in longest. I was alienated from first year flip-cup and beer pong Friday night culture, and Sundays filled with sweat pants, greasy hangover food and rushed essay writing. I didn't belong there. It was okay though, I just needed to make it through the academic year, do well and get my credits. I reminded myself of this daily.

One day, I noticed brightly coloured posters for a group workshop about how to handle anxiety plastered on the walls of my residence floor. Anxiety and depression still defined my life, but I had long since given up hoping for external help. It was now just a matter of focusing on my survival. Some days the goal wasn't happiness or productivity, but continued existence. It was trying to grasp onto something solid when the ground felt like it was moving, and the world was fluid and slipping through my fingers. I was living my life five minutes at a time, just waiting for time to pass. Just because I wasn't always talking about my health issues didn't mean they weren't there. Anyway, what I'm trying to tell you is that I signed up for the workshop.

It was a Saturday afternoon—the first week of December. It was led by two residence dons in the recreation room. They started by saying some pretty generic stuff about dealing with anxiety that I could have easily found online. Then they handed out giant sheets of paper and magic markers. We were to work in groups and talk about recent causes of our anxiety, and together brainstorm how to address it. My peers talked about the stress they felt around exams, and ways of dealing with this stress like healthy eating, exercising and good sleeping habits.

Before my last exam, I was awake all night. I know I needed sleep, but I watched the minutes pass. My body felt physically sick with worry. My stomach hurt and my head was heavy. My mind was stuck in this loop about failure that no logic and reasoning could overcome. Relax, you did well in the class, it's just an exam. But doing well on the exam was connected to succeeding at school. Succeeding at school proved that I made the right choice in coming here. If I didn't do well then I would be reinforcing my parents' doubt about me leaving home, and my peers' comments about me being a failure. If I was supposedly a nerd and I couldn't even do well at school then what did that make me? Derek seemed to do well without really trying. What would he think if I just scraped by? What if he knew how much time I spent studying and worrying, when he treated school as an afterthought and still did well? I was seriously losing it. The next morning I was too sick to eat, my head was fuzzy and I wrote the exam in a half-awake haze, and I had no idea how I did.

All of this is to say that I didn't find the workshop particularly helpful. The other students talked about exams, and financial stress, but I didn't feel like I could talk about my problems as they talked about theirs. I'm not saying that their anxiety wasn't important—but just that once more I was an outsider. This reminded me of when I tried to arrange for personal counselling, and well, we know how well that went. But being around Derek helped with my anxiety and depression. He was so calm and supportive that I felt grounded. I couldn't imagine my first term at school without Derek.

Between school, work, and Derek, I rarely left the downtown core. I just moved between classes, residence, Derek's apartment, and whatever bar, park, or restaurant we found ourselves at. The city was still largely a stranger to me; the transit system remained a mystery. I was confused when people referenced local history, or talked about certain neighbourhoods, as if I was supposed to understand the significance of housing developments in Regent Park, or a shooting somewhere else. It was okay though, I was content with my little life—with school and Derek.

It was the beginning of December when Derek brought me to a Christmas party. It was a big party. People scattered throughout the small house, trying to find space to sit or stand, as they exchanged friendly smiles and bumped into each other. The party was held by some guys that he knew from a local pub.

"Hey, buddy, it's good to finally see you!" one of the longhaired hosts exclaimed, giving Derek a quick hug.

"Yeah, you too! Sorry it's been so long. You know school, it's kept me pretty busy." Derek shrugged.

"Hey, no problem, I get it. Or is it this one over here who has been keeping you so busy?" he commented, putting his arm around me.

"Oh, I'm sorry. Ben, this is Patricia. Patricia, this is Ben," Derek hurried through introductions.

"Nice to meet you," Ben said, just as someone came and pulled him away mentioning something about a beer spill on the rug.

I actually found myself having fun. Most people were busy talking, so the need to make small talk with strangers dissipated. There were sweets and a few people brought instruments and played Christmas songs. It was a joyous environment, and like most Christmas parties there was lots of drinking. One of the other hosts stumbled up to Derek. From the smell of alcohol on his breath, and loud voice, it seemed he was having a good night.

"There you are, Derek! Ben told me you were here. Is that what's her name with you? Amanda, is that who you're seeing? Or is it Lindsey? I can never keep up with you. You're the man! So how've you been?" He didn't wait for Derek's response between questions. I shouldn't have been standing there, but he clearly didn't notice me, so in a way I was safe. I wished I was invisible, but in this moment I kind of was. I was the girl on the crowded subway platform who no one noticed.

"I'm pretty good, thanks. I've been busy with school. And this is *Patricia*," Derek put extra emphasis on my name.

"Oh right, Patricia, nice to meet you. Never mind me, I'm a bit drunk and I can never keep anything straight. By the way, I'm Morgan."

For the rest of the night, I was tempted to ask Derek about his dating history, but I didn't. It wasn't my business. I wondered about *the one that got away*, which he hinted at but never really talked about; a ghost, she shaped his thoughts and feelings, but remained nameless to me.

I forced myself to focus on the party and I had a few drinks. As the crowd slowly cleared, the music was now quiet enough to easily speak. Derek had been drinking since we arrived. I watched the alcohol slowly shape his behaviour. He was happy, laughing and singing along with the musicians, his serious demeanour left behind by the buzz. He was talking about his experiences travelling, skipping all over the place in comparison to the normally logical flow of his words. Derek went to stand from his place on the couch, and Ben stood beside me as we watched Derek lose his balance. A few people took note. I didn't know what to say.

"I think you've had enough, buddy," Ben quietly commented to Derek.

"What are you talking about, man? I'm just having a good time, along with everyone else, just stood-up too fast s'all."

The evening continued as Derek downed some more shots.

"How are you getting home?" Ben inquired, turning to me. A few other people looked in our direction as Derek hummed Christmas carols to himself, oblivious to his surroundings.

"We're going back to Derek's apartment. It's only a fifteen minute walk from here, but I'm not, I'm not really sure if walking is still an option," I said, a bit embarrassed.

"Whatcha talking about? Why aren't we walking? We walked here—it's not far." Derek was suddenly paying attention.

"Get a cab. It's not far, so it'll be cheap," Ben suggested. Morgan, who was standing near us, nodded in agreement.

"What the hell are you guys talking about? I'm fine."

Derek barely made it to the bathroom before he was puking. After a while, I went to check on him. He was half-conscious, slumped on the floor beside the toilet. I made sure he was on his side and left. Ben called us a cab.

When Derek stumbled from the bathroom, he confronted Ben, "thanks a lot for calling a cab on me bro, but I'm fine, I can walk. You should really mind your own business Ben." I called goodbye and apologized to Ben and Morgan as Derek slammed the door.

"I'm done hanging out with those guys. I go out of my way to see them, and that's how I'm treated? Fucking assholes! You should see how much Ben normally drinks!"

I just nodded my head in agreement, realizing there was no point in discussing the matter in his present state. I was a bit startled by his burst of anger. I'd only seen Derek happy, relaxed, or indifferent; I hadn't heard him raise his voice before, and surely not when someone was trying to help.

"And why did you thank Ben and say sorry to him, what the hell was that?"

It was a long night.

The next afternoon, I was still feeling a bit off from staying up most of the night with an uncooperative Derek. I saw Elyse in the laundry room. Well, actually, she saw me; I was busy thinking about the night before. She tapped my shoulder to get my attention.

"Hey you! Where've you been hiding these days? I feel that Derek gets to spend all this time with you, and I never see you anymore," she beamed.

"Yes, sorry, I have been so busy with exams. And yeah, Derek, too." I knew how my answer sounded, but what else was there to say?

"You are so mysterious about this Derek guy. I know how we can fix this. Brittany and I are going to the residence Christmas formal tomorrow. You should come and bring Derek. And don't try and get out of this!" Her tone was serious, but she was smiling.

"That's a good idea. I'm free, but I'll need to ask Derek about his schedule."

"I'm going to take that as a yes. How about you two meet us at my apartment for 7 p.m., and we'll go together."

I felt like I'd neglected Elyse. I knew she was busy between school, working, and dating, but I still should've tried to keep in better contact. I really wanted to attend formal. Plus, I figured from the night before that Derek owed me.

I wasn't really sure what to expect by putting Derek, Elyse, Brittany, and myself together in a room. While I had a close connection with Derek and Elyse, they were such different people. As for Brittany, my verdict was still out, but I was also having trouble placing Derek and Brittany together in my head. Worldly Derek, who loved to talk about politics and philosophy, and then Brittany, who I still felt didn't really like me, and whose interests revolved around fashion and boys. I know that sounds harsh, but it was true.

I hoped they didn't expect me to try and play hostess. I could bring Derek, and introduce them, but that was about it. While some people have the gift of putting strangers together in a room and magically making them instant friends, this was not in my repertoire.

I felt anxious the entire time I was getting ready for the party. This was a bad idea.

What if no one said anything, and we're just staring at each other? What if they expected me to fill in the gaps in conversation? Or, what if Elyse and Brittany are talkative, but Derek doesn't really engage with them?

All you need to do is show up and introduce them; the rest is on them.

By the time 7 p.m. came around, I was so tense that I wondered how I'd manage to eat.

The night actually went better than I expected. I was a bit surprised when Derek arrived wearing a tie, and greeted them both with a firm handshake before I had a chance to collect myself to make introductions. Derek was good at reading people and situations, and was easily able to gain their liking. I knew they weren't necessarily people he'd normally socialize with. I could tell that he was making an effort. I sat back, perfectly happy and content as I listened to Elyse and Brittany ask him questions about his travels. From the look on his face, he didn't mind the attention.

I sat there thinking how happy I was with my life, and to have Derek as a partner. In that moment, I knew he was *the one*.

I'd be perfectly happy if our relationship didn't have an end, I thought as I looked at him talking with my friends across the table.

But you see Alice. Derek and I were always on a different page.

I wasn't the romantic type that believed in happily ever after, but it was so tempting. In those few months, how I thought about and experienced the world, and even who I was seemed to change. I will never be the person I was before him. My head felt invaded with thoughts that seemed to belong on motivational posters about love. I tried to tell myself to get it together and that I was getting way too ahead of myself. I hadn't even known him for that long. I needed to be realistic.

During the dinner, Aashi made rounds to greet all of the guests. She came by our table toward the end of dessert and chatted with us for a few minutes.

"He's a keeper," she whispered to me when I said goodbye.

Derek had an exam to study for, so he said goodbye to me after dinner. Elyse and Brittany really liked Derek, and I spent the next hour chatting with them in Elyse's room, hearing their reviews of the evening. I couldn't explain exactly what she said, but Brittany subtly suggested that she was surprised that he was dating me. I warned you before about my anxiety, maybe it was just in my head and she didn't mean that at all. I was exhausted, and I excused myself before they started a movie.

I lay in bed, feeling extremely happy about Derek. I realized that I only had one week in Toronto before I left for the winter holidays. I was halfway through the year. I allowed myself a small congratulations, and my thoughts faded.

CHAPTER 10

I was dripping wet the first time he surprised me by holding me down. He wrapped his hands around my neck and told me that I was a, "good little whore," again and again. I was stunned and didn't know what to think, but soon realized that I liked the feeling of him being in total control. He broke the moment by whispering, "is this okay?"

I told him it was.

I shouldn't have gone there. Not with this guy who I learnt had no respect for me.

It's hard to explain how this domination and degradation in the bedroom felt like an expression of love, but it did. It turned me on knowing how badly Derek wanted me. I never thought it'd feel so sexy to be used. I loved giving him power over my body. Trusting that he'd stop when I told him to. I allowed him to use me for his pleasure, but he also cared about mine.

That first day he crossed that line, we talked about it after as we made dinner in his apartment.

"I hope that was okay, I just felt so overwhelmed with desire," he offered.

"It's okay, I enjoyed it. If I didn't, I would've told you to stop," I responded. If I didn't feel comfortable with, or interested in something I wouldn't do it. I definitely didn't agree with narratives that suggested that women's sexuality was a performance for men. As if we needed this constant rhetoric about what women can and can't find pleasurable or empowering.

"It looks like you drifted away on me for a minute. I was planning on talking to you first to see if you were interested in experimenting. I wanted to for a while, but I didn't want to make you uncomfortable so I waited, and it just came out." It was hot the way he seemed embarrassed, half-apologizing, half-explaining.

"Well, we can talk more now if you'd like." I was excited to hear what he was going to say.

"I just have so many thoughts about what I want to do to you," he stepped back from the pot he was stirring and gave me a dark look. I marvelled at the things that we could do together and what he was going to say. He just turned off the stove, picked me up in his strong arms, and asked, "Are you going to do as I say, slut?" as he carried me to his bed.

I'm not sure what is appropriate to tell you, but I feel I may have already crossed the polite line. So fuck it. You told me to tell my story however I choose. Want to hear about riding crops and collars, or the colourful array of bruises on my neck that I needed to conceal? Or what about Derek binding me to his bed, and leaving me there all day as his little fuck toy? He secured my arms and legs, so I couldn't move, and when I protested he gagged me. He left me there as he did his homework; I was restless and lonely, but every breath reflected anticipation. I lay there until he got bored and horny, and fucked me nice and hard. The focal point was *his* pleasure, not mine. Sometimes he wanted it to be about me though, and he wouldn't stop touching me—even if I begged him to stop—until I climaxed enough to satisfy him.

Or would you like to hear about being grabbed from behind and thrown onto the bed, hair pulled as I screamed, "no," only to have a hand placed over my mouth so my screams were silenced. Of course, my *no* was really *yes*, and I later cried out, "yes, yes, yes" to him as he made me come. Don't worry; we talked about this. We even had a signal setup if I wanted him to stop.

I spent a lot of time thinking about my sexuality and reading about BDSM. At first I couldn't admit to myself, let alone talk to

Derek about having rape fantasies—never mind wanting to act on them. However, I slowly began to accept my sexuality, and that there was a difference between fantasy and reality. I wondered from time to time why I wanted to be controlled. Why did the idea of him overpowering me, of forcing me to have sex with him turn me on? Was something wrong with me for desiring this? According to the internet, my fantasy was fairly common, but still, I struggled. Maybe something was wrong with me. But it wasn't like I really had anyone to talk to bedsides Derek and internet forums on websites you can probably guess the names of. Kink and BDSM became this hole—this world of two-dimensional distant people just waiting to chat and share their experiences.

I couldn't imagine what Elyse or Brittany would think if I mentioned our increasingly kinky sex life.

Over the next few months, Derek was really insistent on communicating regularly about our evolving sex life. He wanted to know what turned me on, what I wanted to explore, what my limits were—anything and everything. Just talking with him excited me. I knew I wasn't as experienced as his previous mysterious partners, but he made me feel beautiful, sexy, and intriguing, and he told me so. I always felt comfortable talking with him. This is coming from the girl who, prior to meeting Derek likely wouldn't have admitted to masturbating.

I was always the good girl and that sometimes got a bit tiring. In high school, I focused on getting good marks. I worked a job on weekends and summer holidays to support myself. In university, I didn't delve into a world of partying. Honestly, I'd only really been drunk once, and most of the night was spent with my head in a toilet. That wasn't a night I cared to remember.

To tell you the truth, I found my life a bit boring before leaving home and meeting Derek. I was drawn to the sense of adventure. In becoming close to him I felt like I was being introduced to an entire new genre of film after ruling out cinema as dry. I hadn't been this close to anyone before.

Life for me was lived according to my organizer: finish this project, go to this meeting so the next thing in the process can happen. Every day was part of completing a task to finish a course, to get a paycheck. But Derek was a bit of a *carpe diem* seize-the-day type.

He was great at contextualizing risks, thinking things through and deciding what he wanted to do with his body. He occasionally used drugs, mainly psychedelics for increasing self-awareness, but he sometimes used other drugs too.

I have had drinks with him before, and was always careful not to overindulge. I didn't want to get carried away with him, so I normally measured my drinks against his, making sure he at least passed my number.

Derek smoked weed now and then, but he was more of a drinker. On the rare occasion I'd sit beside him on his couch as he pulled out an old grinder and smoked from his pipe, offering it to me. We sat talking and I coughed as it caught on my throat. I never really felt high.

All of this is to explain our last night together before the Christmas holidays. I wrote my final exam earlier that day, and I felt relief that the term was done, but also hesitant to leave Derek and spend two weeks with my family. That night seemed worthy of celebration, so we decided to do MDMA together. The conversation leading up to this decision is long forgotten, but I remember agreeing to it. I tried to ask him when he had tried it before, and with whom, but he didn't really answer. He was good at skirting around questions, changing the topic in a way that I wouldn't realize he never addressed what I had asked. Sometimes I would realize days later, but by then it was far too late.

I was excited for this adventure with Derek, but at the last minute when he took the pills out, I completely froze. Did I really want this? I hadn't really experimented with drugs at all until this point. I was mainly concerned about my health and safety. What if something happened to me? And what about my mental health struggles? Would this alter my brain and send me on an even wilder rollercoaster in the weeks to come?

Derek was good at reading me and sensed my anxiety. He reassured me that he was familiar with the drug, that we were in a safe environment, and he wouldn't let anything bad happen. The pill sitting on his kitchen table was as much about an experience with a chemical as it was an exercise in trust and going on a journey with him.

"This decision is completely up to you. I understand if you change your mind, and we can do something else tonight if you'd like." He was always so considerate.

I took the pill.

It's hard to describe this experience in words when I'm no longer inside of it, existing in a new space, bridge already crossed; forever, wondering how to explain the truth of my history. Maybe as I try and write this down my memory of what happened continues to change. I wrote a few notes the next morning. A distance will forever exist between what I wrote and what happened. I wonder if it was even worth it to try and explain. I can't make sense of it all, but perhaps you can.

I read somewhere that we think in shapes and colours, not ideas and words. Some days the visions in my head were hard to distinguish from dancing shadows and we stumbled as we tried to model the shadows into sounds, words, and sentences. It's funny that even when my words invade the page, sometimes I trip on ideas. Clumsy mouth and clumsy pen. We're all clumsy, I perhaps more than most. Sometimes I just sit here looking at what I've written, amazed at the creation of language—using words for ideas, things, feelings. *Isn't it strange?*

Here's what I scribbled down the next day. Reading it now, I'm blushing:

The experience was amazing, so full of awareness and awakeness (is that even a word? Whatever). We made love for hours. I don't know how many times he made me come…But he kept checking in, seeing how I was feeling, and that was nice. I loved knowing that he was there and cared. I wish I could spend every day with him, but then maybe our minutes together wouldn't be as precious.

But I am this high and low all the time, this feeling of needing to be asked if I am okay because sometimes my entire day is just beyond me, floating on an emotional sea of ups and downs. Being on M, it is okay not to be okay. This is how I feel every day, ecstatic, yet scared and uncertain. Unpredictable like my drug trip. Floating in the sky, in the river on a boat. Holding on for dear life.

After we made love the first time, I was awake. I couldn't sleep. I just held onto him as tightly as possible, wishing we could share a body and that his scars, too, would mark my arms. I think something to him, and he seems to respond without speaking. Our brains meld and anything is possible. I was too tired to have sex again, but I held onto him and it seemed as if we are one being. When he started kissing my nipples I was too tired to react, but I needed him inside me—to be as close as possible. We are one person, and I want him to be in me forever. So I guess Zeus got it wrong, cause this erotic joining doesn't allow us to walk away easily. I'd willingly curl up in a ball and starve beside him, and after a night like last night anything is possible. My brain was hyper, but I felt so connected to Derek as we lay in his bed. I was floating down a river and he was with me. I didn't want to get up because I didn't want to leave his side.

We spent the next morning together. When we said our goodbyes on the subway, I felt like I'd been ripped from another part of myself—like the only other person in the world, torn from Eden.

I've never been so in love. And it's lonely. Knowing I want to be with him forever, but in reality you only ever get today.

Notes from two days after:

I feel like the loneliest person in the world, ripped from bliss. Alone. Ripped from my mother, ripped from the earth. I am too tired to hope or daydream. I'm not sad like crying, I'm sad like every minute goes on forever, with no purpose and all the people I share the earth with can never be reached.

CHAPTER 11

Being home and away from Derek didn't help with my feelings of isolation and sorrow. The first few days were defined by extreme depression and indifference, and the Christmas holidays felt the same as they did every year. Perhaps part of the magic of Christmas was the way that it seemed to challenge the linear movement of time. My world was so different than last Christmas, yet the same decorations, activities, and people surrounded me. It made the last year feel like a dream.

Todd arrived home a few days after me. John was unavailable because he was busy with his family. Besides, John was welcome in theory, but my family hadn't made a point of displaying this. I couldn't imagine how tense their wedding would be, with my family and all. I was hoping I'd have the opportunity to get to know John better. I'd only met him a few times, and always briefly.

Todd had paperwork to do over the holidays, but we still spent a bit of time together. After a few days of being around the house and getting restless in the frenzy of household preparations, we decided to go out. We talked about school and friends. He asked if I was seeing anyone. I never thought I'd be sitting with my brother and drinking a beer, talking about what qualities we found attractive in men. I felt safe beside my brother as the snow fell outside the pub window.

I told him a bit about Derek, but I didn't let the conversation go on too long. I was a bit concerned by the fact that I'd yet to hear from him. I texted Derek when I was on the bus home to thank him for the previous night and say that we'd talk soon. Normally he was quick to respond, but my text went unanswered. It was okay; it wasn't really anything that required a response.

Nevertheless, I was relieved that my parents weren't the type to inquire about my love life. I really didn't feel like mentioning him because they would only try and decide if he'd fit in with our family.

On Christmas Eve the four of us piled into a car and headed to mass. I won't go into my particular spiritual beliefs, but my parents go to church maybe twice a year: always around Christmas and sometimes Easter. Like I said, I come from a household that doesn't talk about politics or religion. I know that if I tried to start a genuine conversation about religious beliefs they'd squirm, and I don't like making people uncomfortable (aside from you dear reader). After mass we finished getting ready for Christmas dinner and went to sleep early, knowing that Christmas would be a busy day.

In the morning we opened presents, and then had brunch. The gifts I received could be described as nice. They were expensive, such as a designer raincoat from my mom. I still wore the raincoat she got me last Christmas.

My mom's parents, as well as her younger sister came over for Christmas dinner. My grandparents and aunt live within an hour's drive, but we rarely saw them. My dad's parents passed away a few years ago. Mom's parents seemed like an older version of my parents: successful and polite, but hard to get close to. Interacting with them was what I imagined talking to my parents in twenty years would be like. We discussed their recent vacation to Barbados, and they asked about school. Christmas dinner was enjoyable, if not a bit boring. At the end of the day they stiffly hugged me goodbye, and in my mind, I checked off another completed Christmas.

There was something, however, that was bothering me. Holidays weren't really a big deal, but still, I should have heard from Derek. I hadn't spoken to him since I kissed him goodbye on my way to the bus. My texts remained unanswered. I wasn't worried about him. I knew he was okay from his social media updates that arrived on my computer, reminding me that even if he didn't have time to talk to me, he had time to post philosophical quotes and lines from books he read for his 200+ friends. I wondered why he couldn't spare a few minutes for me.

Do I sound needy?

I took out my phone and saw I had a few messages and wondered if it was him. I found myself holding my breath as I opened my texts, but the messages were from Kara, asking me how my holiday was going. I responded, and then put my phone away, telling myself to forget it. I didn't want to bother him; I definitely didn't want to be the girlfriend who didn't know when to back off. Women's magazines on their glossy covers declare that we shouldn't let guys have power over us and run our lives, but when I was with Derek it was difficult to remember this.

I pulled on my pyjamas and buried myself in blankets with *The Bell Jar*. It was so nice to have time to read. I struggled to focus on the words, but while I was drawn to Esther the previous night, I found myself feeling frustrated by the story as the question of why I hadn't heard from Derek distracted me.

I decided to call him. I got out my phone: one new text, it was Kara again. I decided to wait a while longer because if he wanted to talk to me, he would. I went to see if my mom needed help tidying the kitchen, but everything was neat.

I returned to my room, and as I listened to the ringing in my ears I thought, *really Patricia, you have so little self-control.*

But it should be okay for me to call my boyfriend on Christmas, right? He didn't answer, and I left him a message.

It was long past the midnight, and I was almost asleep with the book in my hand, when I saw my phone had a new message.

"Hey, I see you called. Merry Christmas, Patricia." I guess it was a comment about our generation when you called someone on the phone, and get a text back. I couldn't really be mad though. He responded, right?

John surprised Todd—or should I say, John surprised our parents—by showing up two days after Christmas. Todd received a text from John an hour before, saying he was on his way. Todd was ecstatic at first, but I watched him squirm as he told our parents about the upcoming visit. They responded politely. My mother, always the good host, made a comment about not wanting to serve leftovers, and that she'd go to the store and make a nice dinner. Making food was the best she could do at suggesting that John was welcome, but I could tell that she was trying. Todd made it clear over the last year that his presence in the family home wasn't to be taken for granted, and that if they were unwilling to accept that he was with John then he didn't feel obligated to visit. I was impressed with Todd's confidence; normally he was easy going, and not one to tell my parents how it was going to be, even in the name of standing up for himself.

Todd dressed, and then sat in the front room for the next half hour flipping through magazines. He absently sipped coffee, and having already finished his drink, continued to pick up the mug to try and drink from it. He periodically looked at his watch and the front door, wanting to be the first in the race to answer it, and perhaps save his lover from the semi-homophobic, awkward dance of our family. Todd asked me questions about my interest in journalism, but then didn't comment on my responses. It seemed like he forgot that he asked me a question. I tried to carry the conversation for a few minutes, and then gave up. I wandered to the kitchen to see if my mom needed help.

I felt like a minor character watching a soap opera unfold. The doorbell finally rang, startling everyone, and Todd rushed to answer. From my station in the kitchen, I heard my dad enter the front room and offer John a drink.

The phone rang in the kitchen; it was my grandmother calling, asking my mom if she had seen her scarf that she misplaced on Christmas. I heard my grandmother ask what we were doing today, and my mom quickly replied, "oh you know, not too much." I guess for the sake of that conversation, that was how John was categorized.

My mom later made up acceptable excuses to tell her family about me, too.

My mom wiped her hands on her apron and went to greet John; they briskly kissed
on the cheek, while I got a friendly bear hug. At least he knew there was one member of the family he didn't need to worry about winning over. The four of us talked for a bit in the front room before my mother and I left to finish dinner. John offered to help, and I was sure he was disappointed in our refusal, as peeling carrots with me would be more pleasant than being interviewed by my dad.

The three of them sat and bits of their conversation drifted my way. I heard pieces about John's career, followed by a discussion of my parents' recent travels. If I didn't know my father, it would've sounded like a friendly interaction. But I could hear the tension in his voice, the forced laughter, and the rush to fill the natural pauses. Todd tried to prompt the conversation, offering comments about what John was up to. John was welcomed to the extent that he wasn't welcome. If that makes any sense. It was going to be a long day.

At least they were trying, I reminded myself. But I couldn't help but think about how awkward the wedding was going to be. Sometimes, trying isn't enough.

The next morning John, Todd, and I went for breakfast before I had to catch a bus back to the city. We were finally able to put formalities aside and relax. John had such a fun personality. He could be serious when needed, but otherwise, he was full of energy, always ready with a joke, and eager to tease.

"So, how's Patricia doing? Breaking many hearts now that you've escaped from home base? Just look at you, I bet my sophisticated college girl has people lining up for a date," he put his arm around me.

I blushed and hesitantly told them a bit about Derek. I never really liked talking about myself. John wanted to know how we met, what he was like. I focused on the good stuff of course; the fact that he essentially ignored me over Christmas wasn't a detail that would leave a good impression. For some reason, I felt defensive. As I listened to myself talk about Derek I became more proud to be with him, and excited to be reunited. This didn't sound like the guy who was so rude to his friends and I at a Christmas party, and barely interacted with me over Christmas. I reddened,

70

remembering our last night together, the tangling of bodies, and whispering of feelings. Connection. Vulnerability.

"Well, it looks like you did well for yourself, kiddo," John proclaimed and Todd nodded. I sat basking in their praise and acceptance.

"Now, tell me more about school," John began as he drove me to the bus station. I hugged and kissed them both, wished them luck with the remainder of their visit with my parents, and began my ride back to the city.

It would be the last time I felt truly content for some time.

CHAPTER 12

The trip to Toronto took just over two hours on the bus, but the journey in my head felt much longer. I never told you where I'm from did I? Ah well, I think I'll keep it a secret. Of course, I've changed everyone's names, and maybe a few of the details, but still, in a place as small as my hometown, it may be obvious. And oh dear, then what would my mother say? *These sorts of things don't happen, if they do, we don't talk about them and we certainly don't write about them. Not in nice polite families anyway.*

Despite the relaxing holiday, as I thought of Derek my stomach churned, my shoulders tensed, and I could feel the stress mounting through the pulse in my head. My brain was trying to tell me that I was okay, while my body screamed that I was far from it. Talk about conflict.

I started to feel dizzy; the bus moving me forward wasn't helping. Then everything felt far away. My phone in my hand was heavy, then light. What are hands, how do they work to hold this thing? And I was sitting there waiting to hear back from Derek— to see if he sent me a message.

People said I was so predictable, but I wondered what would happen if I reach out and touched the man beside me. He was an older guy, suit and tie, brief case, maybe going to Toronto for work or something. What if I just slipped the paper from his lap leaned over and touched his hair. And I didn't even want to. Not really. I don't know why I thought these things. It was just that none of this was real. I'd been brainwashed to follow the orders. Follow rules. Follow the rules.

Derek. Fucking Derek. I told myself that people get busy, and Derek was likely so distracted with his holiday plans that he just didn't have the time to talk. Things would continue as they were, but another part of my brain doubted that.

Don't be the clingy girlfriend, Patricia. He's been nothing but great to you, just give him space.

But then I remembered how he told me, "I was too much," when I was worried about him after he was two hours late when he said he was on his way over.

"Too much," and, "lighten the fuck up." I'd heard those words from his mouth a few times.

I forced my brain, which still felt like it was floating, to try and think of other things. Thoughts were like islands in this hurricane and I was just trying not to get pulled away from land.

I wanted to steal the newspaper, or get up and pace the aisle of the bus. Anything. Sit down, be quiet, and follow the rules. The man in the suit had crumbs on his suit jacket, I thought of brushing them off. Don't do it. Oh, but why not? Human brains are the hardest fucking things in the world to train.

School. School was a safe thing to think about. Was I too shy to be a journalist? And that stupid *do I have what it takes* question resurfaced. I received good marks first term, I reassured myself; unfortunately, good didn't always translate to good enough. Maybe being in the top quarter of the class still wasn't the mark of success. I needed the grades, the personality, and the networking skills to be number one. Yeah, this was okay, and I was decent at it, but could I make it as a career? I really hated competing. So, I not only had to be good, but I also need to prove that I was better than everyone else?

Come on, Patricia, time to clear your head, I thought as I attempted to do some breathing exercises.

But somewhere between deep breaths, my thoughts returned to Derek. Before Christmas we had made plans to spend New Year's Eve together. Did he still want to? Was he even in Toronto? What would I do for the New Year if he wasn't around? New Year's Eve was never a big deal for me; in high school the girls and me went to one of their houses, drank sparkling wine, and ate snacks as we waited for midnight. Like I keep telling you, I had a boring life before Derek. Anyway, spending the night by myself was just sad. Maybe Elyse would be around, but I bet she had plans with Brittany or her boyfriend. I was sure Brittany would be thrilled to ask me what happened to Derek.

Relax, I thought. *The holidays are supposed to be a happy time. Quit worrying.*

I tried to remind myself that I was just making up problems. I needed to deal with things as they happened, one day at a time.

Let me tell you, it's very difficult to win an argument with yourself.

I was exhausted by the end of the bus ride. As I got off the bus, my legs shook as if they forgot how to hold my weight. Downtown Toronto seemed so, so absurd smelling of piss with people sleeping on sidewalks, rows of fancy stores and well off folks rushing past the homeless people. They were careful not to make eye contact, as if poverty was contagious and might be caught by a glance—a smile. It was only 1 p.m. when I got back to my dorm, but I plopped down on my bed, exhausted, and didn't bother changing out of my jeans before entering a restless sleep for the next few hours.

Later that day I ran into Elyse. We talked about the holidays and seeing our families. She asked me what my plans were for New Year's Eve. She was going to a bar with Brittany, but invited me to join. I was tempted to forget about my arrangement with Derek. After all, I'd barely heard from him.

I told Elyse, "thanks, but I had plans already," and spent the next hour wondering why I didn't say yes. I realize now I should have said yes, and went with them, and just classified Derek as a first term fling. He clearly didn't care.

Finally, the night of December 30, I got a text from Derek: "let's go for dinner tomorrow night, my treat. Sushi at 8 p.m.?"

Relieved, I quickly replied. I felt dumb; I waited days for him to text, and I answered within five minutes?

I walked into the restaurant at exactly 8 p.m. I wore my new clothes from Christmas, and spent a bit of time trying to look nice. Derek was already sitting at a table.

"You look gorgeous, Patricia," he stood and took my hand, grazed it with his lips, and pulled out my chair.

"Thanks, Derek, you look so handsome." My heart did a little flip as I looked at him. I wondered if I'd ever get used to his presence.

"I missed you. Honestly, I can't believe how many times I thought about you. And that's not really something I'd normally say." He leaned across the table and gave me a quick kiss.

Well, why didn't he call be back if he was thinking about me? Of course those thoughts didn't escape my lips.

The waitress came and took our drink order and after Derek turned to me to speak. "I'm glad Christmas is over. I always find this holiday really superficial. Capitalistic bullshit used to sell this commercialized idea of happiness and love, and the backstory is about this birth of a religious figure, that statistically most Canadians no longer believe in. I mean, come on. Talk about an empty holiday. People spend so much money, and expect Christmas miracles and united families and justify it using rhetoric that is long out-dated. But anyway, how was the visit with your family?"

"Yeah, I agree. It's hard to oppose something when it looks like it'll continue to be a long-standing tradition though. My holidays were okay, nothing extraordinary. My grandparents came; we had a nice dinner. John showed up for a visit the night before I left. I feel bad for him. My parents are trying, but still, it's pretty clear that they aren't comfortable with Todd being gay. They're nice to John, just a bit stiff. Anyway, I'm really glad to be back."

For the first time, I wondered about what I had to say.

"What about you? How was your holiday?" I asked, realizing how little I knew about Derek's background.

"I actually spent a few days with my sister, Kathryn, in Hamilton. She's a single mom with two kids—eight and ten—so she's got her hands full." he offered.

I wondered about his parents, he had never mentioned his mom or dad. Were they still part of his life, distanced, or deceased? I sensed there were some topics that were off limits and I didn't want to ask too many questions and have him close off further.

"Oh, that's really nice, I didn't realize you had a sister. It's good that she's so close and that you can visit her and her children." I was tempted to ask about his mom, but still, I hesitated. *Don't ask Patricia, just don't.*

"Yeah, it was great to see her. I hadn't visited since last Christmas actually. She works full-time, and with two kids she doesn't exactly have time for social calls. We've always been pretty close, but we don't need to see each other all the time."

A silence fell, but not the awkward someone needs-to-speak silence, rather, we just sat looking at each other, amazed by each other's presence. That was how it felt to me.

"I know I already said this, but I really did miss you, hun," he almost smiled, and I felt my previous worries dissolve. Still, I couldn't just let it go; forgetting about things had never been my strong suit.

"I really wish we got to talk during the break." I was feeling confident.

"Didn't we talk? I kept thinking about you. I thought I called, or I meant to."

I pictured him helping his sister and chasing kids around in a game of hide and seek. It was okay; Derek didn't intend to ignore me. He was just preoccupied being a good brother and uncle.

The waitress came to take our order, and we quickly looked at the menu we had neglected. The rest of the dinner passed pleasantly, and I sat there glowing, basking in his attention.

Oh how I worshiped his attention, but I shouldn't have.

After dinner it was still early. We stood outside the restaurant on Queen West, watching people hurry to important New Year's parties. Two ladies in high heels passed, trendy coats and elegant scarves hugged their necks. White snowflakes looked perfect against the black of their coats. Their laughter created puffs of condensation. I thought about following them, and imagined a fancy condo party, with their boyfriends rushing to get them glasses of champagne as other men flocked to get their attention.

Derek interrupted my musing, "I hate clubs, but I feel we should do something festive tonight. So, I'm willing to put up with the crowd. Besides, I need to show off my beautiful lady, and I want tonight to be special for us."

I agreed to his plan, even though I didn't really like clubs either. Not that he asked how I felt. I didn't really want to go to a club, but what else was there to do? We were dressed up with no place to go.

I think I got the pretty standard New Year's Eve club experience a packed space, with drunken people and glittery outfits. I felt awkward, first because I had a huge underage stamp on my hand, and second because it just wasn't an atmosphere I felt either of us blended with. I worried that people would notice we didn't belong.

Derek bought a beer for himself and a soda for me. Later, when security wasn't paying attention, he bought me a beer. I had my beer, as I watched Derek continually drink. The drunker he got, the more I felt out of place being sober. It was New Year's Eve after all, and I didn't want to get in the way of his party.

We danced a bit, with awkward moves as we tripped on each other's feet, bodies out of place and clumsy. My legs and the music were foreign to me. I wanted to sit, but we stood to the side and watched the dance floor. There was half an hour till midnight.

"See anyone you're interested in?" He asked as we both looked around.

"I mean, I'm here with you. So, yeah, I guess I see someone I'm interested in, and I'm looking right at him." I tried to be cute, but he didn't let it go.

"No, really. Do you see anyone you want to dance with? We are at a bar after all. Like, look at that girl over there—the girl with the sequined shirt, dark hair, and tattoos. She's gorgeous, right? I bet there's someone you want to introduce yourself to. I don't want to leave you."

"Not really," I tried to hold my ground. I was getting uncomfortable, and started to feel panicky. Yeah sure, guys look at other girls, but why was he saying this stuff to me? What was I supposed to say? I thought he was excited to spend New Year's Eve with me.

"Well, if you don't mind, I'm going to go say hi. We are at a bar after all; if we were going to keep to ourselves we should've just stayed home." He walked off to introduce himself before I could respond.

I guess he had a point. I stood there and waited for him to come back. I took slow sips of my beer, hoping that everyone didn't turn to look at the sober girl by herself. I thought of high school, rushing between my locker and classes, desperately hoping that no one would notice me. I felt pretty when I looked in the mirror before leaving to meet Derek, but at a bar my shirt with the high collar and hoop earrings were too formal. And I spilt something on my shirt at dinner. I felt self-conscious about my minimal makeup, flats, and my lack of visible skin.

What was I thinking? It was New Year's Eve and I didn't look sexy; I looked like I was going to an office meeting.

I checked the time: four minutes to midnight. Was I going to bring in the New Year standing alone in a club? I tried to convince myself that this was just some dumb holiday from a made up calendar, created to market fancy parties and gym memberships. I didn't care, but I was trying not to cry. Cry, or yell, or walk away. Something like that.

I watched the girl, accompanied by another attractive female, laugh as Derek spoke with them and draped his arm around the one with tattoos. I felt stupid for watching, but there was really nowhere for me to go. Was I just meant to observe this display? Did Derek actually cross a line? It seemed odd, we were on a date, and he was trying to pick up girls?

I saw him nod at me, pointing. I wondered what he was telling them, maybe that he needed to return to his *friend,* or something. He slowly walked back to me.

"Hi, babe, how are you?" He put his arms around me and pulled me into him, just as the countdown began.

Five...Four...Three...Two...One... and then there was the cheering, the confetti and the drunken, "Happy New Year!" But I'd never felt so sober. We kissed, a lingering kiss against the backdrop of "Auld Lang Syne." I was happy, but not quite content, as we swayed to the music.

"I'm going to get another drink," I watched Derek stumble to the bar and dig for his wallet. As he walked back, he sloshed his beer; my outfit reeked of stale alcohol. One of the girls he was chatting with—actually the one with the tattoos that he first pointed out—made her way over to us.

"Hey, cutie," she said to Derek. She glanced at me, and then her eyes returned to him.

Derek politely introduced me, "this is Patricia." He didn't downgrade me by throwing the word "friend" in front, but he didn't exactly clarify that I was his girlfriend either. She slipped Derek her phone number on a crumpled piece of paper and we left shortly after. The entire encounter was uncomfortable. Didn't she realize I was with him, and not as his wingman? And why did he take her number? Was he just being polite?

I should have taken a better look at her face. I wonder if this was the girl who answered his door later.

As we stumbled out of the bar, Derek took my hand and I was relieved that we were leaving that space. As we walked he commented about how nice the girls were. I just grunted in response. What did he want me to say?

"You can be really awkward sometimes, you know that, Patricia? You were just standing there staring." His voice went up at the end. I couldn't help but wonder if he had something more to say.

"Well yeah, I came with you, and I didn't have anywhere else to go…" I tried to defend myself. I should have told him to fuck off and went home, or went and had a drink with Elyse.

"I know, I know, you were just being really weird and…boring. Why didn't you talk to them? And what's with that outfit? Maybe show a little skin, or get some heels or something? Buy a push up bra? You look like a secretary and not the kind of secretary I'd fuck on her desk," he slurred. I figured there was no point in responding. Seriously, what was there to say?

Asshole, I thought. *Why was I with this guy?* I was filled with rage for a second, I wanted to kick the street sign, to kick the beer bottle on the street, but I ignored the urge.

"What are you going to do? Pout? Got nothing to say, Patty? Come on, don't ruin our night, it's just getting started," this wasn't him talking. Still I stopped to ask myself if I wanted to spend the night, or any other night, with him.

Maybe I should have gone home.

"Are you sure you want me to come over?" I didn't really know what to do. I wanted to spend time with him, but this wasn't him.

We went to his place, and he poured himself another drink, without offering me one. "Hey, Derek, are you sure that's a good idea, I mean you already—"

"Fuck off, Pat! You aren't my mother." He shoved the bottle of rum into my hands, and told me to "make yourself a drink and shut up with the nagging." He was just drunk and needed to be in control. If I did as he instructed we could still have a nice night.

I made a drink. We sat on the couch, and he put his arm around me.

"Sorry, babe, I didn't mean to be so rough. It's just my head is hurting, and I'm actually a bit worried about school because of my marks last term, and I'm stressed about having enough financial aid to pay rent..." Normally he was so articulate and controlled, but the alcohol made him mean and vulnerable.

"It's okay. I understand you're stressed. Just try not to take it out on me. I'm here for you." But was it really okay? Or was that just the easiest thing to say?

Yes I know, Alice, I'm great at making excuses for people.

"Thanks, babe. Again, I'm sorry," he said and kissed my forehead as he left the room.

"Jesus fucking Christ!" I heard him yell from the bathroom.

Great, now what?

I watched him storm out of the bathroom and run around his small apartment, tearing the couch apart, frantically looking for something.

I tried to make myself small, and get out of the way.

"My fucking wallet is missing," he told me. I helped him search, but I was mostly in the way.

"Fuck, fuck, fuck!" he yelled.

He was beyond reasoning, but still I tried. "Let's call the bar, see if they found a wallet," I offered.

"That's dumb. No one would hand over a wallet with money and cards. I'm not that naïve." His voice was still raised.

"Fuck!" he shouted one last time, before throwing a liquor bottle at the wall. Glass shards and alcohol covered the floor. I jumped back, startled by his rage. He never touched me, but still I was scared.

I needed some space, so I moved to change into the pyjamas I kept in his bedroom. And there, on the floor, beside his bed I found his wallet. I silently brought it to him. He was relieved, but the earlier tension didn't dissipate as easily as finding a missing wallet.

We began to kiss, but aggressively this time, hungry, thirsty, needing to rip each other apart. He yanked my pyjamas off and rubbed his cock over me. No gentle petting, no stroking my body, just this electric energy and his throbbing cock. He was sweaty and reeked of rum.

"You like that, you little slut?" he asked and with no warning he shoved himself fully inside. I wasn't wet enough; my body wasn't ready.

A moan escaped from my lips. I wanted him to be gentler, but I was excited by this animalistic desire. He held me down as he fucked me until he was completely satisfied. This was about him; me getting off was an afterthought.

The next morning I got up early, saw my clothes strewn on the couch, and remembered our passionate fucking, but also the things he said to me, and how he flirted with the other girl. I couldn't quite figure out how I felt. As I left I stepped on a splinter of glass that must have escaped his hasty drunken sweeping. I picked it out of my foot, and got a tissue, but my wound left a small trickle of deep red blood on his floor. I didn't bother to clean it.

Derek called the next day and apologized for his behaviour. A simple "I'm sorry" phone call—while appreciated—wasn't enough to erase actions, especially if the words didn't seem to hold true. I guess the old saying about actions speaking louder than words really has some merit.

How did the next month or so go? He was just nice enough for me to stay, to wonder what I'd be missing if I walked away. But he was mean enough for me to start to resent him. He was frustrated with his life, school, or money, or what have you. He was so angry with me. He never touched me, but he continually told me how boring and awkward I was. I got used to the yelling, the anger. I thought this was just part of accepting someone as they were. *Like I keep telling you, this is no love story.*

Don't worry, I don't think that now, but I'm telling you about how I felt back then. I tried to be patient. I tried to have empathy. Every time I thought this wasn't worth the frustration, the hurt—that I was done—some little thing made me hold on. Some kind conversation, some amazing time together. It wasn't *all* bad. I wished it is just a bit worse, so that back in January the decision to leave would've been easy and I wouldn't be in this mess now.

One Saturday in the beginning of February Derek invited me for dinner. I greeted him with a hug, but his arms went limp around me. He was stiff, cold.

"How are you?" I asked.

"How the fuck do you think I am?"

I flinched.

"I missed my midterm because I'm sick and slept through it. My rent is overdue and I don't know how I'm going to pay it!" he yelled.

"I'm really sorry, Derek. I wonder if there's any way you can redo the midterm? Can you maybe get a doctor's note?"

"Seriously, Patricia, you always say the stupidest things. There is nothing that can be done. I just need a few minutes to finish dinner okay? Okay?"

"Sure, no problem. Would you like any help?"

"No, I'm almost done. You just need to get out of my way. Have a seat." He pulled out a chair. I sat down, stayed quiet, and made myself small until he was ready to deal with me.

I sat there, replaying what had been said in the two minutes since I entered the door. He invited me over for dinner, why was I there if I wasn't wanted?

What else should I tell you? I could tell you about how he got got even more stressed because he kept missing class and staying up too late, liquor bottle in hand. Of course, I couldn't have said anything, or he'd get mad.

According to him I didn't understand anything.

By now you're probably thinking I am dumb for continuing to date Derek. The truth is that despite his bursts of anger, I'd never felt such a powerful connection with someone. I didn't like his aggression towards me, but I chose that over not having him in my life. Yes, I know how that sounds. But he was the first person to really see me, to experience me. Hopes and dreams collided to create this chaos that was the two of us together. I'd never felt as high as when I was with him, nor as low.

Don't worry; I don't feel this way about him now. I'm just trying to explain how I got so caught up with him.

I don't blame you for not understanding my actions, but it was the mixture of my feelings for him, and how I'd been raised. Abuse, I was always told, comes accompanied with bruises. He was this angry, viscous creature. I thought maybe, just maybe if I was nice enough, gentle enough…if I treated him like I wanted to be treated, he'd stop ripping me apart.

Me telling you how Derek acted wasn't to say I didn't want to be treated better or that I never stood up for myself. When we were alone, I tried to talk to him.

"I…I really wish you wouldn't get so frustrated with me, hun. You put me down a lot. I want to be there for you. I'm on your side, so please try and be nicer to me," I began.

"Seriously, Patricia, you always want to talk about this stuff. We were having a perfectly nice dinner. I didn't do anything today. And believe it or not, I'm trying, so can you just drop it?" He scowled.

"Okay sorry, Derek, I didn't mean to offend you. I just wish you could be as nice to me as you were when we first met. Or at least show me the respect I see you offer other people. I don't understand why you feel you can treat me this way. Would you have gotten as mad at me as you have recently, or called me stupid when we first met?" I was feeling bold and I needed him to listen, even if it was just this once.

I was remembering the water glass he threw last week in the kitchen. He was pissed at me, or at life, or something, and whipped his glass at the wall near where I was sitting. Shattered glass and water coated the floor.

"Seriously, Pat? I thought we were past all the social bullshit about being polite and I didn't realize you needed the same courtesy I show acquaintances. I thought I could be real with you..."

"You can be real with me, I want to be closer to you, but I just don't appreciate you disrespecting me." I felt dismissed.

"You always over-exaggerate everything Patricia! I don't know what you want anymore, god. Just drop it. I'm stressed enough as it is, without you wanting to *talk* all the time. I think the problem is that you are easily offended and too sensitive."

You can see how the conversation went.

Maybe I am too sensitive.

I wondered what he saw in me.

I was forgetting what I saw in him.

In Journalism class we were given an assignment about inspiration. I listened to the instructor talk about muses and family, friends, or famous people as sources of inspiration. I immediately thought of Derek. He managed to see the potential in me and my ideas, and pushed me. Sometimes, in my half-asleep haze, I spoke of my desire to be a novelist—words that would never fall from my lips had I been awake. Derek pulled this dream from a sleepy haze faraway in a whispered fantasy. He asked me what I wanted to write about and who my favourite authors were. It's funny that he turned out to be the villain in my first novel, or whatever this is. Or maybe I'm the bad one.

Anyway, I was just this plain, small town girl to him. But he helped me see myself in a way that I hadn't even imagined. Yeah sure, I have my family and the friends I told you about, but there was no one who could reside in my head like Derek.

I wanted to be his muse, as he was mine, but I started to feel that I was just in the way.

I hope this doesn't come off as rambling.

In February we had a romantic and sexy Valentine's Day date. Yeah, yeah, it's a corporate holiday and all that bullshit, but it was the first time I felt love was worthy of celebration. I got a bit swept away, getting him chocolates and stuff, and he gave me this card that would make me blush to share. Regardless of how he acted before, I knew—from the smeared pen in the card and what he whispered to me that night—how much I meant to him.

I needed to remind myself of that sentiment the following week. We had plans to do homework in my dorm on Friday. I got a call from him a half-hour before he was supposed to show.

He told me he was feeling a bit down and overwhelmed, and that he was just going to stay at his place that night. I was disappointed, but having depression I understood, and I had a lot of homework; I focused on my journalism project. Besides, at least he was nice and took the time to call me, rather than send a quick text.

Sunday afternoon he called again, saying he was feeling a bit better and asked if I wanted to get lunch. We went to a small café near his apartment that we had been to a few times prior. It was a quaint place, with a nice lunch menu and Paris themed decorations.

I relaxed. Everything was going okay. He was being friendly and we were having a nice conversation. But what happened next will make me sound like a horrible girlfriend.

When he left for the washroom, Derek left his phone on our small table, titled towards me, almost testing me to see if I'd snoop.

I will not look, I told myself and focused on eating. *I will not look. I trust him, and what kind of girlfriend would that make me if I looked through his phone?*

Then, his phone vibrated, shaking the table with an incoming text. The name "Brittany" flashed on the screen. I could read the message clearly without touching it.

It said: *"I had such a good time on Friday, babe. Text me soon."*

Then, as if motioned by an invisible stage director, Derek emerged from the bathroom and took his seat.

He glanced at his phone and new message, and with a perfect poker face asked me how my food was.

What was I to do? I couldn't just say, "Hey, I looked at your phone, and I see you stood me up on Friday for another girl" or, "Is this Brittany my friend?" *I wondered if I deserved it. Part of me knew I didn't. Part of me thought I did.*

I was frustrated and hurt by Derek, a hurt that deepened because there was no room to address it. I couldn't mention the text, but the text led to more questions and wonder about the contents of the rest of his phone. If I said something, the conversation would shift from the text, to the fact that I looked at his phone, and I would become the guilty party.

I recommend never snooping; it's not worth the weight of knowing things and being forced to keep silent. If you ever wonder if people are saying awful things about you, chances are that yes, if you look in forbidden places, you'll find out things you wish you hadn't.

But, hey, maybe I'm the paranoid one. I'm trying to get as much of this down as possible as I fight the drowsy side effects of the drugs they've given me. The hum of the florescent hospital lights rids me of my remaining sanity.

But what I'm actually trying to say is my snooping wasn't really the issue, but regardless I couldn't talk to Derek. I tried to talk to him a few times about different relationship things, like how we could communicate better. He just told me I always wanted to talk about our relationship and it was annoying. When I tried to tell him that I really wanted to work with him, he shot me some vague line about relationships being about trusting one another, and we trusted each other right? So let's not make a big deal about this, and just relax, school and everything was stressful enough without making a big deal about us. I just agreed seeing as there wasn't much I could say. I figured if he didn't think we had things we needed to talk about, then that was good, right?

After seeing that text I was suddenly more aware of how he interacted with other women. He sometimes introduced me to his acquaintances as Patricia, other times he called me his girlfriend. I didn't know if this was intentional. After all, I hardly ever referred to him as my boyfriend; I preferred to call him Derek because it just felt more personal. But still, I couldn't help but wonder what exactly I was to him or if he just defined me according to whatever was convenient.

At a party shortly thereafter he proudly put his arm around me and introduces introduced me as "his girl." I felt that maybe it would be okay.

It was my interest in literature—I always overanalyzed these things.

CHAPTER 13

I realize I don't mention it all the time, but my life still revolves around ups and downs, with the flow of my depression and anxiety shaping my life. I manage to block it out, just barely under the surface. But I'm still aware that at any second it can completely overpower me.

Anyway, my trip to the social worker's office left a bitter taste in my mouth. Abandoned.

I was having trouble eating, sleeping, and concentrating on school. Time played tricks on me, an hour felt like a day, and all I wanted was for it all to be over. It hurt to think, to breathe, and to be awake. I didn't feel like going to class and I definitely didn't have the drive to do anything extra, like go out with Elyse and Brittany. The only thing I even vaguely looked forward to was seeing Derek. But he was dangerous to use as my source of light in all of this, I soon realized.

My grades suffered, but I didn't care. The consequences of passing or failing seemed abstract and distant against the weight of trying to make it through each minute, each hour, each day.

"Name, student number, and health card number," the lady at the front desk demanded, not looking up from the computer.

I dug in my wallet and just handed her my cards, and didn't bother to waste my energy saying my name. I was waiting for an appointment with the school doctor. I felt that he wouldn't be able to do anything for me, but I was in so much pain that I needed to try *something*.

I have no idea how I found the energy to drag myself there. I sat in a room full of my coughing, sick-looking peers, and I felt less legitimate. What exactly did I expect the doctor to do? My eyes felt heavy. I was startled and struggled to stay alert when a nurse called out "Patricia." I sat up and tried not to rub my eyes as I followed her into a small room.

"What brings you in today, dear?" she asked as she looked down at her chart. Her voice was friendly, but hurried. Everyone was always in such a rush.

"Well, I'm really depressed lately." I was unsure where to begin. I never know where to start, that's why I'm telling you all of this.

"Have you been diagnosed with depression?" she asked, still looking at her paperwork.

"Not formally, no."

"Has anything happened to you recently that you feel may have triggered this?" she asked.

"No, not really. It just gets worse sometimes." I was already wondering why I came.

"When did this episode start?"

What exactly did she mean by episode? Feelings were an episode?

"A few weeks ago," I said, though I wasn't sure. The day I was born? Or what about when my parents first stumbled into one another, and I only existed as a raw state of desire? Or maybe it started when I was blackness, not even a thought, before my mother and father were born. This pain, it was so deep perhaps it started before Adam and Eve, and I'm not even religious.

Don't worry; I kept these thoughts to myself.

This timeline rhetoric is weird. It wasn't like I got sick and would get better; my depression didn't seem to work that way.

"How would you describe your symptoms?" she inquired.

"I, I just have no energy. I'm very tired, and I don't want to do anything I would normally want to do. I'm, I'm getting behind with schoolwork. I was usually really organized with assignments, but I find I just don't care about anything." There was so much more to say, but I didn't know where to begin.

"Thanks, Patricia. The doctor will be with you shortly," she tells me as she shuts the door.

It didn't take long for the doctor to arrive.

"Hi, Patricia. I'm Dr. Peter, nice to meet you. How's your appetite been recently?" he asked looking at the notes from the nurse.

"Okay, sometimes I find it really hard to eat when I'm depressed, but—" he cut me off.

"Be sure to continue with a balanced diet and exercise, nutrition, and an active lifestyle, which is important when it comes to dealing with depression."

Dealing with depression.

"Is there anything else you'd like to tell me about your symptoms that you didn't mention to the nurse?"

"I…I feel…" I realized I had no idea what I was going to say and started to panic. A familiar lump rose in my throat and I was afraid I was going to start bawling in the doctor's office. I had no idea what I could say to the doctor to make him understand. I was utterly helpless. Hopeless.

I left with some name brand anti-depressant prescription in hand. I think I'd seen a commercial for it on television. I promised to book a follow-up appointment in a few weeks.

I rushed from the doctor's waiting room full of sick patients and into the comfort of my residence room. I hurried into bed and let my head, heavy with tears, embrace the pillow as I let go.

Now, you may be wondering what happened with the pills. I took them as prescribed, carefully reading the warning label, and then wishing I hadn't read it. Sometimes I wondered if it was worth taking a medication that had a list of potentially fatal side effects. But I guess depression is fatal as well, isn't it?

I tried to make a daily chart that recorded how I was felt, but the lined paper just mocked me. I was so all over that I really couldn't tell if the pills made a difference.

I reported to Dr. Peter within a month. I told him I didn't feel any better. He seemed more concerned with the fact that I didn't feel worse, and since the potential negative side effects hadn't occurred, I should give it more time. More time…everything needed more time, right? If time was the answer to life's problems, doctors and therapists should just give out clocks.

I took the medication for another few weeks and eventually started to forget to take it. I didn't notice a difference on the days I forgot, so I decided to stop bothering. I never saw Dr. Peter again; and I hid the pill bottle so people couldn't see it when they came over.

I tried different things, like exercise, healthy eating, and more alone time; I even joined a yoga class offered at the school gym. These things made me feel briefly better, but I still felt like a sinking ship, and I had no idea how to help myself. I made an effort to spend more time with friends, arranging coffee dates with Kara and Elyse, but they were both so busy with their own lives that plans needed to be made weeks in advance.

"What's gotten into you?" Elyse casually asked one day when we were watching a movie in her room. "You seem different. Are things going okay?"

She meant well, and I thought that sharing with a friend could help, but I soon realized that trying to explain my depression was a bad idea. She could never understand the language I speak, although she tried, which almost made me feel worse. Alice said that only those who have been there understand; only we can really get one another…

I really missed Alice; but I suppose I'll keep writing. I promised her I would write and I already began, so now I might as well continue. I don't know what else to do.

Elyse was a good friend when I was happy. She was a nice person to be around, fun and caring. But she wasn't t like me, even though I wished I could be more like her. I tried to let her in, but I felt more isolated in the end because I couldn't quite explain myself in a way that she'd understand.

"I saw Derek the other day with this blonde girl. Are you guys still together?" she wanted to know. I wanted to know.

I started avoiding Elyse.

CHAPTER 14

erek wasn't really there to talk to either. He was going through his "own stuff" and made it clear that he didn't have time for more stress with me. The only option I had was to be light. We saw each other less and less. Most of the time when we were together it revolved around last minute plans arranged by him, which almost always involved his bedroom. Whenever I tried to arrange one of our late night meetings, he'd be uninterested. I felt dumb, but I knew that even meeting for sex was completely on his terms. I missed doing other things, but the booty calls were a pleasant distraction from my spirals. The chaos Derek brought into my life somehow brought balance.

Our sex life flourished, and it became rare that we had, what's the term? *Vanilla* sex. Just sharing our bodies was no longer enough. The bedroom became this battle for power; but I realized that Derek needed to be in control, so I let him, occasionally pushing his boundaries and then happily submitting.

It was clear that he derived pleasure from being in charge. His instinctual need for me turned me on, and I felt overcome by his desire.

We acted out different roles—the student and teacher; the cop and civilian; and yes, he even pretended to rape me. Play rape, or consensual non-consent was the term I came across online.

I shouldn't be telling you this, but I already started a while back so why stop now? I wish Alice could read this.

Perhaps you'll understand what I experienced in giving him power over me. I really wasn't passive in all of this. The way my heart beat when I would make dinner, and Derek would just look at me and say, "you're mine, slut," and then he pulled me by the hair, away from the kitchen and into the bedroom. I wouldn't have time to wash the tomato juice off my hands as he lead me by my hair to his bed. He would have my hands pinned above my head and I would know I was trapped. Helpless.

There was one night when I didn't feel like playing.

"No!" I yelled, and with my free legs I tried to kick at him. "No!" I cried again, although I know my protest was useless.

"Shut up, slut. You're making me mad. Stop pretending that you don't want my big cock."

"NO!" I screamed again, but with more force.

Derek put his face near mine and looked me in the eye, glaring. I snarled and bit, trying to distract him to get away. I could see his bulge, partly concealed by his tight jeans. He was still fully dressed. My pants were off. My shirt was still on, but a bit dishevelled from the struggle.

"You fucking bitch," he said and for a second removed one hand from my wrist. My heart thudded and I watched, as if in slow motion, as his hand descended on me. Before I could cower, he hit me gently, then harder, and then as hard as he could.

I was so shocked that I couldn't move. My eyes watered from the pain, and I was ashamed of my tears. I tried to ignore the sting, when suddenly I was overcome by another sensation, as I felt the instant rush of pleasure as he filled me in one thrust. I was dripping.

What was the safe word we agreed on again? The fight had left me, and I heard a moan escape from somewhere so deep that I almost didn't recognize it as my own. I lay still and listened to the sound of my own betrayal.

"See, you like it, you little whore."

I grunted again and he put one hand over my mouth. He was still pinning me down. There was no way I could move under his weight, so I gave in and closed my eyes.

"Shut up! This is about me, not you. You are here for my pleasure, got that?"

Of course, I agreed to all of this, and we'd discussed how I'd signal if I wanted him to stop. And we both know I wouldn't want him to stop—didn't want him to stop.

I struggled with all of this. Why did I want this? What was wrong with me? It felt almost disrespectful to people who are actually sexually assaulted, like I was acting out their experience of trauma. Anonymous internet posts made me feel less alone. I tried to stop the internalized shame, but I had so much to unlearn from my small town upbringing, where even my brother's monogamous gay partnership is met with disproval, averted eyes, and hushes.

PART 2

CHAPTER 1

It's funny that relationships are supposed to be about trust, yet how quickly that fades into the art of deceiving. *Alice said this was why she prefers to stay by herself and trust no one. I'm starting to think she was right.*

I can't exactly recall what took place at that point because it became this back-and-forth game, so excuse me if my story is a little muddled. It could be the drugs I'm on now too. But really, I think it's just the blur of hormones and frustration that's clouding my memory.

Derek and I had plans to go to a poetry reading at a café in Kensington Market. We hadn't gone on a date in a while and I was looking forward to spending time with him.

It was 12 p.m. on Saturday when Elyse, who I hadn't heard from recently, texted me to ask if I want to go for lunch. I told her I had plans with Derek.

She asked me if I was still dating him, and then told me that she thought she saw Derek kissing another girl on campus. It wasn't a blonde, like she had seen before, but a girl with red hair this time.

I wondered if Elyse knew anything about him and a girl named Brittany, or if it was the Brittany we knew. Maybe the redhead's name was Brittany. I tried to put this out of my mind, but I couldn't.

Elyse was worried about how I was doing because I seemed to spend a lot of time with Derek. At first I was flattered that she cared, but then her nosy attitude and her questioning our relationship took me aback. I knew Elyse meant well, and I told myself I'd make time to get together with her soon. In hindsight, I shouldn't have ignored her.

"I'm leaving now. I'll see you soon," I texted Derek, as I locked my door.

"I may stay in bed today. I'm not sure if I want to come."

What? I thought. Normally I would make exception after exception for him, but this time I was mad. If he told me earlier I would have accepted Elyse's invitation, or taken my time with my homework and not woken so early. But he assumed that my time didn't matter and that I was constantly available. I was getting used to being so compliant and it was tiring. Did he care about me at all? Or was I just another form of entertainment? I needed to stand up for myself.

It took a minute to work up the courage to write what I was feeling. My text read, "I really wish you told me sooner. I arranged my day around this and could have made other plans."

"Fuck off," was his response.

I resisted the desire to answer. I remembered all the times he told me I was too much.

Just too fucking much. I was sitting on a bench outside my residence building. Did I want to go by myself? That could be fun, but I was planning on going with Derek, and I was worried that I'd dwell on the fact that he didn't come. I couldn't decide if I wanted to cry or yell.

"Hey, Patricia, I thought you had plans with Derek?" I looked up and saw Elyse standing in front of me with her book bag. Immediately she realized something was off. "Are you okay?"

"Yeah, well, I'm not really sure…" I didn't know how to explain it to her, and for a second I felt really alone. Unable to talk, I pulled out my phone and showed her the message instead. Elyse, as expected, wasn't impressed.

"Does he often talk to you like this? It isn't at all acceptable to just tell you to fuck off. He could've given you an explanation as to why he can't make it."

"I wouldn't have said anything, but I feel like my time didn't matter or something. I would have loved to have met up with you earlier for lunch, but I said no because I wanted to keep my plans. He assumes I have no life and that I'll just make myself available for him." I knew that too, was my fault.

"This really doesn't sound healthy. You need to be able to stick up for yourself more and to feel like you are being respected."

"I know, I agree I really need to talk to him. I know it seems like a small thing. He wasn't feeling well or whatever and snapped, but still."

"I think it is reasonable that this bothers you and you have the right to stand up for yourself. I'm just going to get a coffee and find somewhere to work on a paper. Wanna join?"

I was tired and I didn't want to think. I needed someone to tell me what to do and Elyse could do just that. I ran upstairs and got my computer and we found a coffee shop to work. We ate desserts and sipped coffee and talked about school.

She tried to mention Derek. I was actually so annoyed that for once I didn't want to think about him. I heard my phone buzzing in my bag and ignored it.

When Elyse began her assignment, I pulled out my phone; I had four new messages, all from Derek.

The first, "Seriously Patricia, you overreact and get so clingy. So what if I didn't want to go to the dumb poetry thing today." I opened the next message, sent ten minutes later. "Are you not talking to me now? Seriously? I was going to ask you if you wanted to do something later, maybe get a bite to eat." No apology, just his unflattering commentary. The third message, "I wasn't feeling great today. I went out last night and didn't feel up to getting out of bed and then you started texting me, okay?" This is as close to an apology as I was going to get. And the final message, "Fuck you, Patricia, seriously. I try to explain and make it up to you, and you don't bother to answer me. I'm done with you and all your stupid shit. We're done."

I was stunned. Just like that he wanted nothing to do with me? He went from half-apologizing and wanting to go out for lunch to telling me it was over? I It didn't seem real; he would change his mind. I didn't have a chance to answer his texts. What did I do?

Seriously, what did I do? There were so many times when he didn't respond to my texts and I never expected him to get back immediately. I was talking with a friend. I often ignore my phone when I'm not expecting someone and only a handful of people text me anyway. And again, the continual refrain is, I should have been done with him sooner. I *guess this whole story is me telling you the same thing over again.*

I took a deep breath and told myself that Derek was not going to further ruin my day. I breathed in and out—felt the rise of my chest and the fall of my breath.

I refused to accept that we were done. This man I had spent so much time with and opened myself up to wouldn't just dismiss me with a text. That's it, goodbye. You don't even deserve a phone conversation.

I tried to focus on my reading for philosophy class, but I kept thinking of the first time I talked to Derek in the library.

"I can't concentrate. I'm going to get going." I told Elyse.

I didn't show her the texts from Derek. I was unsure what was happening with us, and I didn't want her to know he dumped me. Not like that—at least not now. I figured Elyse would tell me to stand up for myself, and that my life would be better without him. But she didn't know about the beautiful complexities of our relationship. And I wasn't ready to listen to a voice of reason.

Derek and I—two unstable people fighting for power over ourselves and each other. I was a constant storm of anxiety and depression and Derek was in a battle with apathy and alcoholism. I knew then and I know now that there was no way the two of us could be good together.

I wish I had managed to explain this to Alice, but I was always too late. Hell, I wish I had managed to explain this properly to myself.

But I still wanted him. Or at the very least I wanted answers. I wanted to know why I was never going to spend another Saturday with him, or wake up with him. I wanted to know why I would never feel his arms around me again. What happened? Why was he being like this?

Against my better judgement, I called him. It was only around 3 p.m., but it sounded like he was at a bar. I held my phone in my shaky hand. I could barely hear him when he answered on the last ring.

"Hey," he sounded distant, cold.

"Hi, Derek, I'm really hoping that we can talk," I began, with uncertainty in my voice.

"Well, I'm out with my friends now, and I don't feel like meeting…"

"Okay," I responded, unsure if this was the end of the conversation, or the beginning.

"I meant what I said, Pat. We're done. I'm done with you. I need things to be simple in my life right now and you make things complicated. We just aren't the best match. I mean, it was fun, but we're just too different. We'd get bored with each other in a year or so. And besides, we shouldn't get in each other's way of finding *the one*."

So he really did mean it.

"I still really wish we could talk in person. I thought you were happy being with me?"

I was so confused and I needed answers. I felt like I was interacting with two different versions of Derek; one who I really want to be with, and the other not so much.

There was some old saying about only keeping the people in your life that inspire you and who you desire to be like.

Derek, once both, was now neither.

"My friends, who I've known longer than you, really don't think you are good for me. And they're right. Sorry, Patricia, but I've gotta get going. Maybe we can talk more later, but not now," and he hung up.

What friends was he referring to? The guys he didn't really like from the Christmas party? He didn't have any consistent friends. I knew we were done, but I felt pushed away, lacking an explanation that made sense.

I would tell you what happened over the next few days, but it was a blur. We were done, but I still felt like he had the upper hand. He said that maybe we'd talk *later* and I felt like I was sitting around, stunned and moping, waiting to see when and if *later* would come. I held on to some tiny bit of hope that Derek would call me and want to talk and figure something out.

CHAPTER 2

I was slowly starting to heal and come to terms with the fact that my life was about school and survival, and that Derek was no longer part of it. He was so surreal, anyway. As I lay in bed, my pillow tear-soaked and my thoughts heavy, it was almost easy to feel as if I imagined him and our entire relationship. Alice once suggested that maybe I did and I kicked her playfully in response as we sat beside each other in the peer support group.

But really, did someone that worldly—that exciting—that interesting come into my life? I hate to sound so cliché, but we really were from different worlds. If school didn't bring us together; Derek and I would never have met.

Still, things weren't perfectly resolved and I alternated between accepting that Derek and I were finished, to trying to think of how to get him to talk to me. He gave me a bit of hope that there was room to talk and I was having trouble focusing on the fact that my life was better without him. *I know; I know how this sounds.*

I saw Derek in philosophy class. He said, "hi" to me and sat with me just like he always did. It almost felt like before—almost.

We got coffee after class—his suggestion, not mine—and talked about everything.

Well, we talked about everything, but us. It was clear that he didn't want to talk about what happened. Even the question, "how are you?" was met by a quick, "good" before redirecting the conversation to school. I'm sure he could tell I wanted to talk as I squirmed in my seat and bit my lip with anticipation; but he didn't go there, so neither did I.

The meeting left me unsettled. I was glad he still wanted to interact with me, but I really wished it wasn't like that. I needed to understand what happened between us and decide if I wanted to try and move on as friends. I felt like Derek had put a bookmark in me and marked it, *deal with later*. I tried to press pause on my feelings until that conversation.

This was followed by an awful period of waiting; I continually checked my phone and Facebook, wondering if and when he'd message me. We weren't together, so it wasn't like I really expected to hear from him, but still, I hated the way I made myself available. I knew I shouldn't have made myself so open; it was always dangerous to show you care and to give someone power. Lesson learned, indeed.

But where was I?

One Saturday I got a message from Derek, asking what I was up to. I still didn't know what was going on with us and I was feeling raw and vulnerable, so of course I stupidly agreed to see him.

After that things just kind of happened. Without a conversation we resumed our roles and acted as if we were together. The week we were apart was absolute hell, but I couldn't ask Derek how he felt because it still seemed like he didn't really want to talk. We could be together, but he just wanted to enjoy my company, and not reflect as he said before.

I should've gotten out then, as it was clear that he meant more to me than I did to him. But we still kissed, embraced and murmured, "I love you." He was actually the first to whisper it after we split. I needed to be on my best behaviour or else I'd feel like he could walk away from me again without explanation. I think he knew that I loved him, and because of that he could treat me how he wanted. I unintentionally made myself his for the taking. Big mistake.

He was always stressed about school and struggling financially because of his student loans and excessive drinking. Sometimes I felt like I was just another thing he needed to deal with.

And he was always so tense, barely holding it together. This made me a bit jumpy in his presence.

I still loved him, but I admit, I didn't enjoy being around him anymore. I know, I know, twenty-first century women don't need to stick around, and I should have shrugged and kept walking. It's never as simple as saying, "I'm not going to be treated like that," and walking away.

Things got worse, but I knew they would. I guess I just liked watching car crashes.

I won't tell you the names he called me when he was drunk, or the number of times he left me hanging until the last minute to cancel plans. Once, we were having a debate at a bar and he started yelling at me about my privileged upbringing until the other tables turned to stare. I hurried off to the bathroom to escape his wrath and their sympathetic glances. He actually dared to ask if I planned on coming back from the washroom, only because he didn't want to be left at the table.

Whenever I tried to get closer to him, or simply enjoy his company, Derek filled our interactions with his anger. Once we were on the subway and we started talking about if art degrees are useful or nothing more than a social expectation for a certain demographic.

"Someone like you clearly can't understand my position," he scoffed at me.

This conversation ended with him calling me both stupid and privileged. He claimed that he actually had to work to get where he was. There was no room for me to mention all the long hours I put in working summer jobs to save for school and the pile of debt I now have. I almost felt like he hated me, but I told myself that it was just my depression, my anxiety, and my inability to read social situations. But as people turned to look at us, I could see concern and pity on their faces. That was when I knew it wasn't in my head.

He was always angry and looking to fight. I realized I needed to get away. All I had to do was brace myself and make it happen. I felt like I was a smoker trying desperately to quit, knowing that I was hurting my body, but craving what killed me.

I'm going to quit, I kept telling myself.

I decided to risk it all and asked Derek if he wanted to be with me and if he wanted us to work.

I didn't get a, *yes*, but I didn't get a, *no* either. Instead I got a, "babe, you know I find it stressful talking about this stuff. Let's just leave it alone, okay?"

So that was exactly what I did.

I realize that I couldn't be with someone who was both indifferent and rough. This wasn't the Derek I fell for. I didn't want to ruin that memory any further, so I told him that I couldn't be with him.

As expected, he didn't really react. I needed someone who'd bother to react—who would care if we were together or not. Clearly I didn't need Derek and I should've stayed away.

But there's more to tell, so I must be crazy.

And so the game of breaking up and getting back together began.

Forgetting Derek was a full time commitment. Elyse tried to follow up by asking what happened, but I nicely told her I didn't want to talk. She invited me to the bar with her and Brittany, but I didn't feel like socializing with Brittany of all people. I remembered the name Brittany appearing on Derek's phone, so naturally all I could picture was Derek and Brittany on his bed. It didn't matter that I didn't know if it was her specifically. I didn't really know anything.

Finally, I relented and agreed to visit Elyse. I more or less told Elyse what happened. She was an avid and empathetic listener, and a better friend than me. But still, I couldn't help but wonder if she was motivated by the desire to know the latest drama or because she actually cared. I kept telling her that I didn't want to talk about it, yet somehow Derek and I were the conversation of the evening. It actually felt good to talk about the relationship.

As I began to talk about some of the things that happened between us, I became more and more angry. For the first time, I was relieved that we were no longer together. The anger was an easier emotion to deal with than feeling empty, deserted, heartbroken, and worthless. Elyse affirmed that he wasn't a nice person and that I was better off without him. She told me there were plenty of nice guys out there that would treat me with respect.

Yeah, right. Derek was a gentle, interesting, self-proclaimed feminist, who turned out to be such a monster. I had no desire to let anyone else in.

I left Elyse's room feeling a new sense of anger toward Derek, as if the events of the last few months just occurred. I was proud of myself for walking away.

The next day I saw Brittany in the library. She made some comment about how she was sorry to hear about Derek and I. I couldn't help but wonder what she knew, or what Elyse told her.

Elyse asked me over again later that week, but I made up an excuse about having schoolwork.

Kara invited me over for dinner, but I also told her I had lots of schoolwork. I hadn't told her what happened with Derek. I just didn't feel like explaining or acknowledging that we were over. So I pushed everyone away.

Later I realized I had no one, but by then it was too late.

I kept busy with schoolwork as the end of the term approached, but Derek's absence, cruelty, and his indifference are always present. I kept replaying the mean things he said to me. Sometimes I used them to tell myself I was better off without him, other times I used these thoughts to hurt myself.

I was afraid to move forward. I had a strange relationship with time. I wanted to go back a few months and start over with him. Impress him. Sometimes, I wished to go back further and erase him completely.

Since people claim time is the greatest healer, I sometimes wished the next few months away. We could have skipped joyous summer and go to fall. I wanted to be too busy with school to think and to feel. But I was also afraid of time moving forward. I was afraid of the days and weeks passing without Derek in my life. Everyone says that moving on takes time, but how much time? It seemed so simple, but I was in so much pain. I didn't want to move on without him, so I tried to freeze time in some impossible way. I stayed in my room and worked on assignments. I attended the minimum number of lectures.

My fingernails caught on my clothing and ripped, but I refused to trim them—unwilling to accept that my body still acknowledged the passing of time. I lived in my pyjamas. I only washed them when my white top became grey and sweat stained the armpits. My frayed shirt became an extension of my body. It seemed irrelevant if my clothing or hair was clean against the backdrop of what I was experiencing.

I told myself not to let the depression win. Not to let him win; keep going, get by, get up, and finish the school term. But it was so difficult.

I hardly ate; I could only force myself to eat plain dry foods without taste. It matched my life without pleasure. I loved cooking with Derek; food was life, culture, flavour, and pleasure back then. I forced myself to eat when my stomach growled.

My desire to live dissipated. I found myself gagging on plain toast, my body unable or unwilling to perform basic functions. I took hours to eat meals, picking away at soups and stir-fries as assignments filled my computer screen. I got the keyboard greasy, crumbs falling between keys and I really didn't care.

When I ran into Aashi, she commented that I'd lost weight and that I looked good. If only she knew. I missed our conversations—the ones when he was kind. I missed doing things with him. I wanted to know what he was up to.

We avoided each other in class, careful not to make eye contact. Lovers to strangers and I looked forward to the end of the term when we would no longer see each other.

I missed his embrace. It's funny how muscle memory works; I could feel the ghost of his touch, even though our skin hadn't met in weeks. I could close my eyes and remember exactly what his hand felt like in mine and how much space I took up in his bed. I could sense the weight of his comforter and his arm wrapped around my body. I could feel the thickness of his dreadlocks in my hands as I played with them, twirling strands in my fingers, or the way his hair rubbed against my face as we cuddled. I could touch the warmth of his body.

I was overcome by the sadness of his absence. I was still waiting for a sense of relief, but all I felt was emptiness. I was numb and indifferent to life.

I emerged from the dorm shower and looked at myself in the mirror. I was overcome by memories of Derek and I having sex. Not gentle lovemaking, but rough fucking. I sat on the edge of my bed; my body still slightly damp, nipples hard, and began to finger myself. Derek's voice was in my head. He called me a good little slut and that he was going to take me whether I wanted it or not.

I was dripping as I thought about him holding me down, his hand firmly against my neck, as he quickly moved in and out. I heard him whisper that he was going to fill me, whether I wanted him to or not. I climaxed three times, letting out a noise I'd never heard before. I was filled with a mixture of lust, and shame for wanting him.

You can go touch yourself now. I'll wait.

CHAPTER 3

I decided that I was here for school and that was that. Rather than going home for the spring and summer, I'd take classes and get a part-time job. The idea of having any free time scared me.

"Are you sure that's the right thing sweetie? Don't you want a break from schoolwork? Wouldn't time at home be nice?" My mom asked when I called her about my decision.

"It'll be okay, I just want to keep going and get my degree faster," I replied.

"Okay, well good work then. We're proud of you," she paused. "Oh, and by the way, your dad saw this ad for free life insurance with the bank. This special is on for another month. I'm going to send you the number to call."

"Okay, mom. Thanks." Ha, life insurance.

My mom was always so practical. Well, at least she thought I was worth something.

I was by no means happy, but I had accepted my present circumstances and life slowly became tolerable. I congratulated myself for almost finishing the school semester. I reminded myself of my panic attack on the subway in the fall and how far I'd come. I managed to make it through not only the academic year, but also my messy parting with Derek.

I was still having trouble sleeping, either oversleeping in an effort to forget, or too upset to manage adequate rest. Sometimes,

I woke from dreams of Derek that were so vivid that I had to remind myself that he was no longer in my life. I lay awake in the morning thinking about what happened and where things went wrong.

I know, I know; chasing the same thoughts over and over in my mind wasn't helpful, but it was all I could do to make sense of his absence. I still felt the weight of his body against mine as we lay together in bed.

My head was often heavy and I felt dizzy. I continued to mistake dreams for actual events. Real things or imagined, they blended together.

Anyway, I think it was the last day of class and I remember being surprised to see Derek, as he missed the previous classes. I carefully avoided him; I didn't sit near him and ensured that he didn't catch me looking at him. I wondered if he was even aware of my presence in the room, or if I was just some girl he had a fling with, long forgotten.

"Patricia."

I looked up and he was beside me as I exited the classroom. He must have raced to catch up to me.

"How are you?" He placed his hand on my arm and I was torn between wanting to throw it off and walk the other way, and wanting to further embrace him.

"I'm okay," I whispered, as I continued my speed walk, but he easily matched my pace.

"Pat, wait. I'm really sorry about how things ended. I care about you, and I just didn't know how to show it. I'm stressed about school, and money, and was having trouble focusing on us. I know you left because you think I don't care about you, but the truth is that I do care about you. I miss talking to you, miss spending time with you."

"Yeah?" I whispered. I didn't quite know how to respond.

He was looking at me tenderly, and as I looked at him my heart felt like it was going to stop. I had this impulse to just kiss him and hold him, and maybe fuck him in middle of the hall at school. My anger, pain, frustration and sadness were absolved. All the hateful and disrespectful things he'd done dissipated, and he was just this guy that I was crazy for. He was standing before me, telling me he missed me and wanted me. So you can't really blame me. "I love you, Patricia," he whispered, taking my face in his hands. We were standing in a busy hallway as students streamed out of lecture halls, and somehow that exact moment was perfect.

"I love you, too," I automatically responded, and I knew it was game over. I would always be his. I didn't have the strength or will to walk away when every ounce of my body wanted to embrace him.

"I was actually wondering if you wanted to go to the end of term formal with me?" He asked, but I think he already knew the answer. I'd barely said a word since he started talking to me, but in the course of a few minutes I went from avoiding him to having trouble containing my smile. All my sorrow and frustration dissipated, and we left the school hand-in-hand. The rest of the day was spent reacquainting ourselves in his bed.

I know how this sounds. You are likely thinking that I was better off without him and that I just excused him and let him back into my life so easily; but when he came to talk to me and looked me in the eyes, all my will power was gone. The entire month of pain was erased, and I knew that I would gladly live through it again, if only I could be with him longer.

CHAPTER 4

I scrambled to find the perfect dress for formal. I wanted to look amazing. I know this wasn't really Derek's thing, and he only asked as a way of inviting me back into his life.

Elyse came by for a surprise visit, and asked what my plans were for the summer. She saw my gorgeous floor-length dress— a shimmery, aqua gown displayed on my bed.

"Whoa, beautiful dress! Are you going to formal?"

"Yeah, do you like it? I'm not sure if I can pull it off, but I really love it. I feel like a mermaid or something." I picked up the dress so she could get a better look. I knew what was coming next, but it was too late to avoid the conversation.

"So, who's the lucky gentleman?" she asked.

I blushed and then stammered, "Derek asked me."

"Oh no, I thought you were done with him! You're amazing, Patricia. I bet so many other guys would love the chance to go to formal with you."

"I know, but I really missed him. He asked me and I just said yes without thinking." I wanted Elyse to leave it alone.

"I'm happy for you, Pat, just as long as it's what you want and he's nice to you. I really didn't like how he was treating you. Those texts you showed me were awful." She smiled at me and looked at the dress.

"I know, but he isn't normally like that. He was just really stressed."

"Well, I'm not going to formal, but I'll be in residence that day studying, so if you want me to do your hair or makeup or anything, let me know." She offered.

She helped me prepare for formal, and again, expressed her concern about Derek, but I ignored her worry. She made me look beautiful that night. My hair was pinned back, with a few curls framing my face, and the blue dress was complimented by blue makeup. She also lent me a pair of heels, which I needed to practice walking in.

Elyse always seemed to offer more to me than I had to return. I should have paid more attention to her. She was always so good to me.

The formal was a whirlwind of activity. Derek greeted me in my room, and told me how absolutely gorgeous I was. He twirled me around and kissed me, and then pinned on my corsage. He had an aqua tie to match my dress. We looked amazing together—like we belonged.

We arrived at the school bar hand-in-hand, and a photographer took our picture. I still have it actually. I couldn't bring myself to dispose of the photo. It was the first and only picture of Derek and I together. His arm was holding me tightly to his side.

I try to rip up the picture and throw it out several times, but instead I bury it in a junk box. I need to keep it as proof Derek was real, that this was real.

We laughed and flirted and it felt reminiscent of our first date. Sitting at a table with other couples seemed to reinforce our status. After dinner we danced for a bit, although the dance floor seemed unnatural. We laughed as we swayed to the music and I felt so content in his arms. I know, a lot of this sounds like it's from some dumb romance movie, but this was how I felt.

A sense of urgency to touch each other emerged from the energy of the formal. We hurried home to Derek's apartment.

The school term came to an end. As predicted, I was stressed about exams, but I was so distracted by my renewed relationship with Derek, that it seemed I had little time to stress. I said goodbye to Elyse and Brittany as they packed to go home for the summer.

Derek suggested that we go away for a weekend, just the two of us, before the spring term. We rented a car and went to a cabin in the Muskoka area. The cottage was on a beautiful small lake, and we spent those April days sitting on the dock reading, sipping coffee, and wandering through the woods. We stayed in bed cuddling and talking long after the sun rose. We watched the sunset, my head on his shoulder. The sun peacefully faded into the lake, the sky illuminated with leftover pink and purple cotton candy colours. Sometimes we talked a lot, other times, we didn't need to speak, and just the presence of the other was enough. We didn't fight; our interactions and conversations came smoothly. We made love loudly, unrestrained by time or if anyone could hear. We had sex in the woods, on the dock, in the bed, and on the couch. The loons cried to our song, the wolves howled in competition.

School started and things returned to some semblance of normalcy and we fell into a routine. Derek wasn't taking classes because he needed to save for the fall term. He got a full time job as a bartender, which he was relatively happy with. I was only taking one class, so I had a bit of free time and got a part-time job at a café. I daydreamed about my nights spent with Derek as I took cash and drink orders. It had only been three weeks since Derek asked me to the dance and we were inseparable. He would send me cute good morning texts, and we'd do as many fun things together as possible. My previous worry that I was just another girl disappeared. But I did worry that our relationship, as solid as it seemed, was standing on unstable supports. If he was having a bad day, would he break up with me again? What if he started being cruel? Would he listen to me and care about my feeling when I tell him to stop? Was he seeing other people? I had no answers, but I didn't want to ruin the spell, so I bided my time and waited for the ideal opportunity to talk with him. Of course that moment never came and the months passed since we got back together.

CHAPTER 5

It was a bleak, cold, bitter day. I struggled to walk to Derek's apartment. I could hardly breathe. I was weighed down by my thick marshmallow coat. I was weighed down by life.

"Hey, hun, come sit on the floor with me," Derek greeted me at the door. His usually messy hair was even more dishevelled and he only wore rainbow coloured pants that resembled a quilt. He took my hand and pulled me inside. He instructed me to sit cross-legged and look at him.

"Just breathe with me, okay?" He took my hand in his own and closed his eyes, lost in some trance.

I hadn't spoken a word since entering his apartment. I wondered if he noticed the state I was in. I tried to close my eyes. "Deep breath in, deep breath out," he instructed.

I watched Derek's dreads fall in his face as he sat on his floor, eyes closed, surrounded by empty beer bottles and dirty clothes. Laugher threatens to spill from my belly. I fidgeted with my phone and saw I had one new voicemail. I must have missed the ringing as I walked.

"What'cha doing, babe? Put that thing away." Derek squinted at me and reached over to pull my phone from my hand, gently kissing my cheek in the process.

Later, when Derek was in the washroom, I checked my phone and saw that I had two missed calls and a text message, both from Todd. Todd hardly ever called, and never leaves a message. My stomach sank.

"Hey, Patricia, mom was in a car accident. I don't know her condition. She's at the hospital, and I'm just waiting to hear back. I'll call you with an update as soon as I know anything. Don't worry, just wanted to let you know," was the message my brother left.

Oh my god, what if something actually happened to my mom? I hardly knew her, never had the opportunity to get close. What if she was seriously hurt? What if she dies...?

I sat down on the floor in Derek's hall, shaking as a lump rose in my throat. I needed to call Todd, but I couldn't breathe.

What if she's really hurt, car totalled, in surgery, doesn't make it...What if I'm calling too late? All of this was happening when I was fucking meditating with my boyfriend.

I pulled out my phone and tried to call Todd back. My hand was shaking so much that it took three tries for the phone to dial. The line was busy.

Frantic, I tried again a second later. Still busy. A third — busy.

Derek emerged from the bathroom and I told him what happened. He took my hand and pulled me from the floor and back into the living room, by this time I was sobbing. I wrapped my arms around my knees. Derek didn't touch me.

"Well, that's too bad, but I guess the only thing you can really do now is wait to hear back." He told me.

"I know I need to wait, but it's hard and I don't know what happened. And what if it's really serious? I'm not ready for her to be in a coma or die...I don't know if she's okay. If it was only a small accident then my brother wouldn't have bothered calling, at least not until, until he knew what was happening." I had a picture in my head of my mom in a sterile hospital bed, eyes closed, barely breathing, attached to a tangle of cords and a monitor. I tried to think of something else, but my brain flipped to the image of a totaled car against a hydro line, glass and blood all over the street, body ejected through the windshield. Sirens. I shivered.

"Relax, Patricia. You don't know what happened yet, so you just need to wait. And besides, life is in a constant state of change. Bodies age and time moves forward. The earth changes, grows, and expands. Things rot, decompose. We need imbalances to be natural. We need these...these freak accidents to balance out the earth. Nothing stays the same forever. No one dies of old age; we may say that, but it needs to be of something—of cancer, or heart failure, or maybe from a car accident. Statistically, the longer you live the more likely you are to get in an accident. Sickness, car accidents, house fires, and shootings are really about the passing of time, time, time. What is time? So yeah the longer you drive...getting in a car accident is only natural..."

"Yes, I guess you have a point, but still, I'm worried about my mom and that's legitimate." I wanted to reach over and shake his shoulders.

Didn't he get it? What an asshole. He was acting strange today. I tried to block him out and concentrated on telling myself it was going to be okay.

"Here, just listen to this and see if you can feel what I mean," he said. He went to his computer and clicked on something then sat down again.

I was overcome with the sound of running water and the beat of a drum. Derek lit some incense and I struggled to breathe. He didn't notice. I wanted to slam his laptop shut and scream.

"Here, hold my hand, deep breath with me. Inhale. Let the music take over. You see what I mean? It's all about nature. Everything that's happening in your life is about this rhythmic circle. Everything returns to the elements of life. Oh man, just close your eyes. I am in the forest by the waterfall. I am the waterfall. I am the drum. I am life."

I was sweating and uncomfortable. I wondered what the hell was going on with him. Restless, I needed out. Out. Glass, blood, smashed car, sterile hospital, the beep, beep, beep of machines.

"Hey, do you think we can go for a little walk, get some air?" I needed to be out of his apartment away from the drumbeat and incense.

"Oh shit, what time is it? Last night I told Ben I could bring him a few tabs of acid and I was supposed to chill with the guys today. I just got so carried away that I totally forgot to look at the time. What time is it?"

That explained a lot.

"Around 3 p.m."

"Oh man, let me look at my phone. Yep, two missed calls from Ben. Let's go." He hurried me out the door, but had to return a minute later for his keys and wallet. We started walking.

"I think I might just go back to my place. I have school stuff to do and I need to be alone right now."

"Are you kidding? It's a beautiful day! Don't rush off, Patty; enjoy it with me. As you were just reminded, sometimes you only get today…Hey, did you see that tree? Look at the outline of that maple tree. It looks like it blends in with the clouds and is dancing with the other tree…What was I saying? Oh yeah, time…is just a capitalist invention—totally man-made. Do you know how the modern calendar was created?"

Time might be manmade, but my mom's time, our time, would still run out someday. But I didn't say that to him because he'd think I was being silly or too serious. I looked at my phone and still had no call from my brother. I thought about calling my grandparents, but I didn't want to worry them. I tried calling dad, but his phone went to voicemail.

I was so scared. Was my mom okay? Was she okay? And what about her and I? We had a distant, but functional relationship, but were never really close. There was still so much I didn't know about her. I wanted to hear about the first time she got drunk, and if she ever tried to run away as a teenager, and if she thought she'd end up marrying someone like dad, and if she ever really wanted kids or did it because of social pressure?

She can't die. I didn't know her yet. I was being selfish and making this about me, but of course it was about me too.

Derek took my hand and led me down the street, but he pulled away to pick up a caterpillar from the sidewalk.

"Hey, just look at this guy. He's an example of what I was talking about and this circle of life thing. Like, this guy is slow by nature, so he's going to get run over by cars and people, but that's okay. That's the caterpillar's role in this cycle. You see, it all relates. We need diseases, accidents, and disasters, or there wouldn't be enough resources for everyone. Oh, look at that over there! See the way the sun is hitting the clouds and the sunrays are coming through? I'm so happy to be alive right now." He skipped and took my hand again, swinging it with the last words of his statement.

"Yeah, the sun looks pretty," I replied. "Hey, I'm actually not feeling the greatest, so I think I may head home. I'm not really up to partying."

"Is this about your mom? Honestly, I wouldn't worry about her. She's probably okay. And if it's more serious, well, you see…it's like the caterpillar and the trees in the forest and everything in nature is this huge matrix! We all get injured and die someday. And, well, we eventually become the soil and…but really…please, Patricia, stay a little longer. Enjoy the day with me."

I felt my eyes soften and a sob slowly rose in my throat. I realized how alone I was. I used to be able to talk to him. And now I was worried about my mom and he was high as a kite.

I went home and tried to focus on schoolwork.

I read the same paragraph five times. I sighed and shut the book. I moved over to my bed with my laptop and looked for something mindless to watch. Again, I zoned out. Eventually, I was startled by my phone ringing.

"Hey, Patricia. Sorry, I was at the hospital and then my phone died and things were just pretty busy. Mom's going to be fine." Todd's voice flowed through the speaker.

She was going to be okay? She was going to be okay? I struggled to hear what he said next.

"She has a fractured left arm and broken ribs, but that was from the airbag. I guess someone rolled through the stop sign and was on their phone."

"Oh thank god, your message really scared me…"

"Yeah, sorry about that. Dad was panicking and called me and asked to come to the hospital. I didn't know what was going on yet, but figured I should contact you. Then I had to call and cancel all my work appointments for today while I was waiting, which drained my battery. We are settled at home now with mom." My usually calm brother sounded flustered. This was probably the most serious conversation we've had. I could hear the tiredness and worry in his voice. He was probably sitting in the emergency room, thinking the same what if's that marched through my head.

I offered to go home and help since my mom had a broken arm, but my parents quickly told me not to worry. They were both taking a few days off work while mom recovered. She would have a cast on for a while and had to be careful not to fall on her broken ribs. The echoes of what could have been floated through my thoughts for the next week or two, but eventually faded.

Having a reminder of her morality didn't exactly by default make my mom easier to connect with, despite my resolve to try. I called her a few extra times in the next month, knowing that her regular emails may be harder to type with the broken arm. But then the scare faded in my memory. The accident didn't automatically change our stiff history.

CHAPTER 6

Stereotypes about love clouded my judgement about what was taking place. You see, I'd been told that love was about accepting all of someone, and that people don't really change. So I guess instead of standing up for myself, I figured the little attacks toward me came with being with Derek and that was just how he was.

I was just spellbound. I know how this sounds. I wasn't really ready to end things, and a little kick at my self-esteem every now and then seemed like a small price for remaining at his side. I didn't fully realize the cost until much later.

And besides, I didn't really have the language to label it as abuse. The dorm hall was covered in self-help posters. One showed a picture of a woman with a black eye and the number for a domestic violence helpline. But this picture of abuse, that wasn't me. I was reminded of the endless commercials against domestic violence. They showed abuse as physical danger, blood and broken bones. But he never touched me.

I thought I was being empathetic. I understood that Derek's words were not his own, rather his frustration with life and the liquor taking control. No, the longhaired hippy with the feminist politics—he'd never tell me how stupid and boring I was, how he couldn't stand listening to me, or how I was wasting his time. He told me I was ugly, that I didn't dress sexy enough. When I tried harder for him, he turned around, looked at my outfit and called me a slut. He commented on other girls in front of me, almost encouraging me to get angry. He wanted me to fight back, but I was not a fighter. He whispered that he "normally didn't go for girls with tits like mine," and then murmured, "oh look how nice her rack is." I know he sounds like a total asshole, but he said these things in a more subtle way. He just hid his comments enough to get away with them. I was starting to feel like he hated me and I wondered why he was even with me. But I realized that it was his self-hate talking and my self-hate that made me stay.

He had few nice things to say about me, but he had fewer to say about himself. Underneath that carefree mask I could see the pressure he was under. He didn't really like himself, even though he came off as thinking he was all that. He constantly worried about money, and I noted the comments he made about other men's appearances. He was gorgeous mind you, but you might think I'm biased. He didn't look like the guy in the muscle shirt at the gym with the model girlfriend babe, and I think that was starting to weigh on him. He wanted to be everything at once and didn't know what kind of man to be. He loved talking about books more than cars, travelling more than money, and ideas more than people. But his friends laughed at him. We went to a party and his buddy asked if he'd seen the latest action flick, and then someone else commented, "Of course you haven't; all you do is read." They also teased him as they barbequed steaks, asking what kind of man doesn't eat meat. What kind of man?

He was also struggling with school. He was smart, but a bit directionless. He wasn't sure what he would do after he completed his philosophy degree and now he was in debt because of school.

All of this is to show you that he could be a nice partner; we spent weekends laughing and talking, eating and staying in bed for far too long. But he was bothered by other things, and took his anger and frustration out on me. I once asked him during one of his outbursts why he spoke to me the way he did, and I asked if he'd talk to Ben like that? He said no, but that was because of social rules and trying to be polite because he doesn't know Ben as well as me.

You see, it was because there were no longer these social walls between us. I should have felt flattered; he was being real with me, no longer saw the need for social formalities.

I asked myself now and then why I stayed so long. Beyond the obvious recourse of I loved him, I was starting to feel a bit sorry for him. I'm not saying how he treated me was right; it was just that I understood the stress.

There are old sayings about leaving the past behind, but then they also say that the past and the people in it are what shape us. I guess we can consciously leave the past behind, but our ghosts become part of us and they shape our thoughts. They are no longer conscious memories, but part of our DNA. Derek never intentionally talked about *her,* but she was part of his history. She was a secret—a sacred memory that occasionally slipped from sealed lips. I never even learned her name, as though it was too painful or precious to utter. But I caught glimpses of their life together: a passing reference to a shared apartment, a silver watch that he kept in his top drawer and refused to wear, a tattoo of a heart that he shrugged about when I tried to ask him the meaning. These were the prints she left in his present life.

I was left wondering about her. What happened? Where was she? Why didn't they work? Was she even alive? Did she leave him, or did he leave her? Did he love me as much as he loved her, or was anyone after her a second or third best? I tried to tell myself that Derek loved me, and was with me, but I couldn't help but wonder about his silent past and how I measured against the ghost. Did he think about her as he fucked me? When I gave him blowjobs? I couldn't get her out of my head. Who was this mysterious past lover? Was I as good as she was? Was he thinking about her, as he closed his eyes and moaned, yanking my hair? Did he close his eyes and remember her every time another woman touched him? As I stood embracing his naked body, feeling our skin merge, I wondered who she was. Did he love her first? I couldn't help wondering how many women like me came after her.

I realize how this must sound to you, but that's okay, I can let it all out now.

His family was also a mystery. He mentioned visiting his sister, but when I tried to ask him about the rest of his family, he changed the subject. Are they still living, or are they not speaking? Or did he just not want to include me in his life? He answered many questions with silence, which resulted in me creating my own answers. All this is to say that he knew more about me than I about him.

There was a point though, when frustration outweighed the sex appeal of mystery, and annoyance won. I knew all the blemishes on his body, but not his mother's name. I also knew that Derek was nothing, nothing, but bad news, *but you see why I deceived myself, don't you?*

CHAPTER 7

We went out on a Wednesday night in mid-May. He was working at a bar from Thursday to Sunday, and wanted to have some fun before his workweek started. I didn't really feel like drinking, not with him anyway, since I knew how he got sometimes. I mentioned that I had school in the morning, but he suggested that we go out just for a bit. He said that he wanted to spend time with me.

I ordered an appetizer, and excused myself to go to the bathroom. When I came back, he had ordered me a gin and tonic. It was already on the table, so I had no choice but to thank him and drink. We talked about my summer class and his job. He told me funny stories of some of the people he encountered at work. It was an okay night, our words flowed into one another as we shared and laughed, comfortable and happy.

But sometimes Derek was unable to leave "okay" alone. As we left together, he went out of his way to address the girls who were making their way in. He stood talking to them, complimenting them. I was left to stand behind him feeling dumb and awkward. He went just far enough that I felt uncomfortable, but not far enough for me to feel that I could say something. He was allowed to socialize with people at the bar, right?

As we walked back to his house, we passed a group of attractive girls. He made a display of checking them out, and wanted me to comment on which one was the most attractive. He started to tell me which one he wanted the most, and what he'd do to her…

I stopped him. "What are you trying to get at? What do you want me to say?"

"I'm just trying to talk to you, babe," was his response. "Isn't it fun to think about other people?"

I couldn't help but feel like he was trying to provoke me—to push me away. I thought about his four drinks to my two, but I was getting tired of making excuses for him.

"Are you sure you want me to come back with you? I need to go to sleep soon. I have class in the morning." I wasn't sure if I wanted to spend the night with him, especially if he was going to be like this. I imagined the night getting worse: Derek making cruel comments as he continued to drink; me trying to voice my discomforts, while he told me I was boring for not wanting to party, or not as interesting as other girls. But, I was with him after all, and he had been nice lately. I needed to give him some credit.

He interrupted my thoughts. "Of course I want you to come back, I already made us some food. We can eat and watch a show or something and then sleep."

He took my hand and we walked to his house. I was still a bit reluctant, frustrated by how he treated me, but not quite bold enough to tell him to have a nice night and make my way home.

He fumbled with the keys as he tried to unlock his apartment. I quickly kicked my shoes off, in a hurry to run to the washroom. I took my time, splashed water on my face, and tried to wake myself. I was tired and wanted to be home and away from Derek.

I opened the bathroom door, and Derek was waiting for me in the hall with an angry, yet vacant look on his face that I didn't quite recognize.

"Hey, slut," he said and pushed me against the wall before I had time to react. He forcefully kissed me and pressed his body up against mine. I could feel him hard against my crotch. He yanked my hair and kissed me harder. I was trying to get into it, but I was tired and frustrated. I kissed him back tentatively.

He reached down roughly forcing his hand under the waist of my jeans. But there wasn't really room for his hand, and I felt the uncomfortable pull of the fabric as he reached for my clit and then forced his fingers inside me. He seemed unaware of my discomfort. I could tell he was enjoying himself so I let him continue.

"Are you going to be a good little whore and let me fuck your pussy with my bare cock?" He licked my juice off his fingers, and moved both of his hands to my neck. I tried to shake my head, but he was stronger. Normally I trusted him, but with the alcohol in his system and the look in his eyes, I was worried about how strongly he was gripping my neck. Something wasn't right. I moved my head, and tried to pull fingers off my neck. I was seeing stars, and felt dizzy. Finally, he seemed to get the point and removed his hands. I leaned against the wall for support.

"Do you want me to fuck you?" He asked again.

"No," I whispered. I was tired, it was well into the morning hours, and I still felt light headed.

"Say that again, whore?"

"No!" This time louder.

"Say that again, bitch?" He was pressed against me as I leaned against the wall.

"I'm serious, Derek. I'm tired, and I just want to have a snack and go to sleep. I don't feel like it tonight." I tried to push him off so I could make my way to the kitchen.

"That's good, babe, you almost convinced me you don't want my cock. It turns me on so much when you tell me no."

"I don't want you to touch me, Derek! I'm going to go home if you won't listen." I started walking to his front door. I'd given up on having a nice meal and watching a show with him. I felt the need to get away; all my survival instincts were in overdrive. Repulsed. Lover turned predator. I had one shoe on when he scooped me up at the front door. He had a bigger build than me, and had extra force with his anger. I started kicking him, swinging my legs and struggling to get lose.

"Derek, seriously, let go. Put me down."

But he wasn't listening. He brought me to his bed. The next bit isn't pretty. *You can just skip ahead a few pages. I wouldn't blame you. I wouldn't want to read it.*

His physical strength, his dominance—what once attracted me to him— was now used as a weapon. I couldn't believe I ever wanted this—ever wanted him. I felt like I could finally see him for who he was, but it was too late.

I hate him, I thought. *I hate him, I hate him.*

But I hated myself, too. I hated myself for not seeing what he was really like. He only cared about himself. He was willing to hurt me for his own pleasure. I gave him too many chances, and tonight on the walk home I knew I should have left.

He pinned me down, reached for the bedside table, and pulled out some tape. I started to get away as he was distracted with ripping the tape. I remembered all the times I told him he could tape up my mouth, and that he could touch me in this way, but I always gave him permission. It wasn't like this.

"No, no, Zeus, stop, red." My voice came out in gasps, slips of a whispered plea. I didn't care what the word was, I just needed him to get off of me, but I knew it was hopeless.

I made it to the side of his bed and started to stand. He threw me down by the hair, and said, "Oh, you want it nice and rough this time, do you?"

He was having fun with my struggle, turned on by my fight. I didn't have time to respond as he gagged my mouth with the tape. All I could do was whimper. He yanked my pants off, and in his haste, didn't bother with my top. He undid his belt and kicked his pants aside.

I watched as if it was happening to someone else as he thrust his unprotected dick inside me. I wasn't on the pill, and we always used condoms.

Pregnancy, STIs. For a minute I was distracted from the current situation by thoughts of future worries. I was brought back to the moment by a sharp jab. I was dry. I felt like I was being torn apart from the inside out.

He was probably only inside me for two or three minutes, but time seemed to slow down and speed up. I felt trapped in these minutes that replayed themselves over and over.

I struggled, kicked, and tried to throw him off, but I was tired and weak. I couldn't get out of his hold. He slapped my face, and I felt the sting. He'd hit me before, but that was when I wanted him to, when I told him to. It was funny how the same physical act could have a different sting. I tried to think of other things—my earlier conversation with Elyse, the characters in the book I was reading for class tomorrow, anything but what was happening.

I could no longer ignore my body, as I felt him move in and out of me and every molecule of my body was screaming *no*. I couldn't help but think that not only was he violating me then, but he was also ruining all the memories I had of our bodies intertwined when we both said yes.

Stop, Derek! Fuck you! Stop, I thought. *Motherfucker, motherfucker, motherfucker,* this mantra quieted my mind for a minute. My head hurt, I was tired, and my insides were throbbing. He pumped harder as I squirmed against him, still trying to make him stop. *Please don't finish inside me.* I'd told him so many times that I wasn't comfortable with that. What happened to the Derek I loved? The Derek who made me feel like I was special? I hated this man, who was touching me, inside of me, wouldn't listen to me.

Fuck. Stop.

My eyes started to well with tears, but I couldn't let him make me feel this way. I hated that I could feel his entire body pushed against mine. The chest I once found comfort in, the hands I'd held. I opened my eyes and looked at him. It was too late to get out, and the only way to survive the next few minutes was to convince myself that I wanted it. It was just a game we were playing, like so many times before, when my, *no* really meant, *yes.* But then we had words, then he listened, in that moment I didn't matter. I was nothing more than a doll, mouth taped shut.

Shh, Patricia, you want this, I tried to convince myself. *You like being dominated by your man. He's overcome by lust, and wants to make you feel good. You should feel good. You've told him yes so many other times; just pretend this is no different.*

But it was. The hardest person to lie to is yourself and I lay there silently trying to do deep breaths through my nose. I was detached from my body, floating away from this space.

I felt him come inside me, and then he rolled off me and left to wash himself. I was too tired to think, to feel, to cry, to worry about the cum that was pooling from me onto the bed. I could feel my insides ripped open, raw. I removed the tape from my mouth. In a few minutes time was altered, and every previous act of making love, every kind word, and every gentle touch was erased.

I thought about my shoes strewn at the door and realized I could finally escape, but the worst had already happened, and I was too tired to keep my eyes open. My body felt foreign and was turning into a rock. I heard him flush the toilet and I stumbled into the washroom. After trying my best to clean, I started to make my way to the door, but I felt exhausted and defeated. I returned to his room. The light was off, and he was stiff in bed. I curled up in the fetal position, just wanting to be asleep. He reached out and put his arm around me, petted my hair, and kissed my cheek as I drifted to sleep. I cringed under the weight of his arm. I moved as far away from him as possible and he shifted further away from me in his sleep.

A stranger was beside me. I no longer wished to know this man. The last thing I thought as I drifted to sleep was that rape didn't look like this, but that was what this was. There were posters about sexual assault littering the residence halls, but I thought rape looked like someone drugged at a party, or a first-date gone too far, or an uncle who won't keep his hands to himself. Not like this, not like a girl who went home with her boyfriend intending to sleep in his bed. Not like a girl who continued to curl up beside him. But nothing ever happens like how you'd imagine.

I awoke at first light to birds celebrating a new day. Their chorus signaled a cheerful good morning, a reminder of a day I didn't care to celebrate.

Shut up, I thought to the birds. Their happiness deepened my pain. I wanted to run outside and chase them away or throw something at the window by his bed and cover Derek and the birds in shattered glass.

I slipped out of his apartment, careful not to make a noise, not wanting to wake him. Talk to him. Look at him.

Monster.

CHAPTER 8

I'm not interested in trying to capture my experience through some psychiatric narrative about what others think I'm experiencing; yet this keeps being forced on me in this stupid hospital. This writing is mine, so I can tell you what really happened.

I seemed to have entered a space outside of science, outside of time, where logic had no value. It only happened once, against the countless times we touched lovingly. Yet this violation outweighed every other touch. One moment had more weight than another. I could still feel him. I would wake in the night, covered in sweat and wanting to push him off. And then I would flick the light on and see that I was alone in my room. I don't want you to tell me about PTSD, or read my experiences through some first year psychology text. This is my body we are talking about, not some doll, as he seemed to think. My body is not a problem, or a puzzle to be solved.

And it's not about one thing, but rather everything. But *he* took my rage away from me. My emotions weren't even my own, now they were partly credited to *him*.

He called me a few times, but I let it go to voicemail. I hoped he knew that we were over.

I felt his hands against my neck, the tape on my mouth, and his body pushed against mine all the time. I could still feel his forceful touch. I felt it in class, while watching TV, and even walking down the street.

Sometimes the weight of what happened translated into this heaviness—this sadness—in my entire body. I craved his touch, and remembered what his gentle arms felt like during all the nights we lay cradled together. And then I would remember what he did. I wondered how long it would take to forget. Forget Derek, forget his violation, and most importantly forget his tender touch. His hands so familiar in mine, his body so beautiful and comforting. Reminiscing over fond memories of him felt like a betrayal to myself, and to what I experienced.

The whirl of my thoughts continued to circle, and I found myself alone. My resolve seemed to change from hour to hour. Sometimes I vowed to never talk to him again. I said that I was better without him in my life, and I needed to work on healing, on forgetting. Other times I was angry, and wanted to go bang on his door until he came out and ask him, "What the fuck? Why the hell did you do that to me?" Other times I wanted to wish the entire thing away. Maybe I could continue being with him if I convinced myself that it didn't happen, or that I had indeed said yes.

Despite all of this, I did miss him, and desperately wished he was still in my life. Although I couldn't ever imagine trusting him again, respecting him, or inviting him to touch me.

You can't date someone you hate, Patricia, I had to remind myself.

The emotional turmoil his violent love caused was exhausting.

In my last year of high school, classes prepared us for essay writing and effective ways to study for university exams. We were given instructions on how to socialize on campus, and pick extracurricular activities that look impressive on resumes. But never this. They didn't prepare me for this. Sexual assault was briefly addressed during residence orientation week, along with safe partying tips. But the discussion was centred around the buddy system and partying, and to always watch your drink, and how to overcome peer pressure. But I wasn't drugged at some party by a strange guy. I wasn't ready for this.

I felt like I was going to burst. I needed someone to talk to, or it would all just spill out of me. I slowly ran through the short list of people I could potentially confide in, ruling them out one by one. I loved my brother, but I never really told him about my personal life. I was sure he'd listen, and be empathetic and protective towards me. However, I didn't feel like crossing that line and changing the dynamic of our relationship

I thought of Kara, always so kind and willing to talk about anything. But she was home for the summer. I felt dumb even thinking about calling her to talk about this when she was the one who tried to warn me. I heard a chorus of, "I told you so" in my head.

Maybe I was just being irrational. There wasn't anything they could really say that would make any of this better. What exactly even happened? Self-doubt will drive you crazy and make you question your own instincts. "Shut up, Patricia," became the constant refrain in my head.

The dorms were empty because most people left for the summer holiday. The extra space in the communal kitchen and bathroom was appreciated, but the halls were eerily silent. The posters were torn from the walls, the silence created by the absence of music, and the faint whispers of conversations reminded me that I was alone. Utterly alone. Elyse and Brittany were both gone for the summer. Not that I'd really talk to Brittany anyway. I wondered if Elyse was even safe to confide in, or if Brittany would use my misery for gossip.

I began to get to know Aashi a bit better since there were fewer students around. She even invited me over two or three times for coffee in her room. Since she was a don, her room was bigger than the others, and was complete with a couch and a rocking chair. Homesick first-year students often hung out in her room when they were feeling overwhelmed. I tried to picture myself sitting on her sofa, confiding in her, but what would I say? I remembered Aashi liking Derek at the Christmas dinner, and despite everything, I was not ready to change her perception of him.

Should I just tell her that I was upset that Derek and I broke up? Or would I tell her that *he raped* me? Was that too much of a burden? I wondered how she'd react.

What would I tell her if she wanted to know how it happened? How would I begin to explain that we'd role-played this situation so many times, but we both agreed—except this time I didn't agree? Would Aashi be required to tell someone? Was there a code of confidentiality? No, wait; were only social workers and such bound by this code? Perhaps this meant that I could freely talk to Aashi. I wondered if the dons had their own special set of rules. I was hardly the first person to go to her with a problem. She had people approaching her to resolve fights over communal space, and students upset about failing their first exam. But still, I remembered Aashi liking *him* at the Christmas dinner and despite everything I was not ready to change that image.

I ran into her in the hallway, and any thought of confiding in her vanished. She appeared to be in a great mood, smiling and telling me about how she was excited to go on a camping trip that weekend with her boyfriend.

She was a nice girl, but I couldn't talk to her, not about *that*.

You may be wondering about the rest of the social system? I'm apparently part of the generation that advocates to "break the silence, end the violence." Raised with the media narrative to tell someone, tell someone. But they never really did say who to tell, did they? I pictured myself going to the police, and then getting the rape kit done in the hospital when the evidence was still covering my body. Yes, I know how all that works, so I couldn't say that I didn't know. But how do I explain that the old bruises on my body are ones I agreed to, except this time I said *no*?

I thought about my Introduction to Women's studies class, and talking about the statistics around sexual assault in Canada. Yes, sexual assault, not *rape*. For some reason that word had gone out of favor. Go ahead, dilute what actually happened by using legal jargon. I think it was something like ten percent of sexual assaults that are reported have sufficient evidence to go to trial, and even fewer perpetrators are prosecuted.

This crime was something that happened to me. It ripped apart my body, my heart, my life, and my mind. I didn't feel like my body belonged to the legal system. To have to prove that *he raped* me beyond any reasonable doubt—sorry, *sexually assaulted* me. I pictured myself in the hospital and then later at the police station, being asked by kind, but busy professionals to state my name, and health card number—always my number. Sterile rooms: white, grey, hand sanitizer, uniforms. Medical evidence. Onus of proof. Being put on hold on the phone; push this button, followed by, "enter a number if you wish to talk with someone." My cell phone bill rising by the second, yet I wouldn't hear a human voice. Shiny tile floors, manila files containing my life, a second violation by the system that was almost greater than the first violation. Talk, relive, and tell us again and again what happened, let me write it down in this file, and I'll ask you about it again and again to see if you change your story at all. See how credible you are. *No, thanks, I'd rather not.*

I couldn't picture him in handcuffs. He'd find a way to resist—to do his time, but still somehow escape the physical setting, much like his presence at the university. And besides, that wasn't what I wanted to happen to him. I didn't want him to be punished by a demeaning system, but rather I wanted him to understand. I wanted him to feel the depth of how he hurt me. I realized that I had a greater chance of winning in the legal system, than I had of him ever fully realizing what he did.

I wonder what he'd think of me now.

I kept telling myself that I would not think of him. But I couldn't help but wonder if he missed me, or if he hated himself for putting me through this. Or maybe he didn't even realize what he did, the alcohol shaping his memory and helping him forget that I said no.

Still, I needed someone to talk to, even if I didn't know what exactly I would say. I had so much to say and yet nothing at the same time. You may be thinking there are professionals for that, but really where was I to go? Could you picture me going back to the counselling office, the very first place to reject me? They asked me to prove myself, define myself, justify and quantify my need for help. This time, I had something to talk to them about— real issues that they could clearly mark on their charts. I laughed in my head thinking about their paperwork.

Reason for counselling? Raped. How many sessions needed to address this issue? Five. Ten. Or maybe forever, but what did I know? Maybe this wasn't really about him raping me, it was about everything.

Perhaps I'm not being fair, but I could picture myself walking into the overly cheery office with the motivational posters, and having to fill out their paperwork once more. Student number, reason for visit…besides, it wasn't like I just wanted to talk about the rape. I also needed to talk about what I was doing with him in the first place. I would need to tell them why I stayed when he started making me feel so terrible. Sometimes I came up with awful names for him that I think, but don't dare say out loud. After all, survival strategies are needed when interacting with dangerous animals.

I finally decided to call Elyse. I think I knew all along that I was going to talk to her. I just delayed making the call, instead running through the list of imaginary options of people I could talk to. You probably already figured out why I didn't even consider talking to my parents. They'd be uncomfortable, but sympathetic. Then they would offer to pay for whatever, and feel like they did their part by directing me to other resources. You know, like in high school when I told my mom I was depressed.

Elyse picked up on the last ring, as I was trying to decide what I'd say on her answering machine.

"Hey, Patricia," she answered in a cheerful voice.

"Hey, Elyse, how are you doing? How's home?" I was sitting on my bed, still in my pyjamas although it was noon and I was going to be late for work if I didn't get dressed.

"I'm pretty good, it's nice to be home and with my family. I got a job at a camp. It's really fun working with kids, but tiring. Always go, go, go. Tomorrow we're going to a waterpark for the day."

"That sounds like a great job for you, and it'll look really good on your resume." There was a bit of a pause. I wanted to get right to the point and tell her what happened, but I didn't know where to begin. Especially since she saw how he treated me before, and said it was for the best when we split the first time. Back then we talked about how he was a nice guy, but he was going through a lot in his life. And she suggested that even though we cared about each other it didn't mean that we had to stay together. She was polite when I eventually told her that we were back together, but we seldom talked about him. I felt really dumb coming to Elyse, but that's what friends are for, right?

"What's it like living in residence when everyone is gone for the summer? How's Derek?" I was relieved she brought him up, giving me a space to talk about what happened.

"Actually, it's really lonely here, and I'm not doing the greatest. We actually split last week." I was in dangerous territory, unsure of when I'd have said too much and crossed a line.

"I'm sorry to hear that. I hope you're doing okay. I know he wasn't treating you very nicely, so maybe it's for the best."

"Yeah, it's just hard, and I really miss him. But I agree, that it's for the best. He doesn't really belong in my life—never did. It's just that how it happened was awful. I guess there's no good way for things to be over. I had to finally put my foot down though, or it was just going to get worse," I tried to explain.

"Well, I'm really glad that you recognized that he wasn't treating you right and were able to get out. Still, I know how much you liked him, and it must be hard. How did Derek take the breakup?" she asked.

I don't remember what I intended to tell her, the truth just spilled out. Well, not the entire truth, but what does that even mean really? I spared her the details about my interest in kink, while finally stuttering out that he raped me. Then I ended up crying on the phone. I could hear myself apologizing for crying. She told me she had the weekend off, and that she would come and visit me. This was a statement, not a question, and I was happy to let her take charge.

I almost wanted to apologize for being annoying; I hate being in the way. Alice told me I needed to stop apologizing, and to never apologize for what I felt. But then again, Alice was in and out of the psychiatric ward before leaving us for good, so I'm not sure I should be taking her advice if I wanted to get by.

Later, when I first got to the hospital, Elyse tried to ask me if it had anything to do with Derek, and him raping me.

"I'll find him, turn him into the police," she offered. But I shushed her.

CHAPTER 9

Sometimes your own contradictions trap you on an inescapable path. The weekend with Elyse was fine and passed quickly. We watched movies, spent the day down by the lake, and went for drinks, all the while engaging in one endless conversation about why I was better off. This was interrupted by my occasional sobs, but Elyse was there and none of this seemed real so I got it together quick enough. Elyse was nothing but supportive, and I was thankful. But I trapped myself by telling her about Derek, or telling her all too soon, for I didn't realize my story with Derek wasn't over. It was love, or addiction, or something like that, and I fear that you too won't understand me unless you've been there.

My endurance in the weeks to come was shaped by the mere need to survive. I didn't have the time to feel pain, or to process what happened. The spring and summer term was condensed, and it was detrimental to get behind. I toyed with the idea of quitting my job, but the student loan didn't leave me enough funds to pay rent, and eat all year. I kept going to school, but I no longer cared. I was late for class; I wrote mediocre papers that I'd find embarrassing if I had the energy to care. I splashed coffee on the counter at work. I barely looked at customers, let alone smiled. I didn't bother to count back the change. I told myself to smarten up, or I'd get fired, but it was so hard to care. Aside from him, all the things that consumed my mind previously seemed to be of little consequence.

I moved forward by replaying my conversation with Elyse. *I deserve better, I don't need him, and this isn't my fault.* I felt like I was surviving on nineties girl power, mixed with anger and apathy. Elyse called me a few times a week, but I didn't really have much to say, and I felt bad that she worried about me, so I rushed to hang-up. But knowing that she cared was helpful. I felt as if I transitioned from her friend to someone she needed to look after. I wondered why Elyse bothered to call. I barely asked her how she was doing. I tried to keep our conversations short. Listening to her happy discussion of summer camp, waterparks and fellow counsellors felt irrelevant, and I struggled to pay attention. I know what you're thinking, *selfish*, yet focusing on the ordinary details of life seems impossible. I could hardly feign interest in my life, let alone care about anyone else. And then I realized that not only did he violate my body, but he also stole friendships from me along the way.

My parents continued their regular stream of weekly emails, and I tried to reply sounding as normal possible. The process of interacting with the outside world was more exhausting than usual. I added their emails to my homework pile; talking to my parents was one more thing on my tiring to-do list.

I chatted with my brother once or twice since the incident with the ghost; I don't really feel like naming *him*. You know who I mean. I liked talking with my brother; he was kind and familiar. We spoke of his work and wedding plans. I mentioned school and the café, but I felt the need to be positive and energetic. The lightness of our interaction was weighing down on the heaviness of what took place. I was starting to feel the pull of my silence. I felt as if I was lying or pretending with every minute I was not speaking about Derek and, what he did to me. The line between good and poor judgement is slippery, and I was no longer sure why I decided that silence was best. But my thoughts were foggy, and I no longer trusted my judgement.

They say the truth will set you free, but I really didn't know what that meant. I was trapped in a space with no solution. Kara texted me one day, asking how my summer was going. We decided to chat on the phone, and the story just came out, this time with more details than I had shared with Elyse. I felt like each time I opened my mouth more of my truth came pouring out. The words became a river that was beyond my control, and I was out of energy to swim against the current. To be honest, I'm not entirely sure what I said to Kara. I'm trying to tell it to you exactly as it was, but even when telling our truth, aren't we always one step removed? I wonder what I'd be telling you if the end of my story turned out differently. But let me continue; my mind is constantly distracted by the thoughts of *what if.*

Kara was an empathetic listener, and easy to talk to. I tried to share the details of what happened, but she was more concerned with feelings than with facts. She was outraged by his violence, but respected my desire to leave the police out. She thought it was because I was paranoid, but I'm not the first person to turn my back on the justice system.

I really felt like Kara listened and was concerned about how I was feeling and coping, but also how I'd fair with men in the future. I was careful not to tell her how much I missed him and wanted him back. Those words sounded absurd even to me. She made me promise to give counselling another try, and by the end of the phone call, I was determined to give it another shot—if not for me, then for the reassurance of a dear friend.

I signed up once more for school counselling, and the experience in the waiting room filled me with flashbacks. This was exactly the same as last time, except now I had something they would see as legitimate for their paperwork. I couldn't help but wonder if things would have turned out differently if they had accepted my need for support in September. Would I have told an empathetic and kind counsellor about my developing relationship, and perhaps managed to get out before it reached this point? Like I said, my brain was haunted by the word *if.* But that wasn't how things went, did they?

The receptionist asked for my student number and name. I gave them to her, feeling like a zombie, just playing my part in some abstract game. I wanted to hand her my student card and not waste my voice. I filled out the paperwork. Once again it asked for my student number. I attempted to explain myself on these pages, and began to feel more and more frustrated. My need exceeded the three lines available. I was overcome by the feeling that I betrayed myself in entering this space again. I wondered if my concerns would be met by empathetic or indifferent ears.

I remembered visiting this office the first time, feeling like I needed to beg the intake counsellor to accept me. Suddenly, a lump began to rise in my throat. I left the half-completed papers on the coffee table in the waiting room and rushed from the office, knowing that I couldn't return. Sorry Elyse, sorry Kara, I tried, I really did. I was exhausted, but proud that I managed to stay true to myself.

And my yearning for him, it just somehow continued in all of this. How do I describe a love that endured beyond all logic?

Derek was everywhere, and sometimes I used all the energy I had left willing him away. Trying to forget his name, his taste, how he felt against my body. But trying to forget was almost as tiring as remembering. Then I switched and embraced the memories, which lead to missing him and longing for him, and wanting nothing more than to be back with him. Love isn't about logic—not that abuse is love. But for me, they have some kind of perverse marriage.

The city was his. Well, it was his and mine together, but now I felt like I was walking over ghosts. I passed the cafés and bars we frequented and almost sensed him as I crossed the campus for class. I didn't believe in psychic energy, but I swore I could feel him—feel us in this space—lingering. I hurried by his favorite bookstore, and passed his friend's house from the Christmas party. Derek may be out of my life, but I wished I could understand why he was still everywhere. His physical absence made him hyper present. In my head I spoke to him. But it's dangerous talking with ghosts, allowing reality to merge with fantasy.

I avoided going out, but I was so busy between work and school, that I had little free time. I didn't want to run into him. I constantly feared seeing him and I didn't know what I'd do if and when I encountered him. Our meeting felt inevitable. I alternated between wanting to fuck him the minute I lay my eyes on him or punch him—probably both. But in reality, I knew I'd turn and hide.

Derek knew the inner workings of the city, and all the places I had explored were with him. Like a wild animal, he marked this city with his scent, and I no longer wanted to be there without him. Not that I wanted to go back and live with my parents, so I really didn't know where I'd rather be, or what I'd rather be doing. I was hesitant to go explore the city alone. The idea of hidden parks, bars, new cafés, restaurants, and trips to the waterfront on sunny days seemed empty without the potential of his company. And suddenly it seemed fitting that everyone I knew here besides him went home for the summer. I was abandoned in a strange city with no one here I cared about—except him. I couldn't help but think I didn't belong anywhere.

This city confused and scared me. I was surrounded by the backdrop of the honking cars and sirens on my walk to work. The newspaper headlines were filled with stories of gun violence and pedestrian deaths. I guess in a way it made sense that I was in this alien city. I didn't know if any place in the world would feel like a home to me now.

I was in a diverse city, surrounded by beautiful and interesting people, but all I could think about was him. He was the one my body longed for. My sex drive was both absent and in overdrive. I needed to avoid thinking about him in public or I would find myself dripping, mind racing, breathing short. But I tried to remind myself it was wrong to want him.

Never forget what he did to you.

Yes, I know how all of this sounds. I'm embarrassed even writing it.

I neglected my body. I avoided touching myself. I allowed my body to become as alien as the city I occupied. I saved my focus for school and work. I carried on in a numb, zombie haze.

But in the heat of the summer, with my residence room stifling, I got carried away. My body was tense with frustration, stress, and the need for release. I thought of him, and I went to a place beyond turning back. I remembered all the things I wanted to do with him, and climaxing one time wasn't enough. I started to feel guilty, so I continued until I could no longer move, a whimpering wet pile of sex, heartbreak and hormones. If he were there, I'd have exploded for him from a mere touch, maybe just a look.

I had a physical need for him. He was intertwined with my body, my history. I couldn't quite explain. But memories were dangerous things to have sex with, you could never quite fuck a ghost, grasping for someone that you could never quite reach, falling through your hand. A body that slipped past you in the night. I remembered the weight of his body against mine, the throbbing of his cock filling me. I was overcome by the weightlessness of his absence, and I just wanted him there, with me, and I desired nothing more than to feel his skin against my body. My wetness was met by absent fingers, and I realized the despair of fucking my memories. As I lay strewn, panting and spent on wet bed sheets, I wondered if he would have said yes to me. I wondered if I'd have cared. I wondered if he heard me moan his name.

CHAPTER 10

I was filled with guilt for wanting him, missing him, and then, and then this missing slowly turned into self-hate. *Why do you want him, Patricia? You don't need him. You are busy with school, and there are so many people out there that would treat you with respect and kindness.*

But those people weren't him. Love, I tell you, is a dangerous path to follow.

I began to confuse my dreams with reality, or maybe reality was the dream, reality and truth are such slippery things. He spent the weekend with me in residence; we were watching a movie and eating popcorn in my bed. I felt the popcorn crumbs against my skin as I lay in the tangle of bed sheets. But I awoke alone and confused. My mind slowly pieced together why he wasn't there, and for a few minutes I thought, *this can't be true.* He was just beside me in bed, arms around me, head fighting for a space on my pillow. He couldn't have done *that*, no, no, not him.

But he did. Or maybe it wasn't him, some evil version of him, a monster whose body is made of alcohol and hostility. Not *my* Derek.

Derek couldn't have done this, not the Derek I sat with listening to poetry that first night; it couldn't be the same person. No, just no. We like to follow these ideas about linear paths, one thing happened, and then the next. But, but maybe he was this monster all along, existing simultaneously with the Derek that I loved. He did this all right now, and it will keep happening.

I looked everywhere for the fresh strawberries I bought when I walked passed the market stall on my way home from work. I was in a hurry to get home, and curl up in my pyjamas and ignore the world. But I was proud of myself for stopping, for taking a minute to purchase the fruit, to have a farm fresh strawberry melt in my mouth and feel pleasure just for a second. But where were the berries? I could smell their sweet earthy scent. I looked on my counter, in my little bar fridge. Then I started looking in erratic places: under the clothing heap on my floor, in my desk, perhaps I went to do something and absently set them down. They were gone. I was left wondering if it happened. Did I just imagine the fruit vendor? Confused, I look at the calendar. It was a Sunday; I went to work the day before, as usual, right? Dreams and reality continued to merge. Have you ever really stopped to ask yourself what is real?

I felt like I was on a continual drug trip but I was sober. I wasn't really sure what was real. I looked at my face in the mirror, but I couldn't see my eyes; they were black. I was a shadow. I tried to touch my eyeball, but my lids flickered shut every time I got close. I pictured my eyes falling out. I squeezed them shut to keep them in and see the darkness inside of my brain.

When I left my room, everyone's outlines were blurred. The people appeared as black paint that an artist dripped too much water on. People became smudges. I think Shakespeare said "the eyes are the windows to the soul," but I couldn't see anyone, even when someone turned to look at me. Their face was nothing. I shivered. I wanted to ask everyone I passed, "are you real?"

Am I real? Was he real?

I don't want to be here.

But what was I talking about? More downs than ups, just the continued question of how far down the rabbit hole each day brought me. I'm a cross between Alice in a nightmarish wonderland, and Sylvia Plath's Esther Greenwood. I was reading *The Bell Jar* again for my English class, and my foggy brain repeated over and over the line about the universe itself being the nightmare. That damn book, following me around. And what about Sylvia

Plath? Didn't she kill herself in the end? Overdosed on pills, or held her head in the oven? Did she escape the dream? Did the faces that surrounded her become darker, the zombies more real? Nothing else could explain all of this pain. But still, I try and hold on. Alice said that this was my mistake, trying to hold on, and not letting it go. I get dizzy, confused, I cry, I whimper. I'm empty. I become nothing. I am nothing. I'm a body out of context, a character written to occupy a dishevelled storyline that made no sense.

I almost liked the nothingness. It was not the euphoric light bliss of sunny July days spent with beer and friends by the poolside, without a so-called care in the world, this place I'd never known. But, but rather a dark, and yet giddy nothingness. The constant feeling that you were forgetting to do something, yet no longer caring to try and remember what you forgot.

I was out of control, and slowly losing the language to communicate this feeling. My emotions evolved beyond the ability to verbally express sadness, but I wanted to howl like a wolf. I tried to pretend that I was okay, but pretending was exhausting. Elyse and Kara both called to see how I was doing. I had a little visit with Kara when she came to Toronto to see her boyfriend. I tried to be okay for them, seeing as there was nothing they could do. But I needed help, *real* help, and I couldn't even put that into words. Once I asked for help and had the language to express this need, but the words slowly slipped away. What was left was the places between words, between sounds. I could describe a second, the pain, the beauty, the agony, and the inability to comprehend how many more minutes I needed to stay up in order to have survived a day. Survived, and for what? I could describe a blade of grass, but ask me to tell you more about my state, or how I could feel better, and I was at a complete loss. Maybe I was beyond the point of no return, coming out of the confines of the birth canal, or before that, maybe when my parents' DNA collided. Perhaps it was when my grandparents met. Maybe it was when Eve picked the fruit; maybe it was when the world started. Maybe it all happened at the same time.

When the surface was still something I could see, I grasped and struggled to make it to the top. But, I was so far under that everything was dark and murky. To be perfectly honest, I had no idea which way was up. *But I digress.* I was as nice as I could be to Elyse and Kara, but dismissed them by saying that I was just worried about school and work, for this was the language of the world they inhabited. They understood sandy beaches, and rough waves, while I lay tangled in a bed of ocean debris, trapped like a sea turtle in garbage. The more I tried to look at what my leg was caught in, the harder it was to see what was holding me. Elyse and Kara offered continual friendship with a verbal chorus of, "fuck Derek." I should have been grateful.

In the background, the phone rang again and again, but I knew a stranger was on the other end. Perhaps this stranger could have reached me, as I'd slowly become a stranger to myself. Or maybe I was just more in tune to the world, to my heartbeat, to the slow turning of the clock, to the constant hum of the fridge, and this weird circle of thoughts.

I ignored any attempt at contact, letting my phone go to voicemail, texts and emails left unanswered, sometimes unread. I was starting to fear that the only one who may understand me was him, but I still knew that he was the last person who I should let reach me across this polluted water.

Have you ever looked at yourself, and I mean *really* looked at yourself? Not as in being able to describe your hair colour and texture, face composition and eyes. I'll give you a minute, go look, and I mean really look, come back and tell me something new.

I leaned into my full-length mirror, almost colliding with it, greasy fingertips smearing the glass. I looked at myself, and there was someone I didn't recognize. I saw something beyond the brown hair escaping my ponytail, greasy face and eyebrows that in my disarray I'd abandoned. I could see beyond the pale, slightly sunburnt face and pores to anger—a fury that wasn't there before. I was a cross between vacant and rip your throat out. They say it takes courage to look people in the eye, to hold a gaze, but try entering a staring contest with yourself. How do you win?

"Patricia," I whispered looking at myself, trying to touch the mirror. "Patricia, Patricia, Patricia." I chanted.

But Patricia was long gone, I realized. I no longer felt like Patricia, or looked like Patricia, whatever that meant. Something in me hardened, gave up. Who was Patricia? What was Patricia? This body, this person, this mass of cells, this thing. What does it mean to be human? What does it mean to give up?

It's fascinating that people are so interested in watching wild animals, compelled by nature, but they forget we, too, are animals. We assume that humans are so familiar, so predictable, not wild beasts forced to be tamed, cages larger, environments more elaborate. All of us trapped by some laws. Laws of nature, laws of survival, or desperately clinging to ideas about who we think we are. If we let go, there is nothing left.

I lost track of time, staring at myself, looking myself directly in the eye. Time actually stopped, they wanted you to believe that time always moved forward, or it'd drive you fucking crazy. I was safe only because I was already crazy. Trust me, time can start and stop again, and doesn't follow the rules we made. We made time up, no wonder time is a liar.

What animal is it they say never to look in the eye? I wasn't even sure what I was looking for, or why I started staring, but I couldn't turn away. I was fascinated, as if I were watching a tiger in the wild. *Wild.* Why do we hear of shootings and pretend that we humans aren't part of the wild? Domesticated, ordered, civilized, but wild. Dangerous. *You heard me, right?* Dangerous.

It's interesting—this rhetoric about being able to understand others who've gone through similar experiences. Well, not quite understand them, but hold a closer understanding, as if there is a universal experience of poverty, cancer, or heartbreak. Well, perhaps the stories we tell are similar, but we hardly have the language to compare. They say you can't understand or judge another unless you've walked a mile in their shoes. But hell, I've walked so far in my shoes, and yet I can't claim to understand myself. Or how I ended up before this mirror, this judgemental place. I quivered as I looked myself in the eye.

One always loses in staring contests against oneself. I looked at that person in the mirror one more time. Did I like her? Did I hate her? I didn't know. I guess the better question was did I know her? I lifted my eyebrows, and I was surprised that the face in the mirror responded to the movement.

I control the body in the mirror, I told myself. I was in control. But how much power do we ever really have?

I glanced one last time, but I couldn't say I really knew the reflection and this scared me. There was forever a divide between the mirror and myself. I wanted to break it, to pull myself out, but I knew life didn't work like that.

Do you know that technically you can never actually touch anything? There's always a space between you, and other things. I can't remember the explanation; science isn't exactly my area of expertise. You can never be reached. Touched. Held. It's all a trick. This was why I was so fucking lonely. This made me think, if our particles never touched, did he rape me? And what of the semen that came pouring out of me, does one scientific truth contradict the other?

Reality is a slippery, melting slope, nothing but a puddle of daydreams. Reality perhaps becomes the true fantasy.

We all don't see the world the same way. Put me on a gorgeous lakeshore in cottage country, and my eyes will likely go right to the place where the water meets the sand, lapping the shoreline. I'd imagine how my body would feel as I entered the water. But the person beside me may be watching the children playing, remembering their childhood or imagining future families. And what about people who are colour blind? They may see this scene another way entirely. Can eyes really be wrong? Can minds ever be wrong? I think the entire concept is a bit off—like there's a correct way to see colour. Ask the hippies if there is a proper way to see rainbows.

I wonder what other people see when they look at me. Did I look different to others than I did before *my fall, the fall*? Are the signs of love and heartbreak visible in my very anatomy—this biology? Could my experience be captured in *before* and *after* photos?

I wish I could let someone else into my body. Maybe they'd understand. Maybe they'd run away.

All that happened with Derek was a blur, subject to my understanding, my memory, and my feelings. I couldn't help but wonder how he experienced those moments when I told him *no*, and meant it. For the first time, I found myself wishing that I desired his hands on my body that night, creating heat between us. That I had dreamed about the blissful moment when he entered me. If I wanted it—if I said *yes*—maybe I wouldn't be where I was now. Maybe we'd still be happy.

There were songs about blurred lines, and consent that people were outraged by. We are of the, *yes means yes* generation, and anything other than enthusiasm is *no*. Please don't hate me; I'm not trying to justify rape—just trying to get my head around a few things. The problem with this sentiment is that so many amazing things in life are approached with question marks. Trying a new food for the first time, I'm skeptical, but willing. The same logic might be applied to sex. Say, do I want my ass touched? Fuck, I don't know. You can try and I'll tell you if I like it, but please be gentle. *Oh sorry*, was the other person not supposed to touch me at all because my *yes* was tentative—whispered, conditional? A *yes* with curiosity and limits—that involved trust. Trust that they'd listen to me. Trust that they'd stop.

Anyway, all of this was to say that he and I had a bit of a complex sex life; he was my first sexual partner. Well, second if we are counting the awkward fumbling of high school. We pushed each other, more accurately he pushed me. He helped me discover my body, and understand the possibilities of what pleasure could entail.

Don't let my experience deter you from experiencing and experimenting for yourself—no room for judgements here. Just be cautious about who you tangle bodies, ideologies, and feelings with. People are the most dangerous of animals. They wound and kill all the time; they'll rip you apart, not only with teeth and guns, but words, too.

Sorry if I'm jumping all over the place. At the time when I was looking in the mirror, I began to think that perhaps he didn't realize what he was doing was raping me. Maybe he didn't look at his reflection and see a rapist. Maybe he really thought that I wanted to have sex with him, mistaking my clear anger and refusal with previous play. Maybe between alcohol and history, somehow our lines became confused. Where his body ended and where mine started, and what my *no* meant. Maybe for him, my *no* entered the space of *yes*, in that terrible in between space that most things in the world occupy. I'm not trying to make excuses for that asshole, just trying to make you understand what was in my head. How I tried to come to terms with what he did and deceive myself a little.

I tried not to think about him anymore, or about the entire situation. *Fuck him.* "Fuck him, but don't literally fuck him," as Alice would say. I miss Alice. Perhaps this is what happens to sad girls like me with no career plans. Who don't know who they are or what they want and spend too much time apologizing. *But don't worry, I don't really believe that victim blaming crap. And I'm done with saying sorry.*

If this is hard to read, and seems to skip all over, it's because I really didn't know how to feel about him. I missed him fiercely. They say that time heals, or some bullshit like that, but for me time just sharpened my memory, the intensity of the longing. This became too real as the number of days since he held me lengthened. So I missed him, but I knew that I was better off without him. He was always so angry, unpredictable, and fierce in a way I could no longer relate to. I kept a running dialogue with him in my head, almost knowing him well enough to not need his physical presence to talk with him. *Almost.*

I could hardly go on when I thought of this indescribable pain, and looked at the vastness of the pain around me. Kara said that I'd have other lovers, but I couldn't deal with this world-ending pain again, I just couldn't. But this wasn't just me. I stumbled past a shelter every morning on my way to work and saw a line of people, waiting for a meal if they were lucky. I felt small and selfish, as they laughed, cried, or stood still, waiting to see if they'd get a meal or a bed today. The line slowly moved forward and I diverted my eyes. I was horrible to even compare myself to them. I started to cry. It started to rain. I wondered how the world broke them; what abusive partner, or neglectful parent, or fucked up healthcare system left them standing there. What number they were in some caseworker's book. What student number, what health card number they'd also once been reduced to.

I wondered if they could see me, or what they thought of me. On a bench, invisible, I started to shake. I was starting to become familiar with the city, the flow of traffic and crowds, and the panhandlers sitting in certain spots on the sidewalk. There was a girl I often saw on the TTC; pretty blonde hair, often carefully applying makeup. Familiar strangers, I recognized them in the big city, even if I didn't know their names and they looked past my shadow. I wished we were friends. I hoped they were having a nice life, whatever that meant.

I was on the streetcar near Kensington. A familiar man got on he was twenty, maybe thirty. It was hard to tell because of the layer of dirt and matted hair. He had a beer can in his hand, and he didn't pay as he entered the side door and stumbled to stay upright. A stranger approached, placed money in his hand, and closed his fingers so the coins wouldn't fall. The man was too gone to whisper *thanks*, or realize what happened. *Too gone.* That could be me someday. I hoped that man was okay.

And this lost soul made me think of *him*, Derek, ghost boy. I guess all the old songs got it right; you could love and hate someone at the same time. But maybe, maybe, he wouldn't even pay me any mind and just stumble on by, indifferent to my existence.

This city was a stranger to me. Like my mind, it felt safe, familiar, but then... Sometimes, I walked around at night and questioned my safety. This intersection, it didn't feel like the same place where that guy got shot last week, caught in some gang crossfire. There were posters around campus warning students not to walk around alone. But who the fuck was supposed to hold my hand?

Later, in the hospital, Larry whispered about being stabbed multiple times as he worked security for an after-hours club that I'd just walked past. *But where was I?* Oh yes, I didn't even know Larry yet, so I couldn't see his faded blood on the sidewalk. It was late, and I was told that empty streets they too have ghosts, and I could feel the vibration, the secret hum of the train under me. I was walking to the subway at night, and I could go anywhere. But my feet had a way of taking me on familiar path.

CHAPTER 11

So I need to be straight with you. Derek and I got back together. I'd try and tell you what happened, but the details were a bit confusing. Like a drunken night I could tell you where it started, and where it ended, and perhaps some of the specifics between, but definitely not all. Pieces were missing; maybe the most important pieces were at the center.

And in trying to tell you what happened—in summarizing the plot, the events, I can never fully capture the emotional journey of how I end up in this space. But I promised to tell my whole story so I'll take a shot. *But don't forget, this is no love story.*

Sometimes the only thing that fixes pain is more of the source. Maybe that was why I went back to him. Perfect circle, hair of the dog, or however that expression goes. He was real in a way no one else seemed to be, so I needed him in my life. No, I don't want to get into some philosophical discussion about what it means to need versus want, want versus need.

Elyse and Kara, with their normal, relatively happy lives, became blurry visions I could no longer see. But Derek, the rough and raw—he was in sharp focus. Maybe misery really does love company; that, or the entire world felt fake except for him.

I had all sorts of plans about what I'd do when and if I saw him, but life never tends to work according to plan. He caught me with my guard down, and kind of slid back into my life without my full acknowledgement. How many times would I let him come and go?

I was trying to function, dragging myself through the tasks of daily living. The summer term was almost done, and I was sitting in a café near Broadview and Danforth, but I might as well have gone on an airplane because I didn't know this part of the city. I wasn't getting work done, and I wanted to sleep all day, but I forced myself to get up, put some clothes on, and go somewhere new to work. I got on the subway without a destination in mind. I still felt like a bit of a tourist in this city. I went east, but I could've just as easily gone west. I got off the subway, having ventured far enough into the unknown. I was hesitant to move further from the familiar downtown core. I meandered down the sidewalk, looking at happy people settled in bars and café patios, the sounds of careless chatter echoed down the street. After a fifteen minute walk observing happy people, I was ready to head home. I just wanted to be by myself, but I felt the weight of the books in my purse. I was hot from walking in the sun, and my stomach was trying to get my attention.

I was too warm to deliberate where to go, so I walked to the nearest café. It was cute and non-descript, another space that was nothing more than a backdrop to my misery. I picked at the soup and salad that I ordered. I was hungry and yet uninterested in the task of eating. I reread the paragraph where I left off a few times before I settled into the rhythm of the novel. Something about relationships amongst soldiers during WWII. I was trying to brainstorm an essay topic about masculinity and war.

He asked if he could sit as he pulled out the chair across from me, and, like an old acquaintance, I greeted him and told him that he could. I welcomed him while my brain was still in the battlefields of France.

"I'm glad I ran into you. I was here earlier for this lunchtime music session, it's this new series," he explained, gesturing at the remaining equipment on the little area of the restaurant marked as a stage. I was so focused on trying to order and sit that I hadn't look around when I entered. He was here all along. How long was he watching?

"Oh, how was that?" As if that was the first thing I wanted to ask him. As if I cared.

"I actually really enjoyed it. Ben is friends with some of the guys in this group, and told me about it. I had the day off work, so I figured I'd check it out. Some Indie group—young kids, but I think they'll do okay."

"Oh, that's good." I didn't really know what to say. I wanted to talk to him, and yet I was tempted to wave my book in his face and tell him that I was busy.

"So, what are you reading?" he asked tentatively, his voice softer than usual. Out of his territory, not clear if he was welcome. *I wasn't sure if he was welcome.*

I showed him the cover of my book.

"I really miss you, Patricia," he said looking at me across the table, not even glancing at the book. Was this as close to an "I'm sorry" as he'd get?

I half smiled in return, and we continued to talk for thirty minutes or so. I was trapped by the food on my table. I couldn't really flee with my half-eaten meal, nor did I want to. I felt like a character in a movie, detached from the situation, but desperate to find out what happens, waiting for the plot twist. We met again, we briefly chatted and I told him politely to have a nice life? No, that didn't seem like a memorable ending, credits roll.

In the conversation that ensued, like always, most things were left unsaid. He asked how I ended up in a café so far from my neighbourhood. I wanted to know if he realized what he did to me, if he was sorry. He asked his questions, I held mine. He didn't mention all the phone calls and messages that I didn't answer. We were on a balancing beam trying not to shatter the illusion that all was well. That he was welcome. I didn't know if he was welcome. He left, but not before I agreed to go to a poetry show that he had tickets for.

I didn't think about if I wanted to go, I just agreed.

You can get out of this Patricia, I told myself, *you don't need to do this. Don't forget who he is and what happened. Before you spend time with him you need to talk to him. You can't just move forward.* But promises to yourself are so easy to break, and he always hated talking about important things—about *us*. Did I write *us*?

CHAPTER 12

How can I explain that night—that desperate desire to breathe after being trapped in the murky water of his absence? Drawn like exhausted swimmers desperately emerging from the sea, the sun became clear as we reached the surface, gasping, struggling. Discussions of determinism or freewill aside, I had no chance the minute I walked into that bar and I was reunited with Derek.

In the split second after sitting beside him, I knew that any defenses against him would be completely lost. Call it love. Call it insanity.

Condensation lined cheap beer coasters. Beautiful, moving, powerful poetry that for once was a mere backdrop to my inner thoughts. We were forced close to each other at the table because of the crowd, forced close to each other by the world.

Do you believe in fate? Do you believe in magic? I don't know.

I wondered what he was thinking. We laughed together at the words that fell from the mouths of strangers on stage. Electrified by the mere tangling of fingers, we reached for each other's hands under the table.

I wanted him. I wanted him in my life, to talk with him, to share my days with him, to travel with him, to listen to him, and to be there for him. As I felt his dry skin rub against my fingers I desired him with every pore. I was tempted to reach for him under the table. I wanted to touch him, to feel his swell, and to make him so hard that he felt the need to pull me onto his lap, move my dress and let me ride him in the crowded bar. I pictured the entire room becoming an orgy, and I smiled. I squeezed Derek's hand, and he leaned over and kissed my cheek.

I wanted him to kiss me and pull me to the bathroom, throw me against the wall, remove my panties, hold my head against the wall, and pound me as hard as he could. Make me his. It wasn't the time to be gentle—not anymore. I pulled his hand into my lap, wanting him to slip it inside my pants, to feel my wetness. To know I forgave him, wet even if I shouldn't have been.

The rest of the night was a blur, at intermission we spilled outside for air. The slight breeze felt amazing against my skin during the humid summer night. Derek and I embraced. As he held me and we kissed, I felt him thick against me. He wanted me too. I know biology can be misleading, wet and hard doesn't always mean *yes*, but still, my body ached. The next hour passed in an elevated state of happiness and yearning, my desire intensified by the stiff air of the night.

He offered to walk me home, and we began to talk about how great the performance was, about missing each other, about life, just not about us. I was so stupid. I wanted to talk, but even though he was on his best behaviour I didn't want to make him angry. Tonight was too perfect to ruin. We didn't make the short walk to my place; instead we paused in a covered storefront porch, acknowledging the overwhelming need to finish reconciling.

Grey, hard cement. Cigarette butts and half empty beer cans, chewing gum littering the ground, and spray paint coating the grime. The payphone swayed in dead air, just out of reach, covered in stickers that were no longer readable. It was only safe to touch each other because everything else was filth. Had it been another night, it may have gone differently. But this is my story of what happened, not of *what if*s. "Say it like it is," Alice used to say, and don't apologize. *Never fucking apologize.*

He pulled me into him and I felt him against me. He pushed my bra aside and felt my nipples, hard. I'd never felt so alive as when we touched each other's bodies. We kissed as he finally pushed my underwear aside, and he whispered about how wet I was. I'd been wet for him all night; I was surprised my body remained in a solid form. My wetness could fill an ocean. I became fluid.

He shoved two fingers inside me and I gasped. I worked his belt free, stumbling for a second, desperate to have him. He removed his fingers, pushed his cock into me, and I experienced pure bliss. My life could have been over that minute and I'd be happy. He held me with my back against the wall, and we fucked as his sweat covered my face. Desperate, impatient, animalistic. We were beyond reason in this piss-smelling forbidden alcove. I didn't care that we may have been seen by the cars and pedestrians on the street, or the cops, as long as they let us finish. I howled into the night, competing with the backdrop of the constant sirens. I could not be silent. He put his hand over my mouth, but I bit him and continued to cry with pleasure.

After, we continued the journey to my dorm—more content, less desperate— and I invited him inside. We made love two or three more times, more passionate and gentle this time. You may wonder how I was able to let him touch me after everything. I wondered the same thing. My head didn't have an answer; reason and revenge had no say. I guess grudges could be a useful defense mechanism and forgiveness a dangerous path.

CHAPTER 13

We'd never work—and I knew that, if I'm being honest. I loved him, but I didn't trust or respect him. So, no. Love isn't always enough.

I wasn't sure if that evening was a one-off, or the beginning of something new. I was hesitant to ask Derek. He hated talking about us, and I didn't want to ruin the memory of that night. Maybe it was best to leave that evening as it was—a great memory. It couldn't replace, or erase, the previous violence and mistreatment, but at least I could remember that great encounter with a complex individual.

The next time I saw him was a few days later, and I still had no answers. Did he think we were together? Derek—so familiar—was also a stranger. I, a pile of feelings and thoughts, willing to spill open. Derek, deep and guarded, was made further strange by the attack.

We decided to have a picnic on his day off. As we sat on the subway together on the way to the harbor front, he reached over and took my hand, squeezing it. Was this all the confirmation I needed? If it was a one-off and we were just hanging out as friends, why did he reach over and interlace his fingers with mine? I silenced myself. He wasn't going to *ask* if I wanted to be with him, or vocalize that he wanted *me*.

I made it through the picnic and almost back to my apartment before I told Derek that we needed to talk. I wanted to be the carefree girl, living in the moment. But I needed to talk, and I owed it to myself. My stomach was restless, my joints were tense with the wait.

"Uh, Derek, I really need to talk." My heart was pounding and my voice went high at the end. We approached my building. I was fidgeting with my hands and hair, unsure of my body.

"I know, hun. I was meaning to tell you: I didn't mean it, the last night we were together. I was feeling really overwhelmed by school and work and I was being a jerk and just got carried away. I shouldn't have treated you like that. I don't deserve you. You know that, right? I wasn't myself, between the alcohol and just feeling so angry...and things just got out of control."

I looked at him and nodded. I wasn't quite ready to say that it was okay, and move on. Forgive and forget; now that's dangerous.

"I actually scared myself that night, and I've spent a lot of time by myself, working out my issues, writing about it, meditating, figuring out how to do better."

"I'm glad you realize what you did, and that you're working on yourself. You really hurt me, and it's going to take a while for me to trust you again, if ever." I couldn't think of what else to mention, but I knew there was so much more to say. There always was.

He didn't quite apologize, and I didn't really offer him my forgiveness. He didn't ask if we were together, and neither did I. We just fell together again, with a fragment of a conversation affirming our messy movement forward. We kissed and went our separate ways, an acknowledgement of our broken conversation that didn't quite reach forgiveness.

Sometimes, I felt like I was dating a polite actor, never quite sure how he felt, who he was, and most importantly why he was with me. The rude comments he once made about me still hung in the air, perhaps silent to his ears, but ever present to me. But things went on, we continued on this path of being together. Still, I couldn't help but constantly wonder what he thought of me. Did he care what I thought of him?

Mellow days and weeks passed, full of laughter, love and long conversations. He was notably sober, but we were both careful not to acknowledge this. Mentioning his sobriety would play into a conversation about his slip from control earlier, and that he had a problem. Sometimes I looked at him and felt angry, so angry. Rage that was renewed from nowhere by a simple look at him and I knew I hadn't forgiven him. I needed to remember how he could be. I could love him, but I couldn't like him too much, or let my guard down. I wanted to yell at him, to tell him how much he hurt me. I wanted to ask him, "why, why, why?" In his half apology he never used the word rape. Did he realize, or acknowledge to himself that he raped me?

Still, we moved on, my fury barely contained. I asked myself if I wanted to be with him. If I let out the storm inside we'd surely be over.

And his bedroom was always haunted by ghosts of girlfriends' past. Namely the one that got away, whose name I still didn't know. Beth, Jennifer, Amanda, Odessa…black, brown, older, younger, Canadian, Jamaican. I knew nothing of her, but she was everywhere. The occasional comment suggested I was just for the here and now. I was not the best travel destination, for he had seen greater lands, but I was a stop on a journey that hopefully brought him back to the places before me. And as I lay in his haunted bed that witnessed his tangle with other lovers, I wondered if he raped any of them too. But if he raped them, the language of lovers doesn't seem quite right, does it? Rape ruined the poetry of things.

I got angry all over again. For myself, for girls I would never know, for truths that would never be shared. And this frustration was worse because I didn't feel entitled. First anger, then forgiveness, and then bliss. But how would I tell him that I was furious, hell burning in me, over past events relived in my head that he assumed I'd long forgiven him for. Memory can be a curse, and I'd like to forget all this now.

I had to tiptoe around my friends. I had a secret boyfriend, a lover that I needed to hide, for I had betrayed myself. My friends, I imagine, would look at me with disappointment and concern, with whispers of, "you can do better." So I hid him, *hid us.* I swallowed my anger, until it became fury.

Elyse called me one day and asked how I was doing, and what I was up to that night. I was waiting for Derek to come over, so I lied. I said I was watching a movie. I tried to keep the happiness out of my voice; I didn't want her to wonder. I'm not saying you should lie, but sometimes it was so much easier, especially when people don't have the time or the mind for the truth. What could I tell her—about the heat of late July night? About the condensation on the beer glass? The isolation of being in a big city by myself, and no one but him really getting me? With each lie I told I was another step removed from my friends. Perhaps another step into myself, where they couldn't reach me.

August faded in nights spent together, watching movies, eating late, scrambling to work, dreading the inevitable September because I was so happy in the present, but I knew it couldn't last. *It never lasts.*

I was filled with flashbacks that were hard to reason away, I was fine one minute, terrified and transported the next, to another time and space. The weight of his apartment door slammed with the coat I placed on the hook. My arm shook.

It is okay, Patricia, I told myself, but I flinched and needed to walk up to the door to ensure it was unlocked. I needed to know that I could get out. I know how this sounded, fearful of someone I was dating, but I couldn't help but remember what happened in this place, in his space.

We were in bed one weeknight, tired of going out, wanting to just be alone together. I picked a book from his shelf, and began to read, paying as much attention to the author's words as Derek's notes in the margins as if he was speaking directly to me. Limbs tangled happily. Derek had another book open. Now and then we paused to share a thought, a favorite line. I can't really explain what happened in my mind, but suddenly I needed to get up. Feeling trapped, I threw Derek off me abruptly and stood. I needed to be away from him. I couldn't be trapped. I went for a walk and came back a half-hour later, calm. I didn't explain because I didn't feel that I owed him more explanations. I think he was afraid to ask.

And the bedroom, always contested terrain, I found myself surprisingly calm when we had sex. Perhaps in my mind the worst had already happened, so I let go. That or I was overcome with indifference.

Traitor, I sometimes thought to myself, but I told that voice to be quiet.

He was gentle, tame. There was an unspoken contract between us that he'd be tender with my body. I was not sure if he was more afraid of traumatizing me, or afraid of losing control of himself.

He'd whisper, "slut," in my ear as he nibbled my earlobe and pushed into my body, but that was as far as he'd go. No holding me down, no hands against my throat, no belt on my ass that would leave red marks for days. Perhaps afraid of his strength, perhaps seeing me as a China doll, perhaps remembering what the weeks felt like when I was absent from his life. We were too serious now to play. I wondered what he was thinking as he gently made love to me. I looked in his eyes and knew that despite this chivalry the monster still lurked below the surface.

I nibbled him. I wanted him to pound me, bite me, rip my hair out, hold me down, that would seem more real. I loved the tender, kind Derek, but he was a fake.

CHAPTER 14

September rolled around again, and with it a strange feeling of accomplishment. I made it to another school year. I was still here, still functioning...somehow. I remembered the promise I made last September when I panicked on the subway that I'd finish the year, and I congratulated myself. I knew I still had another three years of my degree, but it was one hell of a year. If you told me a year ago what this year would bring, I'd have frozen, limbs made immobile by the weight of events to come. We have a way of surviving the unthinkable. I was careful not to be too proud, school and surviving is more of a long distance race than anything else, and it's about endurance.

The new school year always came with this exciting feeling of freshness, new crisp books and classes full of exciting and inspiring ideas, the joy of new knowledge prior to the weight of looming deadlines and sleepless nights, but that was gone. Instead, I had new document files and electronic outlines waiting for me to explore authors and ideas unknown. Waiting for me to prove that I could think within the parameters set out on a neat rubric. Prove you can conform. But enough about school, we all know I'm a bit of a nerd.

To be honest, I still wasn't sure if journalism was for me, and I spent the summer browsing through other programs thinking of transferring. But I didn't find anything that was really compelling.

I flirted with different options, but I wasn't ready to commit. I actually tried to talk to the guidance counsellor the first week of school, but the appointment left me feeling dumb and directionless. I waited in line with a flock of unhappy students wanting to change their classes. They fanned themselves with their schedules as we stood in a stuffy hall.

The secretary called us one by one, asking student number, and reason for appointment? But I didn't really know why I was there. I had vague questions; how much longer would it take if I transferred to Women's Studies, or maybe English Literature? I wasn't really sure what I wanted to know, just that I had options. I wanted to know where the point of no return was.

I guess that was always my question, with school…with him. The guidance counsellor was overworked and tired, and tried to answer my questions as I stumbled to figure out what it was that I was asking. I expected to arrive in the office and for things to suddenly be clear. I left Journalism as my major, unwilling to commit to changing it, instead continuing on the path of least resistance.

I hardly had the chance to interact with Derek the first few weeks of September. I didn't have time to balance school and work, so I quit my job the second week of school, having saved enough for the term.

I was still busy with the return of my friends to the city. I decided to stay in residence another year. The rooms beside mine filled with first year students and I was proud of my seniority as proof of having survived a year of school, but I felt stupid for staying. Most of the other second year students were excited to live in the city.

I browsed online listings. The apartments in my price range were shabby, complete with extremely questionable landlords. One ad for a crisp, affordable, apartment downtown came complete with an application. *Here fill out your banking information. Drive by and check the place out. The owner is out of the country doing missionary work in Africa. Will mail the keys.* Yeah, right. I was not that naïve. *Was everyone a liar?*

All the places marketed to students in the downtown area boasted about having hotplates and microwaves and no bed bugs. I saw pictures of threadbare lights hanging from ceilings. One advertisement explained that the kitchenette didn't have a sink, and to use the one in the bathroom. The further you go from downtown the more affordable the housing, but I was unsure how far I wanted to travel into the here be dragons part of the city. I couldn't imagine living with roommates. I saw generic advertisements that sought a fun, social, clean, girl to fill an extra bedroom in a creative household. I couldn't picture myself trying to fit in with random girls. I was always the outsider, shy and picked on.

Besides, I'd heard enough horror stories about roommates found online to be wary.

All of this is to say that September was occupied by residence orientation activities, and I was overwhelmed by the commotion after the relative silence in the summer. The building was swollen with the influx of freshmen students, high on their first real experience of being away from home. Whispers of schedules and new boyfriends and kegs floated by, irrelevant. People either assumed I was a first year, or wondered why I was there. Aashi was still my don, and Brittany—although bitter—stayed in residence. She said something about planning to live with a group of girls in a house, but that fell through. Brittany was being surprisingly friendly, inviting me to her room to watch movies and do homework. I couldn't help but wonder why she was being so nice. Perhaps I wasn't giving her enough credit. Unprompted, she offered her sympathies about Derek, and I couldn't help but wonder what exactly she knew. I wouldn't blame Elyse for talking, but still, I wondered.

The first three weeks of school I only saw Derek once because we were both so busy. We went to the movies, and as we walked to the theater I felt anxious. My brain was circling in a flux of *oh no what if Kara or Elyse see us, what will they say?*

I walked quickly, refusing to stop for a patio drink on the way home at a bustling university pub. I was relieved when the evening was done and I was safely alone in my dorm room. I told Derek that I had homework to finish. What was I supposed to say: "Sorry I told some of my friends that you raped me? If they see you with me they may punch you?" No, lying was easier sometimes, whoever said *the truth will set you free* and all that jazz obviously hadn't done anything worth lying about.

Summer vacation was over for our little romance, and the return of my friends led to heightened anxiety and guilt. When Derek and I finally had time to see each other, everything shifted again.

Enter act three of our relationship: *battle to the death*.

Between her summer job and her parents' financial help, Elyse was somehow able to afford a one-bedroom apartment downtown. The night after my rushed movie date with Derek, I went to Elyse's house warming party. I was looking forward to a relaxed evening after the chaos of the first weeks of school.

I arrived early and gave Elyse a fruit tray and she handed me a glass of wine. I sipped my drink as she showed me around her small, but inviting space. Her kitchen was tiny, and the living room was complete with a small dinner table, a couch and a bookshelf. Her bedroom was tidy, with a pink bed cover and photos of friends from high school and a picture of us that she took last year. The best part of the whole apartment was the balcony. I sat outside for a few minutes, looking at the Toronto skyline. Sometimes it was so easy to imagine being someone else.

Guests trickled in: Brittany and a few other familiar faces from residence. Elyse thrived on the energy, running around, introducing people, and pouring drinks. The apartment grew warm and crowded, and I stepped out on the balcony to breathe. Brittany found me a few minutes later, "There you are! Elyse has someone she wants to introduce you to."

I was led back into the packed living room.

"Patricia, over here!" Elyse called, pulling me towards a boy I hadn't seen before. "Patricia, I want you to meet Jake. Jake, Patricia. Jake went to high school with me. He took a year off, and is just starting school now."

"Nice to meet you," I said, shaking his hand. He was cute. Nice smile, green eyes, firm handshake. I looked away, having gazed at his face a second too long.

"It's nice to meet you, too. I was told I should talk to you. I'm thinking about transferring to journalism."

"He's cute isn't he?" Brittany whispered.

I nodded.

"Elyse and I ran into Jake last week, and we thought you'd like him. He's nice and he doesn't really know anyone in Toronto aside from us. Maybe you can show him around, or show him a good time," she winked. *Fuck off, Brittany.*

At first I was annoyed, but then I found it funny. They were trying to be helpful. If only they knew Derek and I were back together. I smiled to myself, the only one getting the joke.

I sat with Jake on the couch, answering his questions, feeling obligated to talk with him to appease my friends. As the night continued, I grew more comfortable, and tried to actually engage with him as he asked me about myself, stumbling over his words.

Elyse smiled and whispered, "I'm glad you are getting along so well," as she handed me a drink I didn't ask for.

Jake got more confident. He put his arm around me, and I moved toward him. And it felt good to talk to a guy at a party who found me interesting, and who my friends approved of.

We said goodbye as the evening came to an end, briefly kissing on the lips. I pulled away, because I wanted more.

I agreed to keep in touch—to find him online or something. But we all know that I didn't untangle my life from Derek's that night. I went to bed thinking about kissing Jake. As drowsiness kicked in, another life almost felt imaginable.

But I was frozen. He wasn't the one my life and limbs were tangled with Derek was, and so with that I gave Jake vague answers about homework when he tried to make plans with me. Maybe I didn't like nice guys. Or something like that.

Jake joined one of my classes. He politely said, "hi" to me, looked at the vacant seat next to mine and then back at my face, but kept walking. I watched him slowly become close with another girl in our class over the course of the term.

Good for them, I thought, *he seems like a nice guy.*

Every class, I noticed them laughing and holding hands, and I wondered what it would've been like if I shared more than one kiss with him. But it's dangerous to build a life of *what ifs* for they are as fragile as sandcastles.

When Derek asked me about the party, I shrugged, saying that it was a bit boring.

CHAPTER 15

I went home at the end of September for my birthday, at my mother's suggestion. We had a nice, quiet weekend. My brother was busy with work, but my grandparents came. We ate cake and opened presents in the backyard on one of the last sunny days of the season.

I blew out my nineteen candles, and I thought, *is that it?* It felt like I'd been through more than could fit into such a number. My life needed more direction. Since the second grade, I'd been serenaded with the chorus of, "Stay in school!" But I was no longer sure about my program, or anything else in my life. Plus, doing well in school was no guarantee of long-term career success. *Life comes with no guarantees.*

I toyed with the idea of going to college to study something more practical and career focused, but Derek shot the idea down, saying that I'd be bored, restless. "Don't sell yourself short," he had said.

I mentioned college to my brother, and he said something similar. I know, I know I can think for myself, but they were right. University was for daydreamers who like to diddle-daddle.

I returned to Toronto, and finally got the chance to spend a night with Derek. That was when everything changed again. I can't quite say what happened in a way that will fit into a sentence, paragraph or chapter so that you'd understand. It was a shift, like feeling the change in air pressure before seeing storm clouds.

Derek gave me my birthday present: a lovely purple pendant, made with some kind of semi-precious stone. I still have it; I can't bear to part with it—material proof that he wasn't a part of my imagination and that we were fucking real. I should have thrown it into the water, like the girl from *Titanic*. Let it sink. He deserves to go down with the ship.

In our limited time and energy, the space for social niceties evaporated. Once, when I asked him to be less snappy, he told me, "You're lucky your parents can help you and you don't need to worry about working while in school. A little privileged *bitch* like you doesn't get it."

He actually called me a bitch.

"Do you talk to any of your friends this way?" I asked.

He said, "I don't, but I'm not as close with them as I am to you. I can be honest with you; don't you like that? Don't you like that, *bitch*?"

I know I sound repetitive, but Derek and I, we danced in circles.

His mistreatment morphed in my brain into compliments. *I treat you like this because we're close.* I should have stopped and asked myself: *How close do I want to get to this creature?* I turned up the volume on what he said, and turned down the volume of what my heart and head were telling me. *I should have done the opposite.*

He still made my heart race, but he kept growing colder. Any little thing could bother him: food that I didn't microwave long enough, a glass of water and a forgotten coaster. I flinched when he yelled at me, then apologized and held me. And during all of this, was a continuing narrative about a girl that I'm not. Mystery girl, the one who got away, the hidden third person in our relationship.

He got annoyed when I hadn't read some book he was referencing, apparently by his favorite author. He cancelled our plans last minute, never telling me why, but it slipped that it was *her* birthday. The ghost's birthday took on more importance than mine. It was an unbearable weight, being punished for not being another person.

If you want to know another person, don't start with their name because it is of little significance. You need to find out who haunts them, and ask if a space in their life is worth it. Just my two cents—as worthless as the Canadian penny. But the ghost of his past lived on. Throw my thoughts in a wishing well. I don't believe in lucky pennies.

I often thought of leaving, like how one dreams about running off and backpacking across Europe—nothing more than a fantasy. I loved him, even if I didn't enjoy his company. Love was a poor justification for staying, but like I said, I like seeing things through. I needed to know for sure what would be next, wanting a better ending, expecting a car crash. I'm the type that goes and looks at the smoking debris. How can you not look?

It was awful being with someone when it wasn't clear if they wanted to be with you—constantly hearing whispered, "I love yous" that felt more like questions than statements. I had never been so lonely. I was unable to properly grieve the loss, as I was still with him. At the same time, I tried to get over him, a wound that would start to heal and then was ripped open again by his vacant looks and silent refrain of *you aren't the girl.* You'll never be her.

"You have too many issues," he told me as he sipped from his drink.

There were hints of other women in his life, but when I tried to ask him, he would just say, "Stop trying to talk about us. I *don't* want to *fucking* talk. "

I shouldn't have stayed, shouldn't have accepted this. Don't worry, I know that, dear reader. I couldn't mention Derek to Elyse or Kara, or even Brittany. They'd already done their part. They were good friends, helped me get over him. *Aren't you over him?* No, I picked this, and I was in it alone. Utterly alone.

As you skim the pages, you might be wondering, *did he rape me again?* The short answer was no. The more complicated answer is I stopped telling him no. There's this mantra of, *yes means yes and no means no,* but we existed somewhere between. Murky water. A voice a little too rough telling me I wanted it. He would slap me in the face and call me a slut in the kitchen while I did the dishes. But I thought that if I didn't say *no,* then what happened before wouldn't happen again. Don't listen to me if this happened to you, this is just the mantra that I repeated in my head as I tried to make sense of it all.

I no longer told him how I like to be touched, or not to touch me, or to be gentler. I mistook abuse and love. I'd lie still while he was on top of me, his dreadlocks falling onto my face as he groaned and panted. I thought about ripping his hair out. He leaned in for a kiss and I flinched, ready for him to hit me. I told myself I wanted him. That we loved each other, that it felt good. But really, I wanted him the hell off me and for him to be more passionate and caring. I guess the middle ground was my silence.

It didn't matter if I was there. I was just this hole to fill a void. This is what you made me.   *MOTHERFUCKER.*

His hands stung, my body became laden with bruises. I didn't say no, I was too tired. He treated me how he wanted and fucked me how he wanted. I became such a constant that I make myself irrelevant. *Backdrop.* It no longer seemed like he cared if I enjoyed it. I didn't think he cared about me at all. And still, I stayed.

Irrelevant. I was irrelevant. Get a fucking doll, you don't need me. And fucking Dr. Jennings, he said to work out my anger. Anger wasn't healthy, wasn't feminine. *Just let it all go,* more like *go fuck yourself*— and not in a sex positive kinda way. Jennings, ghost boy, fuck, go fuck yourself, go fuck each other. I'm so angry now, but my anger is valid.

You locked me up, removed all my choices, what to put in my body, where to be, watch me shit, trap me like *he* did, and then told me I have no right to be angry.

Fuck you. I really didn't matter to you either. Replace me with a plastic dummy to medicate, and your healthcare system can keep ticking, the doctors and the nurses and their charts, survived off people like me. This system, it pretended to have a lack of resources, just spent them paying to trap people who wanted to be free, kicking out people who begged to be let in.

I'll keep my anger and my words, thank you very much. Even if I have to be all zen, to get out of here. *Fuck that*—I wasted all my energy playing games with the ghost; I had no room left to win against the system when I kept getting dealt losing hands. I was told to fake it out there, and the only way to pass a test in here was continue the lie, no thanks, I really couldn't be bothered, sorry Alice.

Not that I didn't know how to act. I just refused to put on a show. For Jennings, for the fucking medial student, for Leah, for Melanie, for Mandy, and Martha for cured Niki and the bloody security guards. The guards were so serious in their white uniforms helping to protect the vulnerable. *You are such a good person,* their partners would repeat when they got home as their hands stroked bodies that were tired from standing all day. The guards probably jerked off thinking about locked girls in cages.

Fuck you, we are the real ones, we aren't sick. That was what I'd say if I had enough energy, but, but I was tired from whatever antidepressant Jennings gave me.

But where was I? Oh yes—I was telling you about how that asshole touched me...

He was on top of me, calling me a slut and I just wanted him to be rougher, rip my hair out, make me feel filthy, bruise me. I wanted to become *his whore*, the version of myself that he wanted me to be. What was left for me? I was alive in his twisted vision, and being around him seemed like the only thing that was real. Maybe I wanted to provoke him. Maybe I deserved this.

I daydreamed about ripping his hair out with my hands, about cutting his precious dreads in his sleep. Snip, snip, snip— scissors can fix so many things. Fuck you, hippie-poser boy. I thought about hurting him, eye for an eye, *Old Testament* shit.

I wanted to hold him down, no, better yet, tie him up while he slept, maybe drug him first, grind up some of my sleeping pills and put it in his food. He'd lie down after dinner, all groggy from the pills and I'd flip him onto his stomach, tie up his hands and feet, and find something to shove into him as hard as I could. I wanted to hurt him. *Needed* to hurt him. As I'd force something into his dry ass, I'd remind him about what he did to me. As he fucked me I daydreamed about destroying him. I warned you, dreaming was dangerous. Don't worry; I didn't say this to anyone. These are the types of comments that'd ensure I'm locked away forever. *I warned you, this is no love story.*

I wondered if other women dreamed of revenge on their rapists. Sometimes, I looked around at the vacant faces and dishevelled bodies on the subway on the last train home on a Friday night, or during rush hour, and I wondered what stopped everything from devolving, evolving into chaos. Look at those faces at 5 p.m., and breathe in the tension over the train being five minutes late, or the bag that hits the stranger. Don't pretend you don't know what I'm talkin about.

Who else was raped by a partner, by a fucking stranger, once, twice, fifty times? Who was thrown from the medial system, from the prison system to the street? Whose family member or friend was shot by the police? Whose best friend just slammed the door in their face and said, "peace," or fucking hung themselves? I was amazed that we somehow managed to get it together, this city, this circus. I didn't know how. I was angry, but this anger went so much further than him and me. I could feel every hand on every single body that said *no* and every person waiting desperately to see if they would have a space to sleep out of the cold as strangers look at them from the TTC, and every tear and all the anger. And, and this was just the pain of one city. And if there was no room in the shelter, we just leave them outside. I heard they found a homeless man downtown, frozen to death in a t-shirt. Best fucking city in the world I read somewhere.

What a joke. In this world class city folks don't have enough fucking food to eat, and no one cares about you unless you are the top of the social chain. Some people commented about the amount of violence in the city. But me, I'm surprised that the only boiling over is the stabbings and the bullets and the evacuation threats and the cheap tabloid headings. I'm fucking amazed we haven't all stabbed each other in the throat with how ugly it all gets. *You can pretend that you don't get any of this, but I know you do. If I'm making you uncomfortable go ahead, slip the bookmark in and roll your eyes.*

Maybe it was better to see this all through some haze that makes it easier to deal with the shitty reality of being human. Some guy called out "hey sweetheart, can I get you anything?" as I stumbled past the park in Kensington one day after a fight with Derek. And, and I wanted to say "everything," all the fucking drugs in the city, and to sit in that park and to be just gone. Lie down in the grass on my sweater and just close my eyes and forget everything, along with all the other people in the park who were busy forgetting. I used every bit of strength to shake my head and look away from the man on the corner. And I already forgot what I was writing about, but everything was about Derek.

My life was defined by this livid pain and anger and joy I experienced when I was with him and this mellow, apathetic indifference I felt about the rest of the world. Indifference can be nice, bearable—not like sorrow, not like anger.

I couldn't be bothered to try. I could barely make it out of bed in the morning. I missed classes because the days were too heavy, my limbs too numb. I'd sleep through it all, and he'd come along and wake me in hell.

I was narrowly passing most of my classes, but I was failing Popular Culture, which suggested nothing about my ability to theorize about movies and cultural trends, but more about the weight of the murky water, of my mind, of Derek. He'd tell me of theories and dead philosophers in this gentle way, but underneath was this chant of, "listen to me, listen to me, listen to me. I know everything."

I thought he was going to breakup with me soon, biding my time. Nothing really changed, we continued on this rough path, but small things shifted. I was compared more and more to a girl long past, little comments, but I knew I was failing in some unknown competition. I tried harder to please him: made him dinner, texted him to ask how his day was.

Pathetic. Never let people know you care, they'll kick you as hard as possible in your weak spot. Love is about a power imbalance. Rarely do two people mean the same thing to each other, and they just go for that frail spot. Loving the other is literally kneeling down; I guess marriage proposals and blowjobs at least got the imagery right.

Still, I didn't, couldn't leave. Logic had no place in my love; you should have realized this by now. Things couldn't go on like this. Silence became heavy. I wanted to blurt out what was happening, but I was gradually losing the ability to talk to other people. One day Aashi greeted me in the hall as I walked home from class, and asked how I was doing, how my midterm went. I looked up from the floor, and tried to give her a passable smile.

"Okay," I said my voice cracking. "I slept through one of them, to tell you the truth." I was tempted to tell her what was going on, but where would I start: Derek, the rape, feeling angry, wanting to hurt him, the weight, floating away? Afraid of saying everything, I said nothing.

Brittany, Elyse and I went for drinks sometime near the end of November. They talked about school and a new guy who Elyse was dating. I tried paying attention, smiling, nodding, offering my comments, but I was a B actor at best.

"Hey, did you talk to Jake again after my party?" Elyse asked me.

Apparently I don't like nice guys. Fuck nice guys.

CHAPTER 16

How was I to say, "no, wait, stop, I want a condom," when I couldn't even whisper, "no, wait, stop, don't fuck me"? I wanted to say something, but I trusted him, and that things would be okay.

I shouldn't have.

Before he raped me, I had always insisted on using protection. We entered this ritual dance of *yes, I know it's uncomfortable and it feels better without, but we are using a condom, end of conversation. Shut up and wear it if you want to fuck me. Don't make me plea.* And I was supposed to be the submissive one, so of course I only whispered, "please," keeping the rest to myself.

I'm sure you know the conversation. The first few times after he raped me there was a layer between us, but as he grew rougher with me, less polite, that stopped. I was bound and blindfolded, trusting, smelling the liquor on his breath. I wondered how much he had this time? Just enough to make me fuckable, not enough to lose control. The first time he slipped inside I was surprised, concerned, but I liked it. I thought about telling him to stop, trying to get his attention through the gag. But, honestly, it felt too good. I'm to blame as well.

Somewhere inside, I felt disgusted, remembering earlier whispered conversations about STI tests and an offended response—the only kind there seemed to be—of, "yes, of course I'm clean."

I didn't say anything the first time, and we acted as if it was our usual routine. The next week, I tried to say something about the fact that we needed to use protection.

He just said, "Yeah, but you worry too much. You won't get pregnant. Trust me."

Never trust a boy when he tries to refute biology.

My breasts felt heavy, swollen, and foreign. I had cramps, and slight bleeding, but it was far too early for my period. I knew before I actually knew, the weight of my breasts telling me more than a symbol on a pregnancy test. White discharge on black underwear, reminding me of the fact that my body was out of my control. I knew, but I pretended not to, wanting to wait until a better time to confirm.

Not now, I thought. December loomed before me with exams and the holidays. *Not now body*, I told myself.

I hurried past the campus drug store on my way to class. I visualized picking a test from the shelf and going to the counter to pay, covering the test with shampoo and chocolate bars and anything else. What if there was someone I knew in the store? And then what?

Alone in the residence bathroom, I would hide in a stall as I opened the test with trembling hands, pee on the stick, and wait. My story isn't that original. How many of us have had shaking hands, nervously looking around in the drug store, hiding behind a closed door? And the sex education lessons of public school—they don't say so very many things. Use protection, period. But they didn't say how to find your voice when your throat is stuck and your words float away, and your mouth can't find the energy to shape the word, "no," tongue tripping on words that are forever unspoken.

I stared at my stomach, hating myself and the weight of my belly. I pinched my swelling breasts, angry with myself, furious for letting this happen. For, for letting this foreign thing takeover my body, a weed, out of my control like my relationship with him.

You did this to yourself, girl, no one but you. You should've stayed away. You could have been sipping wine with Elyse and worrying about exams. I didn't take the test, what good was confirming what I knew?

The weight of this invasion was enough to push Derek into the background, along with school, friends, and my family—who I'd barely spoken to since my birthday. I couldn't believe people did this on purpose—something about love, and desire to re-create. Fucking biology. I didn't understand, but again, look where I am.

I stood naked in front of my mirror, fresh from the shower, hair dripping in my eyes. I spent a few minutes looking at my body. It had only been a few weeks, but I could see the slight rise in my belly, the change in my breasts, and the look in my eyes.

I never agreed to this, I thought, angry, frustrated, willing the truth away. Alien invasion, parasite growing in me. Cancer, tumor growth.

My body became too real. My flesh accumulated this strange weight. My body told this, this heartbreaking story in my bones. I was all physical, every breath too real; every back pain felt—all of it. And yet I wasn't completely there, drifting, floating. This couldn't be real; I never agreed. I had exams to worry about. Maybe this would go away, like horror movie ghosts that could only scare you if you believed they were real.

This wasn't happening to me, not my body. But my body does so many things without my thinking, pumps the blood through my system despite not wanting to be here, so why would it need my go ahead for creating new life? My fault for giving it materials, always looking to be resourceful, these machines. My body did what my mind told it not to do. I guess my story wasn't unique, people get cancer, get old, get sick, without giving their body permission either. Perhaps this was what they meant by mind body divide. Nothing about my story is original.

I didn't consider telling Derek. I saw him a few times, but he was distant, worried about school, worried about life. He said something about starting a new painting project with the theme of urban landscapes. I was nothing more than a pastime for him now, a semi-neglected hobby, like a television show you only remembered when the TV was on.

I wished I was someone else.

So no, I didn't tell Derek, or Elyse, or Kara, or Aashi—and definitely not my family—that I was pregnant. I could imagine how the conversation would go with each of them. My friends would be shocked that I lied about Derek, but also forgiving and filled with concern. I could hardly deal with myself though; I didn't have the energy to tell them and then have to engage with their worry, reassure them that I was fine when I wasn't. There was also the issue of what I would do, and I wasn't ready to think about the medical system: doctors examining my body, paperwork, charts, health card number, waiting for appointments. The doctor was late. I was late. Tick-tock.

Abortion is such a slippery topic that I cringe writing the word. Someties a sentence that starts by saying "I support your bodily self-determination," becomes a statement about *killing* babies, and the conversation of when exactly does a thing—a cluster of cells—become a being.

And I didn't exactly know where Elyse and Kara stood on the subject; discussions about pro-life, versus pro-choice make for poor cocktail conversations. And if they were pro-life, I couldn't stand to alienate myself further, have the pressure of their ideologies further victimizing my body.

And imagine how my family would have reacted? If my brother's love life was met by uncomfortable silence, a pregnant daughter who was single would be met with even greater discomfort. I could only imagine what my mother would have said. Something like: *have the baby it's the right thing to do. But don't let anyone know about this! Go hide while you're pregnant, like it's a previous century. Slip the baby to some white, heterosexual, middle-class couple and then we'll never talk about this again. And dear god, don't let Grandma and Grandpa find out!* Perhaps I'm being too hard on my family, but maybe not.

And my brother, I imagined awkwardly telling him over Christmas. He would have probably been quiet and empathetic, but realized this conversation was outside of his reach. Perhaps he'd have suggested I talk to a professional, and I already told you about my experience with so-called professionals. That was the only advice anyone ever seemed to have: *Talk to someone, talk to someone, talk to someone. Just don't talk to me.*

What the fuck do you want? Are you waiting to hear if I'm actually pregnant, if it was all in my head, if the crazy girl made this up? Unstable narrator, are you going to believe me? I'm trying to tell you my story, but I realize that I'm writing against a backdrop of unstable female narrators. My dear reader, please listen, I'm telling you the truth. I'm just so livid, blame it on the hormones, blame it on this *thing* occupying my body, this alien invasion. I didn't ask for this.

I wanted to eat everything—peanut butter and pickles, salt and vinegar chips, more pickles, and grease. I was so hungry that I couldn't eat. Mouth dry, mind full of hate, belly full of rage. I couldn't eat ever again, stomach sick at the very thought of food. I never claimed to be consistent.

For some reason I bought into the saying of time healing all wounds. So I waited, hoping my body would heal, praying that my body would realize that I don't want this. Maybe my brain could have told my body that I *didn't mean to do this, sorry, it was a mistake. I'll be careful next time.* I begged with the gods, made bargains with entities I didn't believe in.

I wondered how my mother felt when I lived in her, and my brother before me. Had she hated me for taking over her insides? Was I an alien, monster, enemy, or did she develop a bond with me, this thing swimming in her, stealing her nutrients? Was the experience of pregnancy different when it was rooted in intentionality? Had she loved me then in a way that she could never love me now? My mother doesn't like to talk. Pisces, if you believe in star crap and that birthdates have anything to do with things.

I threw myself into studying to convince myself that doing well on exams was the only thing that mattered. I became obsessive, staying up all night reviewing notes I'd already memorized, trying to repent for an imagined sin by being a zealous student, praying again to a God I didn't believe in and cursing myself for it.

My mind filled with half-construed ideas about abortion from the signs of protesters outside of clinics. Blood, so much blood.

But that's my blood, I thought. My brain, it took these images, and ran with them, cold clinic, male doctor, paperwork, health card number, more paperwork.

My mind filled with the questions I would likely be asked. So many questions: *who's your family doctor? Are you alone? Are you sure? Who'll come with you to the procedure?* I envisioned a knife entering my flesh, cutting away at me, in some cold room, while I lay drugged, unable to move, half-naked in a hospital gown, ass exposed, and vulnerable. Always vulnerable. I cracked.

I refused to read about procedures online, not wanting to know the facts. Looking at myself in the mirror, I couldn't imagine anyone ever wanting this horrible thing to happen to their body. You see, I didn't understand the basic premise of biology, how the world continued repopulating generation after generation, and how all these women let their wombs be taken over. And...and, I couldn't help but wonder if all the women before me said *no*, whispered *no*, screamed *no*, yelled at God *no*, and were ignored year after year.

CHAPTER 17

I returned home for Christmas break, and in this safe space, my pregnancy seemed impossible. My parents treated me like I was fifteen or sixteen.

"Patricia, where are you going? When will you be home?" my mother asked.

"Patricia, how are you budgeting for school? Want me to look over your bank statements?" my father offered.

I considered telling them, but again, what words, what sentence could I have possibly used to tell them about what happened to me—what explanation? I knew that I couldn't tell them, but as I sat through a stiff Christmas dinner with my parents, grandparents, brother, and John, the truth was always one sip of red wine away from coming out.

Christmas cushioned me. I was kept busy baking and watching Christmas movies. Time dragged; my desire for ignorance dulled beside my need to know the truth. I whispered to my body every night that *I didn't want this; make it stop.* She didn't listen to me.

The smell of gingerbread cookies turned my stomach. I picked at Christmas dinner.

My last day at home I spent reading a school novel in bed, feeling nauseous, breasts tender, heart racing. I tried focusing on some nineteenth century romance, but all I could think about was my body, how I couldn't ignore a time bomb.

My head had this strange pressure in it that I couldn't quite describe: tense, pounding, almost orgasmic—or the opposite. I don't fucking know. Not this building pressure of pleasure, but this mounting sensation of pain. I felt every pulse in my temple. I rested my hand on my head and I became every excruciating heartbeat. That was all I was. I needed to get up, needed this to stop. I couldn't describe this feeling—only that it defied logic, defied my tolerance for pain. *Help me, something, someone please help me, I can't do this. Water. I needed water. I was drowning.* I crawled out of bed, stood on shaking legs and collapsed, legs crumpled beneath me on the floor, and I became one big pulse, a mass of unmovable limbs. I didn't know how long I lay there, desiring to be one with my carpet.

"Patricia, can you help with dinner?" my mom called. I slowly lifted my pounding head from the carpet, and tried to shake off the grogginess. My head still hurt, but had resolved itself to a dull, bearable ache. I went downstairs and with shaking legs peeled potatoes, for it was easier than explaining why I couldn't quite stand.

I couldn't wait any longer, two days before New Year's Eve, I returned to Toronto by myself and bought a test. I stood with trembling hands in the drug store, trying to conceal the box as I walked towards the cash. I was relieved that there was no line, although it would have delayed learning the answer.

What can I really tell you? My pregnancy was confirmed like just another movie scene and Hollywood had reassured me that I was hardly the first woman to stand there alone.

My experience wasn't original, so I couldn't even give myself that, although I felt so, so, abandoned. I bought the test, prayed to gods I didn't believe in, pissed in a washroom, and waited for the earth to make up its mind about my fate. Peeling pink wallpaper and a fake plant stared back at me—an effort to cheer up the gas station washroom located beside the drugstore. I looked at the picture behind the toilet of children running on some beach. What was I going to do? Everyone other than Derek was gone for the holidays, but I suppose I didn't need anyone. I'd always been the one to have my own back; what was that quote? "Born alone, die alone," or something like that.

I reminded myself that this was my fault, but I didn't really believe it. I just tried to will myself into a space of action, when what I really wanted was to curl up in a ball. *You need to deal with this, hun*, I encouraged myself. *It'll be okay.* Thoughts swirled in my head, hyper sensitive to the dirty, dank bathroom. For a minute the smell of lingering piss evaporated and I felt truly calm.

I'm okay. I looked at the test, and the symbol confirmed what I already knew. Somehow I accepted the answer, for what choice did I have? I felt different, older, changed somehow having been thrown into this adult world.

I've already warned you this was no love story, but this also wasn't some tale about regretting my choices. This was my story about asking for help from a system that made me a number. It was about having people in my life I couldn't quite reach, and an abusive ex that I couldn't rationalize away and who still haunted me with his indifference and told me that I was the crazy one. And this was about how alone I felt with all of this. Don't forget I was just a small town girl, and somehow I lacked the words, the social space to talk about all this, though I've been doing a good job of rambling now for all these pages. I hope this never makes its way into my mother's hands.

It was everything. My mother, my town, the system, the school, counselling, Toronto, him, society, patriarchy. Or maybe it was just me. I don't fucking know. And then the medical system with the neat paperwork, drugs and the doctors examining my body, and you once more made me a number. The girl in room 312. But I don't need to explain any of this to you. Sometimes I just wanted so much to be understood, I guess that was my curse.

CHAPTER 18

It was New Year's Eve again and I'll tell you now it was the last night Derek and I spent together.

It's about time this girl learned, you're probably thinking. I know, I know. Over before it was officially over. I still can't believe I spent that second New Year's with him, a year had slipped by since I realized he was bad for me, and still I stayed. Why didn't I run?

My brain went into emergency compartmentalization mode—one thought at a time, one thing at a time. If I let everything merge, I'd freeze, panic, unable to move. All of this was to say that somehow I miraculously managed to spend the evening with him, and push aside what was happening. We stayed in, spent the night at his apartment, ordered Chinese food, and watched the fireworks on the television. Conversation dull, going through the act of caring about each other, his arm felt limp around my shoulder. He wasn't angry; we were both just apathetic. Dead weight.

I was too plain for him, and he was far too angry for me—stuck on a ghost. I was tired of being not good enough. We slept together one last time, out of a habit more than anything. I wondered if he also realized we were over in that moment. If he cared. There was no passion and little foreplay—just a tentative kiss and roaming hands, a few thrusts and a pool of cum. I didn't care; it was already too late for the worst to happen. I turned over and went to sleep. In the morning, I gave him a quick kiss and then went on my way.

Happy fucking New Year.

I wondered if he'd even bother to call me if I never texted or called him. Perhaps he preferred a fade out versus a breakup. *Ghosting,* I think is the new term for it; ghosting my ghost, there's an idea. We were once so passionate, could we really part without a goodbye? As I walked away, I imagined never talking to him again, knowing he'd care very little. But, but again life it doesn't work like that does it? When do we ever get clean breaks?

I needed this entire catastrophe to be behind me quickly, and I needed this *thing* out of me as soon as possible. I delayed research before the New Year, figuring that community services might be closed with the holiday, but now it was the first thing on my agenda: start the year off right; be gone, lurking ghosts; and be gone, biological ruins in my body from a boy best forgotten.

I was afraid to type "abortion" into the blinking curser, unsure what kind of rabbit hole this would bring me down. Perhaps I'd be bombarded with stories of regret, of *don't do it.* I needed a doctor; I didn't even have a family doctor. There was the clinic on campus, and Dr. Peter. Remember him? But it was more for walk-in type things, not serious issues I learned at my previous visits. When I thought of walk-in clinics I imagined going to a front desk and pulling out my health card, and telling them I had a sore throat, something immediate, but not an emergency. But, this, this was an emergency. I feared that I would end up on this scavenger hunt called "find the resources," first you go here, then here, and here and…Turns out my school doctor's office didn't open until school started in three days.

And then, as I carried groceries onto the subway, absently reading posters, I saw a sign: "Pregnant? We can Help! Call today for an immediate appointment. Free and confidential." I allowed a slight sigh of relief. *I'll take care of this. It'll be okay.*

I thought I had found my answer.

The intercom rang, letting me into a building, and I hurried from the cold street. I received a friendly greeting from the middle-aged secretary, and I felt safe for the first time since this ordeal began. She offered me a warm tea, and I wiggled my hands, numb with the cold. I could take care of myself. It was the small things. One step at a time, right?

I filled out the paperwork and looked around the cozy office. A plastic fetus model sat on the desk; hard, plastic, too bright a colour. I stood and stretched my cramped legs. My heart pounded after my brisk walk and I couldn't be still.

I noticed a poster that read, "life begins at conception."

"Hi, dear. I'm Dianne. You must be Patricia," an older woman with curly brown hair and warm smile came and ushered me to her office.

"Nice to meet you, Dianne," I said as I shook her hand.

The office was small, but cozy. A few plants sat by the window, along with inspirational quotes and a vase of flowers, beside a picture of what was presumably Dianne's daughter and grandchildren: a woman in her thirties had her arms around two redhead twins. They were at the beach, sun shining, wet hair, and water glittering on their skin. Dianne gave me a minute to relax.

"So, Patricia, tell me a bit about yourself? Are you from Toronto?"

"Uh, yeah. I came here for school; I've lived here for a year and a half," I replied, thinking, *Get to the point.*

"Ah! I see. And how do you like Toronto? What you are studying?"

And so the conversation went. I sat back and sipped my tea and she slowly gained my trust. If Alice had known me then, she'd have reminded me to never let my guard down. *Everyone wants something from you. Find out what, my dear Patricia. And somehow, in this process manage to not hate people.*

The paperwork asked me how I wanted to proceed, and for some reason I marked the *unsure* box, the word *abortion* looked daunting. On some anonymous forum, I'd have clicked it without hesitation, but not here. Not with the lady at the desk smiling at me as I filled out the paper. I was vulnerable. I wanted to do what would please these two ladies. I became an actor in they play they were directing.

I soon realized I was trapped in a one sided exchange, as Dianne knew everything, and I knew so little. I guess I should have prepared. I felt as though I was at a job interview for something I hadn't adequately researched and all I could do was agree.

"Do you have a support network for raising a child? Have you considered adoption? There are many families in the area that would love to have a child. How old did you say you are again, sweetie?" She warned me about cervical cancer, breast cancer, and the trump card of infertility. "Do you know how far along your baby is?" She glanced at my paperwork to answer the question. "About the size of an avocado. Look, see this picture?" Then she mentioned something about post-abortion syndrome. *You'll regret this, this will haunt you. This will make you further depressed, you will grieve for your lost baby…It will be hard to make peace with yourself.*

I told myself not to listen, to nod and then get out. Her words slipped into my brain for a moment. Toxic.

I thought you'd help, the sign said you'd help! I just need my body to be fixed, go back in time to a space before I met him, and I need this to be over, now. I wanted to be healthy and finish school. I thought about screaming crying at the top of my lungs in their pristine office. Don't do it Patricia I warned myself, but it was so tempting.

I nodded my way into passivity, somehow finding myself both frustrated and thankful for her time. Like I owed it to Dianne, with the picture of her grandchildren and her assurance that she knew what was best for me. She was older than me, with an air of knowing what she was talking about, and I guess I was used to letting people have their way with me.

I asked for help, and got it in all the wrong places. Story of my life.

I left the office thinking about my boobs and breast cancer, and I hugged my arms around my chest, feeling the cold. I thought of future PAP tests and cervical cancer and further invasion into my body. Remove the cancer. Remove the fetus. Cut, cut, cut.

I thought about the alien as an avocado, and I remembered the avocados sitting on top of my bar fridge, ripe— almost too ripe to eat. I had been waiting to make guacamole—for the perfect time between the hardness and the softness of the flesh—but I waited too long. I always waited too long. Half-rotten, all rotten.

I want to go back and hug that poor girl now, tell her it was going to be okay; I was in so much pain. Never let them shame you or scare you—that's what I learned from this whole thing. Don't let others look at your out of context choices and go, *no, you are wrong.* My body, my choice, old line got it right. *You might not like this next part, but I'm not interested in pleasing you.* I did what I promised myself I wouldn't do: I went to his apartment. The front door was unlocked. I entered, feeling entitled to this space for the first time. I kicked shoes that blocked my access and I banged on the door to his basement apartment.

"Who is it?" a female voice asked in singsong.

"Just tell Derek to open the door."

I opened the door, and was confronted by a girl with a towel around her waist, supermodel boobs in my face. Lots of ink, dark wet hair hanging to her shoulders his type. "Hey, hey, you can't just come in here. Derek—Derek! Who are you, and what do you think you're doing?"

Who are you? I wanted to respond as I stood in the hall, but I didn't bother. I had absolutely no expectations left. He had nothing for me.

"Oh. Hey, Patricia? I wasn't expecting you." He smelled of booze; it was only 4 p.m. His shirt was off, pants partly done up. Classy.

"Evidently," is all I can think to say nodding towards the nameless girl. A few months earlier, I'd have been sad, hurt, and jealous. But this was just proof that he was worthy of all my present feelings. I realized he was lost, and I almost felt bad for the girl standing there.

Don't fall for him, I wanted to whisper, *unless you can compete with the bottle, anger and a ghost.*

"Umm…I really wasn't expecting to see you. Can I help you with something?" He tried to stand in front of nameless, as if I hadn't already engaged with her. He tried to put his shirt over his head, too wasted to be smooth. I was entrained, beyond sad or hurt, just cynical, watching some cheap train wreck drama, $7 bottle of wine.

"Yeah, you already said that. And no, there really isn't anything in the world you can help me with. Goodbye, Derek." I walked away.

"Patricia! Patricia!" he called after me, but I left his house without turning back.   And for the first time in a long time, I really loved myself.

As I hastily made my way back to the residence room, I passed an older gentleman on the sidewalk, weathered clothing, sitting on a sleeping bag, coffee cup out, asking for change in the cold. Usually, I was careful not to make eye contact. I passed this man every time I went to Derek's place. I hate to say it, but he was invisible, part of the sidewalk, another part of the Toronto scenery. And I realized, in another way, I too was invisible: plain looking, average student, mediocre friend. For the first and only time I looked him in the eye, opened my wallet and gave him all my change.

When I got home I looked at the avocados on my fridge, soft and bruised. I tossed them, for they had lost their appeal.

CHAPTER 19

Once again, I did what I promised myself I'd never do, and put "abortion and Toronto" into the search engine. I swiftly clicked on links and read personal tales. *Stop Patricia*, looking at all of this wasn't exactly helping.

Eventually I found what I was looking for, and clicked on the website for an abortion clinic, not a hospital. Again, I was filled with relief when I read: "Free, confidential, all female staff with years of experience." But then I remembered my previous experience. Apparently, I was easy to trick.

I started to read about medical procedures and panicked. I reminded myself that I should be in and out in about three hours. Relatively painless. Relax Patricia, this is happening either way, whether you panic or not. They also offer medical abortions, non-surgical, in theory less invasive, but less accurate, and the medical abortion required three visits versus one. I'd be awful to have an abortion and later find out you were still pregnant.

The website mentioned bringing a friend along, but there was really no one I wanted to invite. "Hey, Elyse, hey, Kara want to come with me to see a movie? I mean come to my abortion?" *Wait, what?*

I called and made an appointment for the next day. I'd miss my first day of classes, but all they really do in the first class is hand out the course outline. I'll tell you right now that I went through with it.

The time before the abortion was more stressful than the time during, I built myself up to this state of panic, but then it was over. I walked in the door and, walked out three hours later, free to continue with my life, and to keep my secret, for it was my story to tell or not. No wonder older people have so many wrinkles, weighed down by all those swallowed stories.

I entered the office: name, and health card number. I panicked as I dug for my health card.

What if I can't do it today because I don't have my damn number?

I filled out the paperwork, met with a counsellor who confirmed that I wanted to do this and she told me what the procedure would entail. She asked if I had any questions and I asked her about my chances of getting pregnant in the future. She assured me this would not affect my chances. *Like I'd ever want to have a baby.* I really don't know why I asked. I didn't mention the pro-life clinic I stumbled upon, and I brushed away her questions about a partner. This was about me, not him. Blood test, then an ultrasound to determine how far along the pregnancy was.

Then there was the procedure itself. I closed my eyes as the nurse asked if there was anything I needed. I was awake the entire time, local anaesthetic. There was some cramping as *it* left my insides. I felt everything, wondering if I was supposed to feel this much, but it was fine. Like my period cramps, but worse. Maybe this happened to you too, and you know what I mean.

I waited in the recovery room for half an hour and assured them that I had a ride home. I lied. I was getting better at that. I wanted to walk, to clear my head, and celebrate my freedom. But instead, I stepped into the January air and hailed a cab. I felt the thick pad in my underwear I was given for the bleeding.

That was easy, I thought—in and out. It was about a simple medical problem with an easy fix: Patricia McCormack, five weeks along, quick cramping, body inspected, medical gown, drugs, done, rest a bit, over.

No one ever really asked how I was. Perhaps I was selfish for wanting people to ask. I spent the rest of the day pampering myself, I forgot about finding the outlines for the missed classes online. Instead I put on my pyjamas, made popcorn and for the first time in a while I forgot about *him*. I was celebrating, a weight lifted like the end of exams. Three hour exam, three hour procedure. Light. My future restored.

CHAPTER 20

I f you are one of those pro-lifers and are waiting to hear about how I regretted my choice, and how the grief destroyed me, well then you are going to wait forever. Shut the damn book, you can't possibly understand me. No one does, but you don't have a chance. Good for you, I can hear Alice saying, finally learning how to stand up for yourself.

Sometimes, I day dream about what would have happened if I had the baby quietly, and just banged on Derek's door a year later, and handed whatever chick who opened the door a screaming infant and went, "Here you go. Thanks for checking in on me, buddy. Here's your worst nightmare—my flesh tangled with your flesh, and it's too late to stop."

The girl would be like, *what? Who is she?*

One of your ghosts came back, Derek. Even if I don't haunt you, here is a real breathing, crying, shitting kid, complete with childcare payments. Can't deny my part in your old life now, can you? I smiled at these half-asleep thoughts. I wondered how he would've reacted if I had actually told him. I didn't know if he would have believed me then, or if he'd believe me now. He'd likely not acknowledge what happened at first, and then be pissed that I went and took care of things without him. *Feminist and equal* my ass. That guy always needed to be in charge.

Hell maybe you are reading this Derek, going hey, she got it all wrong. But I have nothing particular to say to you, I no longer care what you think.

School kept me occupied. After my struggle the last semester, I was determined to do well and stay organized. I relied on my schedule like others rely on the Bible, and I believed that if I followed it everything would be okay. But I was still one missed appointment or deadline away from slipping off the edge.

Three weeks after the last time I saw Derek, he called me. I guess he figured I'd have cooled down and that he could try and smooth things over, brush it all away. My mistake, I'm always so passive, so forgiving. I answered the phone because I wanted to hear him out and be done.

He said something along the lines of, "I'm sorry, Patricia. I was really drunk when you saw me a few weeks ago, and I don't know what to say. Sorry you had to meet Kristine like that; we're more friends than anything. Anyway…me and you…we just kinda got back together…never talked about if we were exclusive, you know? But I'm sorry if I hurt your feelings at all. I'm going to be really busy for the next while with school and work. But if you still want we can chill now and then, hangout and hook up and stuff. I'm down. I still like you."

I let the conversation trail out. A few grunts and a goodbye, and his conscience was clear. He kind of apologized to me. He was right; we never said we were exclusive. But then again, he never wanted to talk at all.

I still missed him as I walked around campus, and I thought of him as I passed a bar we went to, and as I walked near his street. He wasn't dead, but I thought of him as such. I was busy missing and mourning a person who was still alive, still willing to see me, but I knew he was gone. I didn't feel like fucking him, and he made for dull, yet infuriating company. I could see through his narrow guise of a loving, caring, gentle soul. I knew him enough now. And I no longer liked him. But, I did miss who he was, or rather, who I thought he was. Something like that. One time I cracked, I sent him a nice message asking how he was doing; inquiring about school and work, and all I received back was, "sup?" I doubt he bothered to read what I wrote. I was never worth the effort. I didn't bother to respond.

I believe that was the last time we spoke, but my memory was a bit foggy during this period, with circles of anxiety and depression, daydreams and nightmares melting together.

So I'm sorry; there's no movie scene breakup, no epic bar-fight-style "fuck you" with drinks in his face and me telling him to go fuck himself and have a nice night as I storm out. We didn't go like that, he just faded out. I think we both realized the other wasn't worth the effort. Not even worth a last fight. And so he went, and I let him.

It's so clear now how awful he was. He raped me. He raped me. He raped me. Before, I wasn't quite ready to admit it. My unclear understanding of our interactions was shaped by my feelings of infatuation for him—by my feelings of lust, and my lack of self-confidence. I was so stupid and naïve. How could I let it get that far? How could I think he gave a damn about me? Lesson learned the hard way, unfortunately.

I'd given up on engaging with people, but that wasn't to say people had given up on me. I was tired, with no energy left to care, but I responded when people reached out. After all, I didn't want to draw attention to myself with the weight of my silence. Fragmented conversations and bits of floating texts were my only interactions.

My brother sent me a text, asking how I was doing, how was school. I replied that I was well, and school was busy. I suggested we talk on the phone sometime soon, and asked about the next day, but he didn't get back to me until a few days later. We arranged to talk on the phone on the weekend, but the conversation never happened. I called him, but I didn't bother to leave a message when he didn't answer.

It wasn't our fault—it was just the way communication went these days. Sure, people talked to each other all the time, always connected on Facebook—cell phones out, pressing "like" buttons, replacing heart emojis for feelings. But we only really have time for the "everything is good" type answers, don't we? I could barely make sense of how I was feeling, let alone type it into a three or four sentence message—the longest socially acceptable text—

before one becomes a burden. And, what if I wanted to call one of my friends to talk? We don't really do that anymore, do we? We need a good reason, like a birthday, or a notification of sickness.

I actually called Kara one lonely Saturday; I wasn't sure what to say. Maybe I just wanted to distract myself from my life and hear about hers. Or maybe I wanted a friendly voice, or to ask if she was free this weekend. I didn't really know. I didn't want to talk about me cause what was there to say? That I was okay, but my anxiety and depression were chasing each other in circles, and I somehow got left in the middle? That some days I woke up okay, and then later in the day I was so sad, and so tired that all I could do was sit and try to read, but the words slowly became meaningless, and by then I just didn't care. I was numb and gone in this vacation space, limbo between alive and dead. It was a good space to wait for my body to decide what to do, to have the energy to continue living. I waited for the weight to lift.

Even as I write these words I feel heavy, tired, writing in a book that no one may ever see. The long term goal of having someone read this in the next month or year seemed irrelevant against the burden of pouring the words from my aching body especially now that Alice is gone. Words slipping out, messy, disordered, and I'm too exhausted to be responsible for my narrative. My head hurts, but my heart hurts more.

I've explained all of these things to you, but there's a distance between these foggy thoughts in my head and the paper. But my anxiety tries to make up for all of this. So I go from caring about nothing to caring about everything and thinking about everything: school, him, my body, my neglected assignments (for I'd fallen behind again), my future, jobs, what people think of me, my messy room…I considered all of these things at once, and it was too much. My head was dizzy, my stomach upset, rushing to the shared bathroom to shit my guts out—because my body couldn't take this. Oh sorry, was that too much? Alice said to tell it like it is, keep it close to the heart, keep it real, or don't even bother. But when Elyse, Kara, and my brother texted me to ask how I was, I told them I was fine. It was easier than saying, "I'm too sad to move, and I don't care about school or life, or you for that matter, and then later I care too much and my chest hurts."

I saw Aashi in the hall and she asked me how I was doing, and my carefully constructed poker face slipped. It got tiring repeating the same mantra of, "I'm okay," when I wasn't. She ushered me into her place, gave me a hug, and we talked for a while. It was safe to show her bits and pieces. She mentioned maybe going to see one of the counsellors at the school, and I laughed to myself. I half-heartedly agreed, not having the energy to bother explaining the situation. I wondered if she referred many other desperate students to the counselling department. Had she been herself and sat there, filling out her student number and reason for being there while trying to desperately justify her need for help? Regardless, I was glad for Aashi's kindness, and the brief half hour of feeling the warmth and safety of another's company.

I headed back to my room alone. I hated being left alone.

CHAPTER 21

I can't really explain the next part of my story well. Incoherent logic, plus a foggy layer of film covers sections of memory. The anxiety and depression stopped chasing each other, and I was left with just the depression, with an emptiness that echoed and echoed. I didn't want to feel this way; I needed something to make it stop.

I took a handful of pills that the school doctor prescribed me months ago.

Maybe I need a higher dosage to feel better, I thought.

I took too many, and then I stopped bothering to take them at all. No one was there to follow up anyway. Like I said, the school doctor's office was designed more as a walk-in clinic, not really for long-term patients. They welcomed urinary tract infections and the flu, but shuddered at the words "mental health."

"Tell us your symptoms," they said. "No wait, tell us *some* of your symptoms, don't waste our time telling us everything—no time for that." Then, the experts, with their years of medical school will tell us what was wrong. They understand our brains with their scientific lingo and discussions of chemicals far better than you or I ever could. Don't read too much; don't know too much.

Alice used to talk about how long dead authors grasped her struggles much better than the doctors examining her. There are so many little things that resonated with me after she was gone. I want to tell her I get it. I imagined poets in doctors' chairs, and doctors writing poetry. Would it be all about the rhythm, the science, the perfect beat? Maybe that's what I need, a doctor of poetry. Maybe that's what we all need. But these are just the half-awake ramblings of a crazy chick.

I hibernated in my dorm room. I stopped eating and stopped sleeping, too. Or maybe I was constantly asleep, I don't really know. No more restful sleeps, and no more mornings that left clearly defined boundaries for my days starting, and crisp nights marking the funeral of days gone by.

No, I was half-asleep, dreaming of the ghost, worrying about my future. I got up and tried to eat, groggy, head hurting, heart heavy. I curled up and went back to bed, holding onto my pillow. Too broken to deal with the day, I let my sheets and pillow embrace me. I could only stomach crackers, applesauce, or a dry piece of toast, before returning to a sleep that was far from restful. My mind drifted, my body faded. I felt heavy. My hair started to fall out in clumps. I missed classes, and tried to continue with assignments, but I was missing more and more lectures, and I couldn't be bothered to catch up. Alarms set on my radio and phone, but my body only heard what it wanted to. I was unable to deal with the day—with getting up, putting clothes on, bringing my books to class, sitting, talking, smiling.

It wasn't that I wanted to die; it was just that I was too tired to live. There's a difference, you see. One day, when Kara tried to talk to me I told her that I was too tired for life. She thought that meant that I wanted to kill myself. But that's not what I meant at all. I didn't have the energy for death either.

Everything just slipped into pointlessness, for what was the reason for making meals, of staring at food and swallowing it, when one needed to do this day after day? I felt redundant, or maybe the entire human experience was, I don't know. And schoolwork—why did professors want my opinion on classic dead authors or contemporary politics, when the internet and libraries were full of opinions on these subjects? Academia made a project of trying to teach me to think, to be original. But what I really learned was that so many other people have strong opinions; you don't need mine as well, now do you? *And still, I'm writing this down.* I no longer saw the point in trying to fill my head with knowledge determined by a syllabus. And I hated fun things. I didn't want to go for drinks or read a girly magazine or watch the latest films. I was exhausted by the effort of trying to engage with so-called entertainment. Entertainment became work.

I was too broken to have fun. Laughter was foreign. I didn't want to die; I just no longer cared about anything.

I was a failing student with few friends, a cold family, and no job. Who would notice if I just slipped away? I thought of running off, traveling the world, and all those fantasies of backpacking through Europe that are supposed to feed the imagination of my generation. But I was too tired to dream. I could barely get up to go to the washroom, let alone imagine going on a plane across the world, buying the tickets, planning a trip, going by myself, discovering new lands, new food, new cultures.

They say "it's an adventure. Showing you are wild, experienced, and worldly!" But I was none of these things and I knew it. Perhaps that was why Derek found solace in me: the plain, nurturing girl. Maybe two dreamers in a relationship take up too much space. But perhaps this was also why he didn't want me.

I'm just rambling now, watching my hands move as thoughts float from somewhere in my head to the paper, with little awareness of what I'm writing. It is past their enforced bed time, but I can't sleep, writing by the light of my flashlight. All I can see is my hand and the paper, nothing else.

PART 3

CHAPTER 1

One day, I woke from my daze, and all that was there was anger. A rage deep inside that could only come from being so still and so silent for far too long. The most dangerous part of the ocean is not where the waves rise, but the spaces between the swells that look calm. That was how you got pulled under, drowned, or carried off course. A primitive cry emerged from somewhere inside me—my soul, if you think like that and it reminded me that I was a wounded animal, crying out during my last breaths—and it made me wonder why we humans bothered to try and control ourselves with laws and reason.

After a few weeks of not bathing, I managed to drag myself to the dorm showers, and came back my room wrapped in my towel. Like I said, I was too tired for everything, including modesty.

As I kicked off my flip-flops, the towel slipped away, and I found myself once more confronted by the mirror. I was taken aback for a second by the material reality of my body, the presence of a person I was even further removed from than the last time I encountered myself. Before, I was shy; now I stared at the girl in the mirror and thought about all of the different people I'd been since coming here. Derek changed me, or maybe this city changed me.

All of a sudden I was mad—awoken from a sleep, furious at him for loving me, and then not caring how he treated me at all.

Mad at myself for falling for him. Mad at my parents for not being supportive types I could talk to. Mad at everyone for being so superficial. Mad at the social worker for making me beg for help. Mad at this city and Dianne...

I stared at my body—this thing that briefly held life. My bones were showing, ribs poking out from my ribcage; "good job," I was sure some fashion magazine intern would whisper.

How'd you do it?

Oh you know, get your heart broken, abuse is good for the figure. Oh and be too depressed to get out of bed, so anxious the sight of food will make you nauseous. But be weary, you might not be able to stop.

My hair hung around my shoulders, long, feminine, and wild. It was a matted mess. I hadn't brushed it in weeks, and I needed to condition it twice in order for the comb to make it through the tangles. I didn't need this jumble of hair that my mom and grandmother said was nice and feminine; it was such a nuisance, really. I couldn't care less about being attractive or pleasing anymore. I remembered all the strong girls in the movies, with their short hair and kick ass attitudes. Something about long hair being fuck me hair, short hair being fuck you hair. I don't understand why society made such a big deal about hair length.

I went over to my desk and looked for scissors, frantic, overcome by urgency. It took me a minute to find them, and I dumped my pencil holder in my haste. I returned to the mirror and started to snip. It felt good. My hand, my arm, my entire body was shaking. I had a vision of what I wanted my hair to look like, but as the sobs took over my hand just worked to cut it all away. I wanted it gone. I guess the final result was some hipster looking haircut, uneven, but edgy.

Whatever, I thought. *I like it.*

I stared at myself in the mirror. I wasn't some innocent looking girl anymore. People will be more hard-pressed to refer to me as cute. I was the girl with the *fuck you* haircut. I felt empowered, as if cutting my hair helped me feel entitled to my anger.

I really hope I'm still making sense, that this doesn't get misconstrued.

I was shaking, furious to the core, anger and hate radiating off every inch of my body. I was a heat wave on a winter's day. I

DANCING WITH GHOSTS

thought of Derek and his fucking hippie, poser-feminist stance. And his damn dreadlocks and I thought about cutting them. I wish I could find him now, hold him down and snip, snip, snip. I had the scissors in my hands. Or better yet, I could rip them out with my bare hands until he whimpered from pain. And I'd say fine— *don't want me to pull them out? Cut them off yourself as I watch. Fuck you, Derek!* And I'd let out some howl that only those possessed by rage like mine would understand.

I touched my new hair, rough and uneven in my hands. And somehow, I found myself both angry, and wanting to apologize to myself, reach out to touch my reflection in the mirror and whisper, "you're beautiful." And the glass somehow broke, and then I was glad when the glass shattered. I picked up the largest shard that fell near my bare feet and I threw it to the ground. I wanted to break into more pieces, more reflections of me. There was blood splattered on my leg and dripping down my hand. I don't really know how I cut myself. Everything was a bit blurry. I was so focused on the words in my head, that I lost track of the outside world.

I should wash this off, I thought, as I struggled to put on clothes.

I headed out of my dorm and to the washroom. Not realizing, or maybe not caring, that I was leaving a trail of blood. Then, I ran into Aashi in the hall.

"Are you okay? What's going on? What happened to your hair, and was that you screaming? Why are you bleeding?" she asked. And at some point she asked "do you want to die?"

I said, "No—but I don't want to live either."

She brought me to the washroom, got her first aid kit and applied pressure to my cuts. It didn't really hurt. I couldn't really feel my body.

After my wounds stopped bleeding and she covered them in gauze, she left me alone in the washroom, assuring me she'd be right back. But I was exhausted from the ordeal, and felt my eyes closing. I wanted to sleep on the washroom floor, with its piss smell and shit particles. I no longer cared, my body was sliding.

I forced myself with my last ounce of will to get up and return to my room. The hall was empty, and I clung to the wall for support, too tired to walk unaided. I locked my door and crawled into bed, falling into a numb, deep sleep.

Aashi contacted my parents; she found my home phone number at the residence front desk and spoke with my mom. I guess she told her that she was worried about me. Of course my mom wanted nothing to do with it. She probably told Aashi, "Do whatever you think is best, go ahead."

I heard someone knocking on my door—a pounding. But the cries of, "Patricia, it's Aashi. Are you okay? Please open the door!" didn't coax me into moving. Soon, this faded to the knocks of happy trick-or-treaters, a little unicorn and a princess.

I tried to stand, but my legs hardly worked. I was floating on water, floating on clouds, and I needed to concentrate extra hard to stand. I started to tell them that I had no treats, but I found a bucket of candy by my door, and they were happy. They smiled and waved as they made their way down my steps. Then a policeman and a firewoman arrived, and I gave them candy, too, but secretly I liked the unicorn and princess costumes better.

What month is it? It must be October. I was so confused, but I smiled. I liked the fall.

The knocking continued, it was a busy night. Turns out my house of horrors for the evening didn't revolve around children, costumes, pumpkins and dollar store decorations, but police officers and psychiatric hospitals and, doctors and nurses.

Trick or treat?

Reality or drugs?

Fucked either way.

Don't open the door.

And you know what? Like I keep telling you: I was tired, so I went along with it. I didn't say a word the entire way to the hospital. The cops in the front tried to make small talk and pretend this was a normal occurrence.

"And where are you from, dear? And what are you taking in school?"

But I just stared at them, and then out the window, at the people on the street. I stared at them from inside my place of captivity. I no longer needed to pretend to care about anything, about what people thought of me. It was okay if the crazy girl was silent and rude. Finally, I was free. Going on a holiday from needing to pretend, from doing anything; meals would be brought to me, and my laundry would be done.

Maybe it's not such a bad deal, I told myself. *I was ready for my vacation. So I guess, thank you, Aashi?*

The officers escorted me inside. Well, kind of; they guided me to a small desk inside some weird kind of hospital. They started to say something to the secretary about my *episode*. Normally I'd be ashamed, flanked by cops, dragged to a hospital, but I was *gone*, and what happened next didn't matter to me. One of them got a call and they quickly left, and the secretary motioned to the chair.

"It'll be thirty minutes or so. Just have a seat, sweetie."

I didn't really know if I was free to leave. I think I was waiting to see a doctor. I wasn't sure what I'd say. I stared at my surroundings absently. I thought of standing to leave; slipping through their system—that was my chance. But I was tired and indifferent and I just wanted to sit. I didn't feel like venturing back outside to face the night alone. Was it night?

Numb. I was stuck waiting in a dreary room for the minutes to pass, for five minutes to pass, just waiting, always just waiting. I still didn't even know what I'd say to the doctor, but I guessed I'd think of something. It didn't really matter to me what they wrote in their file beside my name. *Actually, all of this mattered, I just t didn't care about anything then.*

What did they write about me, what did they whisper about me? Paranoid, maybe, but they are literally collecting fragments of what they think of me and sticking it in a file, to share and to keep forever. Why wouldn't I worry?

I glanced at my file once when Jennings stepped out to take a call during our appointment. They got my overview right, but they got all the little details of my life wrong. How could I trust them if they didn't even get the basic facts of my life right? It was like playing broken telephone with my life. But hey, I should be grateful they didn't lose my file.

The chaos of earlier was gone. I was far away, watching this happen to someone else. Half interested, I watched a lady, maybe forty or so, stagger in from the street; damp, red hair covered her face.

"I need help. I'm going to kill someone! The voices are telling me I need to kill someone..." She shouted.

The secretary moved from behind the desk and guided her to the registration. "What's your name again, dear?"

"Pam. I was in here earlier today, and I just need to see the doctor again. It's getting worse and I'm afraid I'm going to kill someone if you let me out." The woman looked desperate as she pleaded with the nurse. The red headed woman's hands shook and her voice cracked.

"Yes, but we just need to fill out the intake sheet again. I'll see what we can do. It says on the file you voluntarily left eight hours ago, so I'll have to check that I'm permitted to get you another appointment." The nurse replied calmly, checking her shiny gold watch and gesturing for the woman to have a seat.

"I'm going to kill someone!" She cried again as she paced in front of my chair. I didn't flinch when she finally took a seat beside me, done with her nervous pacing. I wasn't afraid of her. I was afraid of *them*. Security came, along with a young doctor. The doctor's long, dark, ponytail swayed. She stopped and put her hands on her hips as she began talking. I listened, half-roused from my fog.

"I already tried to help you and you left this morning. That was your choice." The doctor told the red haired woman.

"Yes, but I wasn't hearing voices then, and now they are back, and they are telling me to kill someone. If I go out there I'm going to kill someone. I don't want to kill someone and...and I can't go back to jail. I can't, I just can't." The woman trailed off as she looked at her trembling hands, on the verge of a breakdown.

"Well, you should have thought of that this morning when I tried to help you. If you want to go to another hospital today, just pretend you didn't already come here." The doctor left no room for debate.

"It's not safe to let me out. If I kill someone, and go back to jail, I'm going to sue this place." There was vengeance in her eyes now, and she shook a fist at the doctor.

"You've already been in jail once, Pam, so you know what it's like. Look, we can give you a list of shelters if you need somewhere to sleep tonight. That's what this is about right?" one of the two big male security guards suggested.

"Come on—get up," the other guard said, hovering as Pam slouched against the chair.

The doctor was paged and slipped away as the two masked guards escorted Pam out; only her face was visible as they left; it looked as dark as the night sky. I wondered what would happen as she went into the night. Maybe she'd kill someone—another newspaper heading about a mentally ill person, but missing the essential tagline of "Rejected when desperately seeking help from psych hospital." Tell the shareholders how you really treat people.

She can have my spot, I wanted to tell them, but I was too tired to speak.

The security guards walked past me as I sat, still waiting for my appointment. "Sorry about that, miss," one said, nodding towards the exit.

Oh god, what had I gotten myself into? On another day I'd have been outraged at this sight, panicked and angry. But tonight, I just sat and waited.

What will they do to me?

I got called into a room and chatted with a young nurse. She asked me a few basic questions. She tried to understand why I was in that day, but my answers were jumbled. I felt like I was underwater, or on sleeping pills, struggling with that half-awake feeling, and people were trying to talk to me and I couldn't make sense of what was going on. I pinched my arm. Bright florescent lights were trying to penetrate my head, but I was gone. Maybe it was better this way.

"Do you fantasize about dying?" she asked.

Who doesn't? I almost responded.

She told me that I was going to see a social worker and then a psychiatrist. I nodded. She let me out of her little office, through another door, and into a bigger room with about twenty patients. They were all either standing, pacing, or staring at the blank walls. I saw a large glass window and behind it the medical staff were working, typing notes, meeting with other doctors, and watching us on big TV screens.

I sat in a chair and closed my eyes. I was tired already. I didn't care what happened; I just wanted somewhere to rest.

I couldn't sleep, although my eyes kept closing. I was in this half-awake hell, consumed by nervous energy as the others waited to see what would happen to them. I'd join their anxious pacing, if only I cared about my fate.

"I need my medication; it's in my bag that you took, and I was supposed to take it an hour ago," I heard one person comment.

"My daughter told me to call her. She sent me here because she knows I need help. She wants me to get admitted. She keeps saying only you can help me. I'll get admitted, right? I'm ready. I really want them to help me this time. I'll do anything. *Anything*." Another person desperately pleaded.

My eyes slowly turned in the direction of the voices and I saw an Aboriginal lady, maybe early sixties pleading with a young nurse to get admitted. Something stirred in me, and I found some shred of empathy for the people around me, from somewhere deep in my daze. We were trapped, animals in a zoo, political prisoners, at their mercy—waiting to see what fate they would decide for each of us. Pretending, pretending that we were in control.

"That's up to your doctor sweetie. We have limited resources so we can't just follow what everyone suggests as their treatment plan. There are rules and regulations that determine who is admitted," the nurse told the Aboriginal lady.

A middle-aged man stood against the door that trapped us, at first wiggling the doorhandle, then desperately flinging himself at the door.

"They just told me to come through this door! They didn't tell me the room was locked! The nurse never told me. I didn't do anything; please don't lock me up! You're just making my anxiety worse." His eyes bulged out of his head, his eyebrows raised to the top of his forehead.

Security called some code. They yelled for the others trapped in the room to "get back," but it was not clear where we were to go. And then the same security guards in masks dragged him somewhere upstairs. I was not afraid of him—he was harmless. Once more I was afraid of *them*.

"Let me out, let me out!" I heard the man cry as *they* dragged him away.

I watched the Aboriginal lady get escorted by the young nurse to the door that led to the street. She turned to look back at the waiting room as she slowly walked to the door. Face fallen, I wondered what she'd tell her daughter.

"Good luck," the nurse said as the lady left.

I was called to see the social worker. I repeated most of what I said to the intake nurse. It was tiring saying the same thing again.

"Yes, I kind of want to die today. Yes, I'd like to hurt myself. I don't have a plan, but I'm just really tired. Yes, it's getting worse. Yes, I've stopped eating. What day is it? No idea. No, I don't want to hurt others. No, I've never been in jail. Yes, I'm a student."

"Supportive friends and family?" the social worker asked.

"Well, I don't really know. Yes, it's my first time at this facility. No, I don't have a formal diagnosis. It just feels like I'm in a dream and all there is, is just this pain—pain that I can't put into words and..."

The psychiatrist got similar answers when I was called to see him, and I repeated myself for the third time.

I watched as the social worker and the psychiatrist hovered over my file. I could see them through the glass screen. I wanted to bang on the glass. Instead, I watched them talk about me.

I must have fallen asleep, but I awoke to cries of, "No, no, but I'm not crazy, and locking me in here like a crazy person is going to make it worse! You have no idea what you're doing. Stop, please stop! I had a plan, and my therapist said I could just come and get help if things got really bad, and that I could come back and get admitted another day. I have a bag of my stuff and clothes at my house, and I need to call into work. I need to tell the new receptionist what to do with my customers. And my daughter will be looking for me." I watched a frantic middle-aged lady in a suit surrounded by security guards and the same doctor that I saw with Pam earlier.

"We have your best interest in mind. You are coming with us," the doctor told the lady. The guards sounded excited as they called code red, and they put her behind a locked door.

It seemed that they do the opposite of what you ask in here. I wondered what was upstairs.

Normally, I'd have been careful; you see, it was all a language game really. English class should have prepared me for this day. Say certain words and they'd help you—other words and they'd never let you go.

Anyway, I guess the problem was that I hadn't decided what verdict I wanted as I began to play their word game. First time players got an advantage apparently, no strikes against me for already using their resources, and so they decided maybe they could help me.

CHAPTER 2

Luke warm apple juice in a little plastic cup with foil on the top. Lumpy mashed potatoes. Yellow walls surrounded me, the paint trying too hard to be optimistic. I didn't like it, but I enjoyed the simplicity. I was free of any responsibility. It was no longer my fault I wasn't happy. The food was horrendous, but I had no choice since most decisions were taken away from me—from us. When to eat, when to wake, each hour of the day was lay out nice and clear for me. Now it was peer support time, leisure time, outdoor time, craft time, relaxation time before bed, you get the point. If elementary school teachers, with their neat day books, and craft time plans could cure the world of sadness and mania, then surely we'd all be saved.

I remembered watching *Forest Gump* for the first time. I was sitting in the rec room, curled up in my pyjamas, already knowing it would become a favourite. Later in bed I replayed the scenes, thinking about one of the main characters, Jenny, taking off at whim. I wanted to be more like her—the wild child with the flowing hair and a white dress, running through the Lincoln Memorial Pond to greet her lover. I've never even been to Washington.

Anyway, some details from that first week are clear, but most blurred together. I'm not sure if at the time I really knew what was happening. The fog of that week was briefly punctured by the swish of the doctor's long ponytail in the emergency room, and the security guards' footsteps as they forced people in or out against their will. All I was was anger and clouds, gone or filled with rage.

The fact that I was there was so surreal. I was a struggling university student one week—locked up in a psychiatric ward the next. It was hard for the logical part of my brain to comprehend. I don't think the pile of drugs they assigned helped my problems with clarity.

I had a very brief meeting with another doctor, and to be honest, I can't really remember what was said. He came by and woke me from my slumber, and asked me a few questions. I wanted him to leave so I could return to my sleep, so I gave him the quickest answers my groggy brain could muster.

So there I was with a load of unknown drugs in my body, sleeping pills and anti-psychotics, I believe.

I tried to ask what they were and if I really needed them, but the nurse just told me, "Doctor's orders. Hush now, sweetie. Take the glass of water."

And so I did just that. They did some internal transfer after admitting me through emergency to some temporary ward; that was how I wound up with Alice as my roommate.

My mom sent along the information about her medical insurance, so I had a semi-private room. I didn't talk to her directly, but someone from the hospital contacted her. I think I gave one of the nurses her number, so they could talk with her about health coverage. And my dad, well, my dad acted as if he shared a brain with my mom. They were a political party of two, with my mom the spokesperson, and my dad abiding by her direction. My brother called me on the landline. His voice seemed more distant than usual. We both desperately tried to pretend the situation was normal, talking about everything but the present and what was happening with me.

Aashi came by with a bag of my clothing from the dorm.

Elyse and Kara visited as well, bringing chocolate and books. Security ruffled through my boring things. They came to visit together, and I wanted to stop and say, "wait, do you even know each other? Or did you reach out to each other on social media, united through a mutual dysfunctional friend?" Their messages to each likely read: "Hey, do you know what's going on with Patricia, that poor girl?"

I don't remember much of their visits; they didn't belong in the forced cheerful space of the psych ward, scheduled under visiting hours with their hospital assigned passes. They belonged to the outside world. I shouldn't have been mad at them, but somehow I was. I was mad at Aashi for putting me here—though I should be grateful, and Elyse and Kara for their roles as witnesses—though they'd been nothing but kind. They came a few more times, visiting briefly, making small talk, bringing me chocolate and magazines. They didn't belong in the room with Alice and I. They gazed at her with curious expressions and she stared back at the invaders.

"I wish you wouldn't try so hard to understand—to get it." I wanted to tell them. "Stop pretending to be my friend. Stop pretending that we even live in the same world. You visited, you did your duty; I absolve you of social responsibility. Run along home." But I didn't say that. Instead, I gave brief answers when they made small talk, and responded angrily when they asked me how I was doing and what the next steps were.

"You'll be out in time for school in September, right?" Elyse asked. I looked at her blankly and didn't even respond.

They started to contact me less frequently. I jumped every time the phone rang.

I didn't want them to like me.

I could tell you more about the friends I'd made in well-thumbed novels than I could about my interactions with the "outside world" during that point. It was spring, but as far as I was concerned, the seasons ceased to exist. I looked outside the window, but all I saw was the grey of the road, other buildings, and parking lot. Maybe they should add a season called *grey*. and name it after me.

They hardly let us out, an hour a day, under the guard's careful watch. Adult playtime; replace the teacher with the guard, and swings for benches. The other inmates paced impatiently, rubbing their hands together, lost without their cigarette distractions. I heard something about new legislation that banned smoking at the facility.

Alice claimed this was "total bullshit" that the government and the people at the facility really wanted what was best for you. Alice said they were worried that the smokers were busy planning a way to overthrow the upper class, as they huddled together in circles to guard against the wind. She claimed it was another attack on the poor. I wasn't sure if any of this was true. I made a note to look it up, but it just ended up being another conversation with Alice left unfinished.

Alice once lit a cigarette inside the room.

"What do you think you're doing?" The nurse, Leah I think her name was, stormed in, and took the cigarette from Alice's yellowed hand and extinguished it.

"Well, I'd smoke outside, but since you banned that, I figured it doesn't matter where I smoke. So, I decided I'd save myself the trouble of freezing and enjoy my smoke in my bed." Alice could be mouthy when she wanted.

"Alice, we've been over this before; you can't smoke in this facility!" The nurse shook her head.

"I know, but you've taken away all else, and I'm just trying to enjoy my day. You can have one with me if you'd like. Your job looks stressful." Alice offered the young nurse the pack. The nurse half-smiled and shook her head, rolling her eyes as she walked away. But she didn't take the pack, and Alice threw the smokes and lighter back into her drawer. I tried not to giggle. Alice taught me about pleasure, the joy of a half-smoked cigarette that made the day worthwhile.

Alice, I forgot to *really* introduce you to Alice. Perhaps I put it off because she's the most important one in my story, and I could never do her justice. Ha! And you thought this was about Derek? Alice is the only reason I'm writing this, after all. She's the one who told me I needed to get it all down.

She was there after my transfer, sitting on her bed, book in hand but her eyes wandered around the room. Her blue hair slowly came to focus as I oriented myself to my new surroundings.

"What did you do, girl? Why are you here? So blunt, such an Alice-like introduction.

Who are you? I thought. I looked at her closely, smudged black eyeliner, brown roots made way to blue hair. Arms and neck covered in ink. Ears pierced: a nose stud. I stared at her as if she was the first person I'd ever seen, and perhaps she was.

I knew I didn't need to answer, but I wanted to. "I'm really not sure, one of my friends called the hospital or something, and I just sort of ended up here." I knew I should look away, but I couldn't. Something compelled me to look into her hazel eyes.

"It's okay, I'm just asking, but you don't owe me any sort of explanation. I'm Alice, by the way, or Allie. Call me whatever you'd like. I've been here for a while. Well, in and out to tell you the truth. I can tell you a bit about how this place works. I like your hair by the way, it's real edgy." And that was that. Suddenly we were friends, comrades, sisters in arms.

After the stuff with Derek, I told myself that I wouldn't let anyone in again. I wouldn't make myself vulnerable for another person to come dispose of me. He started out so kind and look at the way he turned out. Why should I assume that anyone in the world would be better? Deep down I feared that he just showed me some raw, essential, carnal and savage part of human instinct. I was scared that everyone was like him inside, and some people just hid this abusive nature more...That was why Elyse and Kara were appalled by him and what he did to me. Maybe because he represented this monster that we all kind of see in ourselves...

So after this, after all of the things I'd went through, I was afraid of bringing out the Derek that lurked in others. Of ever getting too close. After everything with him, it was hard to just let go and trust. I wondered what Alice really thought of me as she sat across the room. Why would she, of all people, like *me*?

But life has weird turns. Just when I settled into the hospital, ready to sleep and ignore the outside world, inquisitive Alice somehow made her way into my life. Alice, with her rebellion and beauty and this fierce, but gentle presence that I am failing to explain. I wonder why it's so much easier to describe abuse than love—violence than, than magic.   It was through Alice that I realized I was wrong about Derek and my ability to love. Alice made me realize he wasn't even worthy of having his name in the same line as love. Perhaps he only served to break my heart, to bring me to into myself. To bring me to Alice. Something along the lines of that.

I hear we struggling warriors, we find each other.

When I looked at her, and we tentatively offered wavering smiles, there was this wave of electricity and recognition. I realized immediately that we somehow spoke the same, rare dialect. It was as if we were saying, "I don't know who you are, but I see you and you see me. I know you, and you know me."

In that hospital room, in my bed next to Alice's, I learned to question everything I thought I knew about myself. I'd only cared for men before, and then I turned around and loved the woman in the bed next to mine with such intensity that I'd never known. Everything I understood about the world changed. And for a minute, it was beautiful, and it was worth it. We loved each other in a way that only two women could. Gentle. Fierce. Beautiful.

I learned Alice's story in fragments. In and out of the hospital, filled with rage, or wanting to die. It was much later, when I dared return the question she asked me on that first day, "what are you doing here?"

"Trying to stay sane enough to live in this world. To understand the laws." She smirked, "You know, like the laws of gravity."

Her mom, she too was angry. She'd so much anger and sorrow that she passed it between the generations. I hear that trauma is part of DNA, built into our genetic code, not lay to rest in graveyards. Her mom, whom she seldom spoke of, was in and out of jail during her childhood. In and out, just like Alice.

She just shook her head when I asked where her mom was now, so I let the question fall. When her mom was sitting in a jail cell, Alice floated between the foster system and her aunt's house, where she lived along with her two cousins. I asked about the cousins, and she told me that they were good people and had their shit together, so to speak. She said they didn't really talk.

She ran away from her aunt's house, but something always brought her back; she left the hospital several times, but again, always turned and walked through the door again.

Then she left for good.

Her friends would visit and make references to drugs and long nights of partying, but when they left, Alice would tell me how she was so much more than that.

Don't get me wrong, I love wild nights, and the music and the colours. I can tell you of the drugs and the men and after-hours clubs. But that's not all I care about. I want to paint it all; the colours, the sounds, the feelings. This, this is all Alice again, not me. *Ah yes, the feelings. I wanted to paint the words, and the words between the words. I want everyone to taste what music is, to find the sound between the notes. The space where the colours blur, and there is colour that exists somehow between the colours, between what we can see.* I'm just trying to recall the fragments of the thoughts Alice left me with.

Another time she explained, *I'm mad at my mom, at the world, at the doctors labelling me as this crazy, traumatized chick.* **They**, *they put me here. Them and all their labels. It's this big money making system, to label us as* **traumatized, as crazy, as victims**. *It's all for profit. Yeah, maybe I'm something, but they made it worse, throwing us into this for profit recovery industry, trying to cure the world of folks who aren't normal. An outlier in societal math. That's me.*

Dr. Jennings wanted to know why I was angry, but he'd need to ask my mom, and my aunt, and all my elementary school teachers, and the ex-boyfriends. But it isn't even them; it was this fucking structure we were all trapped in. "Hey Allie, who are you angry at?" Capitalism, patriarchy, sanism. Yeah, I guess that more or less translates to the world.

Fuck the world. *That's what I want tattooed across my knuckles.* Again, this was all Allie. I'm just trying to give you a picture of what she was like.

I'm so much more than my anger, than my pain. I'm not some dysfunctional chick, like a damsel in distress that needs saving from herself. I have dreams; I want to write and travel, get out of this place, paint more, hell, even finish high school and maybe work here someday. I don't need saving. It's not that I don't get things, it's that I understand too much.

But hell, I'm angry at the world and that anger is only wrong cause they keep telling me I shouldn't be so angry. Women are friendly. Women are gentle. Women don't have the right to be furious at the cards they get in life. Punch it out at the gym. Pretend I don't hear the girl in the next room at a party being raped, just do another line with shaking hands, because I'm too high and too small to stop them from touching her—from touching me. Like the cops ever believe fuck ups like **me. Like us.**

That's the Allie you should know. I don't do her justice, but you should know what she was like.

217

And I was fucking angry, too. Maybe that's why I'm so angry—because some of her rage transferred to me, and somehow I was infected with her fury before we even looked at each other for the first time.

She said, "I don't wish this on anyone. I really don't."

CHAPTER 3

They watched me, and I watched her, and I think Alice watched me back. The professionals, they all had time for me now. Every week I sat at Dr. Jennings' desk, a friendly male in his thirties the type of guy my mother would've liked me to date in a few years, had my life taken a different turn. He had a perpetual tan, as if he was always just getting back from some sunny holiday. He had a firm handshake. He was handsome in an I-play-tennis-three-times-a-week way, and had an I-have-my-life-together smile. In other words, so not my type. He seemed like he genuinely cared, but I hear they train great actors at medical school. I know I sound so cynical, but it is what it is. I looked at his desk, a neat pile of papers, and a computer to the side, as if to suggest I was what mattered. There were photos on the desk, but they were facing away, and I wondered who was in the frames; his wife, children, or perhaps elderly parents? Was he the good son, taking his parents on grocery store trips and cutting their lawn?

Between the psychiatrist, psychotherapist, nurses, recreation leader, peer support worker, the occasional student, and the security guards, I was closely observed. And us inmates, trapped in here, we watched each other closely as well. But I had no answers for Dr. Jennings or any of the others, and I stared at them glassy eyed, giving brief answers, tired of trying to explain.

I asked for your help before, I wanted to say. Well, not their help particularly, but still, I asked before and was turned away. Why didn't they want to help? Now I was worn out and weary, so I remained quiet. The team of professionals, with their condos, and their subway escape route from this place every night, how could they possibly understand? I was a new species of human, captive versus free. I wasn't angry anymore, just resigned; the child who was complicit in their education, but happy giving the briefest possible answer on a test, for this was all a test, right? I never mentioned the ghost, or the abortion. This was all about me; he didn't belong in this space. I didn't mention my family either, or the bullies in high school, or how I was turned away when I asked for help before.

I think I scared them by treating the hospital like a final destination versus an airport lobby, a space to pass over before moving on to greater places. They couldn't help me, I know, but I still wanted to stay. It was like having gone on an exhausting trip only to realize the destination is drab, and I spent all my money and energy getting there. I didn't really think about the outside world, my former friends, or my family.

I don't want to bore you with the minute details of the day to day, for it was dreary enough to live through. But that's not really true; perhaps it was just painted grey from my depression. I'm just tired. I finally understood the expression bone weary, and I really didn't care anymore for my thoughts, let alone trying to write them down.

I told Dr. Jennings as he went through a standardized list from some DSM chart that he'd never understand me. He cut me off when I tried to explain my answers.

"Do you want to die? Do you feel hopeless? Do you feel high, any rapid thoughts? Yes, or no?" He interrupted me midsentence when I told him it wasn't as easy as yes or no. "Are you compulsive?" He tapped his pen. He only had an hour session and needed to get through a list of questions. I shook my head.

Bold Alice leaped through my mouth—they say you become like those you hold dear. I explained that they could never understand me with all the, the framed questions, diagnostic testing, scientific terms, and fancy medical jargon. I actually told him that there was nothing specifically wrong with me. I told him that I just wanted to talk, but that no one would listen to me before all of this. I heard myself and I sounded like some white, middle-class spoiled brat and I hated it. He smiled and tried to agree, but I don't think he grasped what I was saying.

I told him again that he'd never understand me, but perhaps I was being harsh. He said that I wasn't bipolar like the team originally thought—something about me sleeping too regularly and my highs not lasting long enough. I was *just* depressed and had anxiety.

I could have told you this, I thought. The two "conditions" were forever chasing tails with each other, two competing versions of reality.

He mentioned cognitive behaviour therapy, and that after I made progress on my recovery I could leave. I was told I would see Mandy, the psychotherapist, and work on controlling the heavy, the dread, the sinking feelings and the racing thoughts. Basically work on controlling me. On controlling life.

I had regular appointments with Jennings to check on my medications. That, or he was really checking to see if Mandy was doing her job to train me, coach me, fix me. But we all know I'm unfixable. Managing illness, skill-building, mindfulness, coping-strategies, recovery, there was an entire industrial complex built around me being—around me staying—sick.

Sick.

I wondered what Jennings and Mandy thought of me, of all of us. *Patricia, sick girl, no personality because everything about her could be reduced to this illness. She thinks this way, because she's sick, acts this way because she's sick. Sick.* Maybe recovery is about turning people into *things* they don't recognize. Maybe that was why Alice proudly called herself a *lifer.*

Anyway, so yeah, I met with Jennings, he suggested one medication, and asked me what I thought. I felt compelled to say something intelligent as I agreed with his suggestion. But all the drugs were the same to me. I just wanted the rollercoaster to stop. It slowed down in the hospital, numbed by the routine of the place and the drugs that made me sleepy. He tried me on some drug I'd seen advertised on television, but it made me nauseous and I couldn't sleep, and the anxiety got worse.

I tried something else, and noticed no difference.

"Well no difference is better than side-effects," Jennings said. "Just wait, wait a little longer."

Eventually, I was given something that kind of numbed the highs and lows, but I found it harder to smile, to laugh, to stay awake, to cry, to *anything*. I guess this was what I wanted. Was it though?

In my spare time, I talked to the others, but we were all rather lost in our own worlds. That or I sat on my bed, reading the paperback books I collected from the small library. Bending page corners, writing in the margins, marking favourite passages as if they mattered—rebelling in small ways, for I'd never written in books before. And Alice sat on her parallel bed, wearing a nineties style headset, moving her head to music only she could hear. They may have let me rest, but Alice refused to let me pass without an explanation, whispered one sentence conversations weren't enough for her; they weren't enough for me either.

The hospital could house all the drugs in the world, but then there was Alice. I remember sitting on her warm bed on a warm spring day, our legs dangling. She called me over. "Hey, Patricia, I want to show you something." She handed me her sketchbook, and opened it on her lap. I commented on the drawing she just finished, some woodland scene with fairies and elves. Art wasn't my area of expertise, but I told her I liked it, and struggled to say more as she waited for me to comment.

"It's good, Alice." I could have gone back to my bed, but I didn't. I just looked at the drawing and looked at her, and she saw me and smiled. My heart was pounding. I felt like a young teen who'd never been kissed. Terrified and exhilarated.

I moved my body so it closed the small gap between us, and our skin touched shorts and bare legs. I looked at Alice again, and I was calm as she reached for my face, hands in my hair, hands tracing faces, lips touching gently, at least at first. Eyes closed. Nights that followed filled with long talks, and good night kisses— never more, but that was enough.

I'm not even sure that Alice was her real name. I heard the nurse once call, "Arianna, dear, time for your medication."

"My name is Alice," she quickly replied.

I never asked, for it wasn't my business. She was whoever she wanted to be. Whoever she was in the moment. She slowly offered me the small details of her life. I warned you—I'm intrigued by a certain type, and she seemed like she had an interesting story.

One day I asked her what she was listening to and she handed me her headset. It was a mixed CD of nineties hip-hop—a genre I'd never listened to. She tried to explain a bit about hip-hop, power politics and resistance. I actually enjoyed listening as she talked.

"What kind of music do you like?" she asked. But I shrugged. There was so much I still didn't really know about myself. I'd rather talk about her, not me.

Before all of this, Alice was a waitress and an artist—like there was a time before the present; the hospital seemed like the only space that could possibly be real. But I feel strange writing too much about Alice. I'm afraid I already told you too much about her without her permission and all. And besides, she told me to write my story, not hers; it's just that her story seems to merge into mine.

Sometimes she sat by the window, drawing; she even did a portrait of me. I told her it didn't look like me; she made my features sharper, my hair more defiant, eyes more engaging. She turned me into the type of person I'd want to know.

"Oh, but you look like this to me," she responded.

"I see the resemblance, and it's a beautiful picture, but it's not me," I answered.

"Maybe you'll see it once you look at yourself closer, Dove." I really don't know why she called me that. Something about me being like a timid bird, but needing to know my strength and how far I could fly and how my song could carry in the wind. I didn't mind the name when it came from her.

One day, as I woke from an afternoon nap, I looked over and Alice had this blue-green glittery dress on. She had a collection of makeup dumped on her bed. I watched as she finished adding blue sparkling eye shadow that complemented the green eyeliner. She had a crystal around her neck that had something to do with good luck. Her blue hair shimmered in the sunrays that streamed in through the window. She was the most beautiful person I'd ever seen. The most beautiful person I will ever see.

"You look like a mermaid," I commented, my voice sleepy. If I was trapped underwater she'd be the most fascinating sea creature, and it wouldn't matter if I made it to the surface.

"I like that name: Mermaid. I think that's a good name for me, my little Dove."

And so it was.

I watched her interact with Felicia, the girl across the hall during craft time, I hoped her hidden secrets would continue to give way to a portrait of who Alice was. I was totally spellbound, overcome by her magic, and I wasn't going to try and hide it. I grasped at snippets of her conversations during the peer support session, watching how she interacted with the others. I can tell you more about the others another time; Felicia, Jasper, Joyce, Larry, and Carl. I'd make the list longer, but you'll likely forget who I've mentioned by the time I get around to writing about them.

Oh, and there was Niki, too, the peer support worker. I watched Niki and Alice's warm interactions, smiles, and laughter. Alice told me that Niki was actually inside with her during her first time in the psych ward. But Niki followed the treatment path suggested by Jennings and the others.

"Hell, you should have met her that first week she was brought in, but she got *bette*r." Alice told me. "How can she pretend to get it when she's different from us now, professional, cleaned up ironed clothes? Divide...I can't really talk to her like I could before, or like I can talk to you. She's one of *them*. I like her, I think she wants to help and is a good facilitator, but she's one of them and needs to play by their rules."

There was also Joyce. Sweet Joyce was an older lady full of wisdom. She used to be a sex worker, and lived on the street at one point. But she found God, and spiritual podcasts. She was eager to talk about pressure points on the body and coming to terms with your past and ways to cultivate spiritual energy for healing. I'm not laughing at her, really, she taught me about being okay with where I was in life.

Then there were Alice's friends. They scribbled false names in the visitor's log, I think there were restrictions on who she was supposed to see, or maybe they just enjoyed breaking the rules.

"This is Dove," she'd say, smiling and I'd greet them. Dove was as good a name as any, and I was tired of being Patricia.

"How are things going at the bar?" Alice asked one silver haired girl—Fern, her tattoo artist—I believe. Ripped skirt and an airy purple top; she reminded me of a fairy.

"Oh you know, business as usual. Ed, Ryan, and a few of the regulars keep coming by. They always ask where you are."

"Ah, yeah, eh? Well, thanks for not telling. I don't exactly want people knowing where I am."

"It's cool, I got your back. Your secrets are safe with me," she smiled at Alice.

"Thanks. Probably just looking to pick up and everyone is watching me so closely. I bet they are even listening now. The nurses are such snoops. Besides, I don't want anyone else labelling me as the crazy, unstable girl." She looked around the room, but I was the only one there. I couldn't decide if Alice's suggestion made her paranoid or brilliant. Probably both.

"That or they want another photo-shoot."

"Yeah, man, you never know," Alice nodded.

"So, how you keeping anyway?"

"Ah, same old shit. Glad I got a new comrade—this one over here. The doctors aren't happy with what I'm telling them. I guess they don't see things as I do, challenging their perception of reality and stuff. But I've shown them enough progress that they can tick off the notes they need in their books. I think I'm getting out soon. They're getting impatient with me, I can feel it. Taking up their resources and showing the new people around. I guess they don't want anyone to get *too* familiar with this place. They're afraid I'm gonna end up running this hell hole on them." She cleared her throat. She had this dry raspy smoker's voice, it would've sound sickly on anyone else, but on her it was sexy. She slipped her arm affectionately around me as she spoke.

"Yeah, eh? Well, it'll be good to have you back," the fairy replied.

"I'm not ready to get out yet, but I'll see. It's bullshit being stuck here, but I still have a lot of things to set up for when I get out. They still haven't actually told me when I'm getting out of this joint."

"Yeah, man. Hopefully soon though, eh? Any thoughts on what you'll want to do? I bet you can still get some hours at the bar," Fern offered.

"Nah, I think that's a bad scene for me. Maybe I should go back to school, take some writing classes or painting. Or I could become a social worker or psychiatrist. I think I get what a lot of these people are going through more than the talking heads they keep sending." A mixture of bitter feelings and hopefulness echoed in her voice.

I met more of her other friends, and they all offered me fragments of who she was, little pieces of Alice, different personas she slipped into. She always introduced me to them and included me in the conversation.

CHAPTER 4

The psychiatric facility managed to do something I thought was impossible; turn back time and return us to the 1990s—back to my childhood of enforced bedtimes, and parents handing out food rations. Not that Alice and I actually followed these rules. We pretended to sleep at 9 p.m., but lay awake talking, whispering, and sometimes reading with flashlights. Hidden under the covers we were safe. We weren't allowed to have cell phones, or laptops. There was no Wi-Fi, and only a landline phone that rarely rang, but still, Alice was all I needed.

We made plans for when we got out. She continually referenced some restaurant or bar, and I looked at her blankly, and she responded by telling me that, "we'll go together— you and I— when we're free."

She was born in the city, and kept forgetting that I wasn't native to this concrete empire. She had the dirt of this city under her fingernails. We planned a day trip to the Toronto Islands, and also spoke of going for a bike ride or stroll along the Beaches. I happily daydream about these adventures. We dreamed more than we had time for, but I guess that was the sign of a healthy interaction, the desire to spend time together outweighing the ability of calendar days to fit royal plans.

I don't mean to make it sound like I was magically happy, and that Alice fixed everything. It wasn't that thoughts of the ghost and the heaviness of life magically disappeared. But Alice and the numbing routine of this place distracted me. I forgot about Derek for a while, and then something made me think of him; one of the paperback books, or something the doctor said. And then I'd missed him, even though I shouldn't. I'd be left wondering why he treated me as he did. But that boy, he didn't make sense in this space any more than I did, and days drifted by without him occupying my mind. I still stewed in my discontent, unsure what to do with myself in this strange space. Sometimes I'd just stare at the walls, not saying anything for hours. And then sometimes I'd cry. Some little thing would set me off, some passing word or thought, and I'd feel deeply miserable and start to sob, and then once I started it was impossible to stop. And it made it worse that I had no idea why.

"Sorry, Alice, I didn't mean for you to see me like this," I whispered to her once as I sniffled, wiping snot on my sweater sleeves.

"Hey, girl, you don't have to apologize to me for being real. There's so much to be sad about. I don't know why they think there's something wrong with you for being sad." Her hand grazed my shoulder and she smiled. "Come here, hun," and I went limp in her arms.

Sometimes Alice went into this artistic trance, drawing, working furiously in her notebook.

"Shh," she'd say if I tried to talk to her. I learned when to leave her alone. Nurses called us for activities, and she'd refuse to go. There wasn't much they could do to force her. They asked me about her and I just shrugged.

Sometimes Alice seemed panicky, overwhelmed, hyperventilating, overactive, ripping her hair out and biting her nails, trying to do everything at once, even though it was leisure time and there was nothing she really needed to do. All we did was follow our tedious schedule, group, art time, rec time, sign-up to use the gym, go to bed now, eat now, and take your medication now. They wanted to terrorize us with the same daily rituals so we could go further crazy, or pretend we were okay enough to no longer be here. We either got locked in the loony bin forever, or pleaded that we were okay enough to get the fuck out.

"What do you do?" Alice asked me one day as I was putting on my pyjamas.

"What?" I responded, having no idea what she was taking about. I'd known her for a month, and we spent the majority of each day together, yet here she was asking a question of introductions.

"What do you do? What's your calling; what's your purpose?"

I wondered where this was going. "Ummm, I don't really know. I'm still figuring that out. I'm in school. Or was in school, I should say—taking journalism. Sorry, I don't really know what I'm doing. Not very exciting, am I?"

"Stop doubting yourself, Dove. I'm just trying to understand you. Do yourself a favour and stop apologizing unless you mean it, and stop saying *I guess*. You're a strong woman; you just need to realize that." She was right, and I tried to listen. "I see you reading a lot, scribbling notes in books. You are a dreamer. Maybe that's what your role is: a story teller, keeper of history and dreams. Maybe your calling is to write, to imagine, and to see things in a different way. To deconstruct, to reinvent. You're really intuitive, thoughtful. I can see it in your eyes. You have this really strong presence—this energy about you."

"Thanks Mermaid. But I don't know. I love to read, but I've never given writing any thought beyond essays and newspaper articles, and a bit of poetry," I responded, wanting to shoot her down, but afraid to hurt her feelings.

"You write poetry? I'd love to see it."

I thought back to him and the spoken word, and that all seemed so far away. How could the same word dawn on both their lips?

"I don't have anything on me, sorry. But maybe I'll write something." I had a natural inclination to please everyone, but it was stronger with her.

"I'd like that Dove. Now, I need to tell you something if you have time." She pointed to her bed and I sauntered over. "It won't be easy, us artists aren't valued—not in the same way as the doctors, scientists and teachers, but you've got important things to say. I can sense it. There won't be the pay or the respect that comes with other careers, but don't forget that what you have to give is important."

"Okay," I responded, and that was enough for her.

"Just try and get it out. The likes of us don't belong in this world, in, in capitalism. I think that's really the correct diagnosis for both of us: *sees the world differently*, feels *too much, refuses to hide, isn't productive according to societal values.*"

"I know, Allie. I can just imagine what my mother would say. Besides, I don't really know what I'd even…What I'd write about."

"People hear the doubt in your voice, your words, your tone, and they use it against you. Write me a short story, hun, as a place to start. I'd like that. Maybe you can be in it. Really, this is about writing *your* story."

I smiled at her and nodded and our eyes met.

She put her hands on my cheeks tenderly, and our lips collided, and for a second I thought *what am I doing?*

And then I let go. I won't tell you about the rest of that night—maybe later, but not now. Some memories are too precious to share.

I wanted to give Alice a parting gift, as she had given so much to me. But I had nothing to offer. Maybe I could write her something. I stayed up after she slipped into sleep, trying to think of something worthy of Alice. I looked out our window, stroking her head in my lap as she peacefully slept. Nothing, vacant, no thoughts, blank page. And then a poem appeared, anger and politics and ideas that I was not responsible for. Ideas from my classes that better fit poetry than an academic journal. I scribbled it down. Manic, needing to get the words out that I didn't know I had in my body before they slipped away again. My hand smudged the ink of the torn notebook page. I tucked my poem into Alice's packed bags. I hoped she liked it. Maybe I'll show it to you later. Peaceful, I curled up beside Alice and had a restful sleep.

CHAPTER 5

I'm growing weary of trying to tell you this story, and I've gone on for a while, so I'll try and skip to the highlights. They let Alice go. She told them she wasn't quite ready—that she felt safe here, and wasn't sure about the temptations of the outside world, but they just reminded her to have confidence and embrace routine. The caseworker checked that she had suitable housing, and another job—this time as a barista—and sent her on her way. She was to follow-up bi-monthly with the peer-support group. One-on-one was ideal, but again, everything was about the budget.

She tried to ask for more supports, but they told her that group was all they had. "There's free short-term counselling around the city, but they are to teach you survival skills which you already have. Besides, there are lots of people on the wait list. If you want long-term supports you need to pay yourself."

She was to meet with Jennings once a month, but that was really for a medication check, nothing more. They told her they were trying to focus on positive community reintegration, not segregation in hospitals. Personal growth was about meaningful community involvement.

"But I'm scared," she uncharacteristically whispered to me. "My liberation is more about their budget than my freedom. They just frame their funding crisis as part of their anti-oppressive practices." For some reason this made us both giggle. What else were mad girls to do, but laugh at the state of the world?

I never even knew how old she was twenty-four maybe? Too young, I know that much. Her last night at the hospital we spent sitting on her bed.

She looked at me and said, "There's still so much I don't know about you."

"Well, I'm not sure what you really want to know about me. Oh, by the way, I forgot to tell you the doctor decided I'm not bipolar—just depressed and anxious. Not that labels count for much." I told her.

"I mean there's a lot I want to know about you beyond some frivolous labels. Like, where's your family? Why'd you stay with that loser? Who are you? What drives you, and how exactly did you end up her? It's a fascinating question. How'd you end up here? That's what I think when I look at everyone; the old men waiting on their drinks at my bar, the doctor scribbling prescriptions, *why are you here? What roads lead you to this moment?* The men who…" she faded out, deciding not to share her last thought.

"I don't even know where I'd start. But I'll see you in the city, it's not like we aren't going to talk again," I promised her.

"I know, I know. It's just not the same. It feels good to let it all out. The doctors with their brief time slots, neat spaces to fit you in. And friends only half-listen; ask you a question, but their minds drift if your answer is too long, too complex. It's not our fault people have short attention spans. And even others like me…we get bits and pieces of each other's narratives, grasping at the little parts that make sense to us. Shared pain. I think it'll help you to understand yourself to try and write your story. It doesn't all need to be true; make shit up, and only share the parts you want. Hell, you don't have to show it to anyone. I'm not trying to pry. Just be real with yourself, figure out your truth. Sometimes, I watch you eat through this pile of books, making notes on other authors and I wonder if you give yourself credit for your ideas—your story."

"I don't know, Alice, that seems like a huge project. It's a good idea, but I might feel like I'm talking to myself for pages and pages, and then I may feel lonely, talking to myself about nothing, about everything."

"Well, if you'd like you can pretend I'm there. What would you tell me if I had forever to listen to your story, babe? Look, I got you something." We were curled up on her bed, and she shifted her weight to reach into the table drawer and handed me a beautiful diary with a built in bookmark. "Just try okay?"

She made me promise that I wouldn't stay in the hospital forever, that I'd try and get out—be okay enough out there. And I wondered why it sounded like she was saying goodbye for good, even as she promised to come and visit.

I thought about the tone of her goodbye as we gently kissed, with our hands on each other, gentle yet eager, needy and devouring. I traced her tattoos with my finger; tucked her blue hair behind her ears after as we went to sleep, tangled, smelling of each other. Alice. Magic. And it was enough for a moment. Leah opened the door to check on us but didn't come in the room.

Thank you, I silently thought to Leah. Maybe I'll tell you about the rest of that night another time.

Alice left the next morning. She visited a few times, but it was never the same. Our interactions consist of fragmented conversations, and future plans; fingertips and lips of distant lovers brushing past, the moment gone. We talked about how she hadn't been anywhere, trapped in this city all her life. We spoke of going to Montréal, just jumping on a train and taking off. She mentioned her dream to hitchhike out west and see the world. Across Canada to British Colombia, then down to California—just wherever the world and people would take her. I was not sure if she was really serious or if she was just trying to remind herself that there was something to survive for; keep going, keep going, another mile to travel. I smile thinking of us going to Montreal, staying in hostels, wandering the streets and sunny bar patios as we awkwardly tried to speak French.

She spoke in pieces about her life in the outside world, struggling to be real and raw in a place where everyone wanted you to act — to put on a smile, to say something appropriate. I guess she had enough of being fake, maybe her dreams weren't quite strong enough to pull her back, and maybe it killed her to pretend. And so she left.

I don't feel like telling you about how she did it, and how I found out. It's too awful to dwell on. Her being gone hurts too much to think about. *I warned you, this is no love story, at least not one with a happy ending.*

Alice and I were outsiders and we understood each other, because we shared this, this rage and sorrow eating away our insides. Maybe that was why she left, taking her bloodline with her. I wonder if her mom is still around. Or if she visits Allie's grave and if Allie can feel her mom's steps on the soft earth as she walks over her. Does pain seep from their cores meeting at some middle place under the earth? I wonder who hurt her mom, her grandmother, what pain united them. *What happened*, I'd ask, but she didn't like that question and now there was no one left to ask.

In high school I had a nose ring for a few months, but it got infected so I took it out. The little hole healed. This was over two years ago, but every time I take my shirt off I'm careful not to catch the ring. I can still feel the pool of dried blood and puss in my nose. This is to say that Allie is still here, became one of my limbs, gone in a way, more present in another. I wonder if the evergreen tree near her grave can feel her trauma and grace in every limb, in every stroke of the wind, in every creak. *I can.*

I think of her body, nestled in a casket under the ground. I imagine her tattoos, carefully etched into her skin by her friend Fern. I see her and Fern plotting the layout for the artwork on her body, a beautiful illustrated picture book. Fairies, elves, unicorns, deer, birds, a fox, a bobcat, trees, mushrooms, a squirrel, a mermaid, fish and other creatures of the sea. Oh, and a dragon —must not forget the dragon. I caressed them all as we lay together, and I felt the magic in her skin. I think of Alice looking down at her arms on her bad days, dreaming of death, but seeing art.

After she left, they came to life in the forest, staying with her through the funeral, but slipping away before her physical body began to decay. She wouldn't have wanted that. The ink rose from her skin, floated through the cracks in the coffin and began a new life, swirling and spinning into life-sized creatures. Some left for the forest, others made their way to the ocean, a few even dive into children's dreams and story books. Maybe this is what they mean when they say tattoos are forever. I was there, I saw it. *Don't ask me how.*

Alice wasn't meant for this world. She wasn't meant to just be one thing. Maybe that's what Jennings meant when he called her borderline. A person and a tree, deep rage and sunrise, struggling and yet still beautiful.

Dust.

CHAPTER 6

I'm still breathing, waiting to care, waiting to die, or to want to live, wondering how many minutes, days and miles need to pass until I forget them both. I now understand the different people we become after our hearts get broken.

I spent most of the summer in the psych hospital, proving to them that I was no crazier than anyone else, and with a pile of drugs, I was released back into the world. It was either that or I wasn't sick enough to stay. I'm stuck in a space between *okay* and *fucked beyond all help*, forever in a purgatory of my own making. I promised to come to the regular peer support sessions, where we discuss our lives and struggles. Sometimes I'm quiet; sometimes I talk and talk, refusing to stop after the ten minutes designated for each health-card number that participants get. I got my own apartment in Toronto, and started school again in September. Maybe I'll tell you more about this later, if anything exciting happens.

They didn't really help me. No one really helped me. They gave me an assortment of drugs, and some counselling, but they didn't really care about me as an individual. I can't help but wonder if things would've turned out differently if the social worker had actually wanted to interact with me in that first week of school. *Whatever*, I don't really want their help anymore—*fuck them*. Besides, how could they really help me when all my problems are so intertwined with other things, other systems of power? As I keep telling you this isn't just about me.

My mom visited me once, when she was on a business trip to Toronto. She seemed so out of place in the psych ward. We tried to ignore the setting as we ate the deli lunch she brought, and skirted around the topic of my dad's absence. She chatted nervously with my new roommate, Dolly. My mom never really asked what happened, probably too afraid to know, wanting the minimal amount of information so she could pretend this wasn't real. I think she knew *something* about me being raped, but I was so out of it, I really couldn't be held responsible for what I told her. I'm really not sure what my father knows or thinks—that man is forever a stranger to me. As for my brother, well, he called me a few more times and visited with John when they were in town for something, but we were always so polite with each other. I loved him too much to share the cruel details of my life with him.

My mom never said that any of this was my fault, but still, this was one more conversation off limits for the dinner table. There's always a delicate balance between stiff, polite silences, and the uncut truth, isn't there? My parents actually went out of their way to come up with a story to tell my grandparents and aunt about me going on an exchange program to England for the summer term.

I felt even more alienated from my friends from school, who made a greater effort to reach out to me when I returned to the city. The more they tried to empathize with me, the more I wanted to scream, "You'll never get it! You can't possibly understand what happened, and I don't want to talk about me, so please, let's talk about you." Yet, for some reason, I still tried to tell my story. I guess we all desperately want to be understood. I know they were trying to be kind, and I'm thankful for them, but I was still filled with apathy, mixed with rage and sorrow. I maintained friendships with the others from the psych ward, and made new friends; the crazies and the so called criminals are my kin, not university students. I eventually dropped out, but that's another story.

I always keep my promises. I started writing this the day she got out, scribbling down my story in bits and pieces, only when I felt compelled to write of course. Once, Alice came to visit me when I was writing, and she asked to see, but I told her to wait until I had the entire thing down. I wanted her to understand what happened; if anyone could understand it would've been Alice. I'm not sure what I'm going to do with this now. To be honest, I wrote this to explain it all to myself, and for Allie, but I no longer feel the need to hide anything. Hiding involves too much energy. Do with it what you will. Hell, you can even mail it to my mother—although that may give her a heart attack.

What happened to Derek you may be wondering? I heard that school wasn't for *him*; he dropped out, floated into the abyss, to continue travelling or whatever he was doing before. His sister might know where he is; perhaps he sends her postcards from destinations he has long since passed by the time they arrive in her mailbox.

In a lot of ways, I feel like I don't exist. Everywhere I go I wonder if I'll see him, even though I know he's gone. Every subway door that opens, every coffee shop, his ghost is everywhere. I keep wondering if he ever really existed, or if I simply imagined him. But I still have that old picture of us and the birthday necklace, material proof of what once was. His presence and everything that happened with him seems so surreal, so long ago now. The time in the hospital aged me.

Sometimes I dream of Alice, but these are welcomed dreams. We are together, hand-in-hand on some Toronto street, commenting on the people who pass and stop to stare. We are exploring coral reefs, swimming among brightly coloured tropical fish. Miles below the world, the Mermaid is swimming by giant sea turtles and we chase dolphins.

It's not that I like women in general—I just loved *her*. I guess the same can be said about me and men; it's not that I'm interested in guys in general, just *him*. I loved Alice, I wanted to be Alice, same difference, but love isn't the right word if I said I loved him too. I guess they were like two different drugs. I wanted to comfort them both, but I couldn't help either.

Now I look for the shadows of both Derek and Alice everywhere I go. Derek taunts me, while Alice leads my freeing dance. Derek haunts the city and the places we went together, and Alice the places we never went, plans forever broken. She's in the forest, with the dragon and the fairy that live there and in the ocean, in all the creatures that she became. I can feel her everywhere. She lives in more places than my body could dream of going.

Once, I swear I caught a glimpse of Allie and Derek across the platform at St. George Station. I saw them leaning into each other, his dreadlocks concealing part of his face as he moved towards her. She was whispering in his ear and they looked up and right through me, but I knew they saw me. Then, they both started motioning for me to come to them, but the approaching train and the tracks were in the way. I know that if I just stepped onto the platform I could talk to them. Fucking ghosts.

This is my scribblings, the poem I put in Alice's bag when she was leaving.

> *Not my Culture*
> All my dreams are pipe dreams, but I'm not dreaming of pipelines. We said *no* again and again, yelled it on the street.
> *We didn't consent!*
> But then we're met with silence and fences
> Remember G20? Stay, stay away from us, don't touch our golden fence, or you'll be meet with defense.
> We said *no* again and again
> Don't touch my body, all you'll ever be is a wanna be, stop fucking up the economy, I'm so tired of all your dishonesty
> But instead you spill your mess on our body
> The same man who made a system to legally enforce consent, and look what he does, he didn't really listen
> Put your faith in the hands of a man who ignored the cries of *no* over and over again
> And no I don't use man as a figure of speech – just look at who governs you, still lacking representation, it's true

But what can I expect form from a system that stole you away and cut your hair?

Tried to wash your mouth out till all that was left was their language

And then I wonder why so many people ignore the word *no*

The word taken as an invitation to negotiate,

Now, you say times have changed? It's all behind us, said and done, a government funded apology means it is over, right?

But some little things— they haven't changed…

I don't even know what you did to my drinking water, yet I'm supposed to watch my drink at the bar?

Cause it's on me to stay safe, baby. If you don't want bad things to happen to you, better hurry up your pace, carry some mace, didn't you realize if you wanna stay safe in this culture you gotta race?

You tell me my food has natural flavour, but the ingredients are a secret

Make me say *yes* when I don't even know what my *yes* is to I didn't consent to this…this…

Oh and the thing about rape culture is this is *our* culture. And why did we consent to this culture? Trust me you don't want to appropriate this shit

My body, my choice

But how can it be my choice if you keep trying to take my choice away from me?

My body, my choice,

Right? Right?

Acknowledgements

This book is dedicated to my father, Jack Gillespie. He has a passion for both reading and social justice and encouraged me to be different. People are defined by their stories and the lives they touch, and in that way, we continue forever. Thanks for the love and support.

To my mom, while this is probably not the first novel you imagined me writing, you encouraged my love of books, patiently teaching me how to read. The love of reading was probably the most powerful gift you could have given me. To my sister Meghan, who was always eager to recommend a favourite book. Some of the best childhood memories I have are of the four of us sitting together reading, each lost in our own adventure.

I would like to thank the students at Leaping Lion Books for their hard work and creativity in the publishing process. This book was conceptualized in my eight-year-old mind when I was determined that someday I'd be an author. I didn't know what I'd write, but I knew I had many stories to tell. Authors truly are the heroes of my world. I am so grateful for shared creativity and the kindred spirits I've found in novels, which provided needed escape for hours and days at a time.

I'd like to thank my friends, particularly David and Deb who were the only ones who knew that between cover letters, I was drafting a novel. Without friends who believed I was creating something worthwhile, this book wouldn't exist. I'd also like to thank my friends who witness and support my struggles, and who love me and believe in me when I'm ready to give up, particularly: terah li, Kimberlee, Allyson, Anna, and Aggie, among others. I'm also grateful for the love of my new furry friend, Aslan, who makes a great editor.

This is to everyone who is told that they need help, but are left trying to decode a healthcare system that cares more about paperwork and budgets than the human at the other end of the desk or phone. To everyone who is left going, "now what?" To those who have never tried to access this mental health system, it's not as bad as I suggest—it's far worse.

And to every person who is told they are not enough, who stays in abusive relationships for reasons that only they may understand, but are still very real. And mostly, for every person who asked for help, but didn't make it.

My life's journey is to untangle what it means to engage with, to bear witness, to challenge, and yet still dance and find magic. Thanks for those who on a daily basis remind me that with the pain and sadness, there is always beauty and art. This is to all my mad friends, the ones I love and the ones I have yet to meet. Stay raw, stay real.

Emily Gillespie was born in Welland Ontario. She completed a degree in English and Gender Equality and Social Justice at Nipissing University in North Bay. She moved to Toronto and completed a Master's Degree in Critical Disability Studies. She currently resides in Toronto.

She is a passionate advocate for mental health rights. She works at a non-profit organization that does education and advocacy work to end gender based violence. This is her debut novel.

LEAPING LION BOOKS

CPSIA information can be obtained
at www.ICGtesting.com
Printed in the USA
LVOW10s0340280417
532486LV00013B/81/P